A MAN W̶ A PAST

"My name's Tom Easterwood. They said I was to bed here tonight."

"Yes, yes, come in, come in. I'm Professor Asahel Greenslade. I've been waiting for you." His voice was a hoarse whisper. He was on his feet, but had to look upward to see Easterwood's face. "They told me you were a tall one."

Easterwood dropped his saddlebag on the floor. "Which bunk is mine?"

"Take either one. I say, sir, you look like a man who's been running from something."

"I was." He frowned down at the professor. "Maybe I still am."

Yellowhorse

Dee Brown

A Dell Book

Published by
Dell Publishing
a division of
The Bantam Doubleday Dell Publishing Group, Inc.
666 Fifth Avenue
New York, New York 10103

ISBN: 0-440-20246-9

Printed in the United States of America

Published simultaneously in Canada

February 1989

10 9 8 7 6 5 4 3 2 1

KRI

The strange story of the balloon Intrepid *and how it was used to defend Fort Yellowhorse against an attack by Sioux Indians has been told in various conflicting versions. I have heard it related by old Indian fighters, by gold prospectors, and by pioneer cattlemen of the Yellowhorse country.*

None of these tale spinners, however, was present in Fort Yellowhorse when the incident occurred. Soon after I met Tom Easterwood, I heard the true story from him, told reluctantly at first, then willingly and with great frankness in its personal details. Not only was Tom Easterwood there when it happened, he was the principal actor.

This is Tom Easterwood's story of the Yellowhorse incident, with added details supplied by Chief Spotted Wolf in the last year of his life, and with some official data obtained from the dusty files of the old Army Balloon Corps.

1

The horseman was alone under a vast sky unbroken by clouds, his blue Appaloosa moving in a slow easy canter. After a quick glance back at the lonely miles of black-sage plain which he had been crossing all afternoon, the rider began urging his mount up the steep slope of a pine-studded escarpment.

Halfway up among the boulders and stunted pines, he halted to let the Palouse blow. He slid easily out of the saddle, removed his crumpled felt hat, and slapped the dust from it against his leg. The hat was official United States Cavalry field issue, but it had turned a drab gray and a hole was torn in the crown. Instead of a regulation officer's blouse the man wore a beaded buckskin shirt upon which a pair of captain's shoulder straps had faded to colorless tarnish. A bright yellow silk handkerchief was knotted around his neck above a blue flannel shirt, and his wide belt supported both a revolver and a hunting knife. His feet were shod in moccasins instead of cavalry boots. His face and everything he wore was filmed with gray alkali dust.

The man was taller than most, the tallness exaggerated by his military bearing and his habit of holding his chin high. A stranger seeing him once would remember the height, the leanness, and the hawklike nose of this man.

Except for the heavy breathing of the horse the empty land was silent, and there was no movement anywhere upon the plain from which he had come. He glanced back once more, and then looked to his right, studying the rocky range that blocked the eastern horizon. If there was any life there he could not discern it.

It was then that he heard the bugle, thin and broken by echoes, but the call was unmistakable. Before the last note was gone, the man was in the saddle, loosening his carbine and forcing his horse up through the low pines. Somewhere on the other side of the escarpment, a cavalry trumpeter was sounding the charge.

When he was near the bare flat-topped summit he checked the Palouse and dismounted. Crouching low, he ran forward until he could see the spread of valley beyond.

Far to the west, on his right, a pine forest pushing upward against a mesa was split by a curving river. At the point where forest, river, and mesa joined was Sun River Cantonment. There was activity in the cantonment now. But the bugle call had come from closer at hand. The man on the escarpment crawled forward until he could see a road running below him, and then he saw the charging cavalry, a platoon of about twenty men racing along the road from the west. He jerked his head back to the east where a stagecoach was running crazily, half on and off the road, careening and bouncing against stones and sagebrush clumps. He had heard no shots, and saw no attackers now—but from a hundred yards to his left he heard the Indians and their mounts coming up from the valley through the cover of pines. They were climbing fast. How many there were he could not tell. He guessed them to be a small party if they were fleeing a twenty-man platoon.

He moved back quickly to the Palouse, and led the animal into a thick bunch of frost-yellowed bitter-cherry bushes, waiting there quietly until the Indians were over the ridge. He saw them in flashes of color and movement as they drifted down and away from him, and then he mounted and walked the horse slowly to the summit. He then rode quickly down the slope to the wagon trail.

The soldiers had stopped the runaway stage, but the men were alert for danger, and a second after he came out into the road one of the troopers had a carbine raised on him.

"Hold it," the horseman said. The young lieutenant in command was staring at him now.

The tall man rode forward slowly, glancing at the stage driver sprawled in death across the seat with more than one arrow in him. Another man, the guard, was lying on the ground. Two troopers were ripping off his coat and shirt.

When the lieutenant took a step forward, the horseman saw a girl leaning against the stage door. She had yellow hair. Her face was pale and frightened.

"You were a little late, Lieutenant," the tall man said.

The lieutenant started to speak, but saw the captain's shoulder straps on the rider's fringed shirt. His young face colored slightly. "I don't believe I know you, sir."

"Easterwood. Captain Tom Easterwood." He stayed in the saddle, nudging his horse forward slightly. "Is the young lady all right?"

The girl's frightened eyes saw him for the first time. "I'm all right," she said. There was a breathlessness in her voice, but Easterwood liked the sound of it. She was the first white woman he had seen in two years.

They heard the relief platoons coming then, in a whirl of dust up the road. Captain Frank Knowlton, commanding at Sun River, was leading them; he nodded a greeting to Easterwood as the troop pulled up. Knowlton took charge, and in a few minutes the troopers had the wounded man resting easily on the stage top, and the yellow-haired girl was back inside the coach. Blushing slightly, the young lieutenant got inside with her.

As the cavalrymen formed to return to the cantonment, Easterwood turned his Palouse in beside Captain Knowlton at the head of the column. "I was expecting you," Knowlton said, reaching over to shake hands, "but not with the stage."

"Lucky I wasn't with the stage," Easterwood replied. "I saw the last part of it from up there." He motioned vaguely toward the ridge. "This sort of thing happen often around here?"

"First time." He added grimly: "But I'm not surprised."

"Sioux," said Easterwood. "Oglalas probably. I saw some of them."

"Lots of wild bucks been around in small parties. All stirred up. Since early September I've been sending out escort troops to meet the weekly stage. The driver must've been ahead of schedule today and got jumped just before my men showed up."

"Could've been worse."

"Yeah, that girl. A female's got no business traveling through this country by stage right now."

They rode on in silence for a few minutes, then Easterwood said: "It wasn't this way two years ago when I was down here. After we signed the big treaty at Yellowhorse, this country was as peaceful as a New England meadow. What's changed it?"

Knowlton turned in the saddle, frowning at his friend. "Your orders ought to tell you that, Tom."

"My orders tell me to report to Goldfield for temporary assignment as Signal Service officer. That's all I know. We don't get much news up at Frenchman's Creek."

"You don't know about Colonel Quill?"

"We heard he was at Goldfield in charge of the depot."

"You *are* behind the times. 'Horse-Killer' Quill is commanding the whole area now. Political influence from Washington, the story goes, over General Sheridan's head. Quill put a cavalry squadron in Fort Yellowhorse a few weeks ago and is rebuilding the stockade."

Easterwood's fingers tightened involuntarily on the reins, and his horse jerked sidewise. He brought the Palouse back in position alongside Knowlton. "The man's crazy. If he reopens that fort every Plains Indian in the Yellowhorse country will be back on the warpath."

Knowlton shook his head solemnly. "You and I both were at that treaty signing, Tom, and we made some rather strong promises. We promised the tribes if they would go on the reservations, we'd never occupy Fort Yellowhorse again."

"Who's backing Quill and why?"

Knowlton had turned to wave a sergeant forward to the cantonment gate, now only a hundred yards away. He hesitated another minute before replying. "Out here we get only rumors. But the telegraph line to Goldfield is still open and we pick up a hint here and there. I hear some ranchers want to turn the big buffalo grazing lands below the Yellowhorse to cattle range."

"That would fit," Easterwood agreed. "The grass country was promised to the tribes for hunting so long as they remained peaceful. The ranchers know there'd be trouble if they moved cattle in there. So they make a deal with Horse-Killer Quill."

Knowlton smiled but there was little humor in it. "I guess you get the idea. And here is Sun River Cantonment. My quarters are straight across to the right of that headquarters hutment. I've got business with the surgeon, and I'll have to see about taking care of that female passenger. Call the duty sergeant to take care of your horse, and go on in and wash some of that alkali off. You'll find a bottle of rye whiskey in the cabinet behind my bunk. Make yourself at ease."

Half an hour later, Captain Thomas Jefferson Easterwood was pacing back and forth, his moccasined feet making no sound, in the narrow room that Frank Knowlton used for living quarters. He had brushed the dust from his irregular uniform, and his face was red and shiny from soap, water, and toweling.

He was thinking of Brevet-Colonel Mathew Quill, a man he had known for a dozen years, a man he had served under briefly in the Army of the Potomac during the later Virginia campaigns, and then again in the Sioux Wars when Quill had earned his Indian name of Horse-Killer . . . the Sioux under old Spotted Wolf had come in for a peace council, and Quill had seized their horses without warning, several hundred of the finest Spanish mustangs on the plains. Instead of turning them over to the Army Quartermaster for remount use, Quill had ordered the mustangs herded to the end of Box Canyon to be shot to death. *That will take the fight out of Spotted Wolf's band,* Quill had boasted. But he was wrong. The slaughter of the horses had aroused all the tribes from the Missouri to the Platte—Sioux, Cheyenne, and Arapaho.

The dead horses of Box Canyon, their bones bleached white under sun and rain, had become a sacred medicine place for every warrior in the Territory, the gathering place of all the ghosts crying out for vengeance against the invading white man. Quill had been recalled to Omaha, but the Army of the United States had marched and fought another winter and summer before peace finally came to the plains with the signing of the Yellowhorse treaty.

And now Horse-Killer was back in the Indian country. The man to whom Easterwood must report for duty after another three days' journey. Serving under Quill meant seeing Mellicent again, the colonel's wife—Mellicent Sheffield who had become Mellicent Quill ten years ago . . . he tried to shut her from his thoughts . . . so far as Tom Easterwood was concerned she was dead. He had dwelt enough on memories of Mellie Sheffield Quill.

Easterwood stopped his pacing long enough to down another drink from Frank Knowlton's bottle. He could not understand the meaning of the orders recalling him from Frenchman's Creek to Goldfield for assignment to the Signal Service. He was aware that the Service had no field officers, that Signal Service telegraphers and weather observers assigned to military posts were noncommissioned officers, usually sergeants. In his early months of Civil War duty with General George McClellan's staff he had been assigned to the Balloon Corps, but he was later transferred to the cavalry branch, and had served as a cavalryman ever since.

Was this some trick of Quill's, a move to strike back at him by ordering him to some petty duty and then holding him up before Mellie as proof that she had after all chosen the better man? Easterwood knew that Quill disliked him. But he decided this reasoning made no sense, that perhaps Quill had nothing to do with the transfer order and would rescind it as soon as he reported for duty. Chances were he'd be on his way back to Frenchman's Creek in another week.

He was standing in the middle of the room, the bottle in one hand, a glass in the other, when Captain Knowlton banged on the door and stepped inside. "You look like old times," Knowlton said.

"It's good whiskey. You want a swig of it?"

"I've got some news for you first."

"I hope it's better than the last I heard from you."

"This ought to cheer you up. It has to do with a pretty female. You know who she is, that girl?"

"The yellow-haired miss?"

"She's Baird Stuart's daughter."

Easterwood looked surprised. "On a stagecoach coming from the *west?*"

"She's been to San Francisco visiting her aunt and buying a wedding trousseau, she says. The trousseau is in that big trunk you saw on the stage. And the gent she's going to marry is Lee Bowdring."

"I never heard the name."

"You'll be hearing it often down at Goldfield. He's the Texan rancher who wants the buffalo hunting grounds."

Easterwood's lip twisted slightly as he handed Knowlton the bottle.

"Wait a minute," Knowlton said, drawing a sheet of crumpled paper from his blouse. "You haven't heard all my tale. She's Baird Stuart's daughter, and acts it. She ordered me to put a telegraph through to Colonel Quill in Goldfield. The telegrapher's scrawl on this piece of paper is an order for Captain Thomas Easterwood."

Easterwood sat down on Knowlton's bunk. "Read it."

" 'As soon as practicable after receipt of this order and no later than October 16 Captain Thomas J. Easterwood and one platoon of cavalry will proceed from Sun River Cantonment to this headquarters as escort troop for Miss Alison Stuart. A suitable ambulance for the comfort of Miss Stuart will be furnished by the commanding officer Sun River Cantonment.' "

"No later than October 16," Easterwood said. "That's tomorrow. I can hardly wait."

2

At dawn Easterwood was mounted on his blue Palouse in front of the cantonment stables, waiting impatiently for the escort troop to form. The dry air had an October chill in it, and there was a briskness in the movements of men and animals.

Captain Knowlton had assigned sixteen men and a lieutenant for the march to Goldfield. The lieutenant's name was Bridges, the same young officer Easterwood had met at the stagecoach the afternoon before.

An ancient yellow ambulance was backed up to one of the storage buildings where a corporal was supervising the loading of grain and rations. Easterwood edged his horse closer. "How many days' rations are you loading, Corporal?"

"Captain Knowlton said three days' rations, sir."

"Make it four, just in case."

He heard footsteps coming across the grassless hard-packed parade, and recognized Frank Knowlton in the gray light. The cold violet sky was swept almost clear of stars now. "Where's the girl, Frank?"

"She'll be ready in a few minutes. I forgot to tell you I'll have to give you mules for that ambulance."

"Good mules?"

"They're good mules. If I give you horses I'll have four men unmounted here."

"Mules will slow us down."

"You can still make it in three days."

"If we ever get started."

Knowlton chuckled. "The sergeant is bringing the team now."

Harness chains rattled and a sergeant and two men swung around one of the stables, backing the mules into the ambulance shafts. Lieutenant Bridges came trotting up the parade on a bay mount. He gave Easterwood a sharp salute. "Miss Stuart's trunk is ready to load, Captain."

"What trunk?" Easterwood stared at Bridges. In the light of morning, the lieutenant looked as if he were sixteen years old. The chill air had flushed his cheeks.

"The trousseau trunk," Knowlton explained.

Easterwood glanced at the range running above the forest west of the cantonment. The higher peaks had sunlight on them. "Where is the trunk?"

"In the Winters' hutment," Knowlton replied. "She stayed the night there."

"I'll go along with the ambulance," Easterwood said. "Lieutenant Bridges, form your platoon and have the men ready to march in ten minutes."

Thirty minutes later, Easterwood was still waiting outside Surgeon Winters' hutment. The trunk was loaded and strapped in the ambulance; a trooper acting as muleskinner was mounted on one of the mules; the platoon was assembled with Lieutenant Bridges on their front sitting stiffly in his saddle. Upon Easterwood's urging, Captain Knowlton had just gone inside to speed up matters.

Finally they came out, Knowlton holding the girl's elbow as she came down the wooden step, the Winterses following behind. "Captain Easterwood, I believe you've met Miss Alison Stuart."

"Only briefly." Easterwood removed his hat and bowed.

"Good morning, Captain Easterwood," she said, with more sweetness in her voice than he had noticed the day before. She was wearing a frilly green dress and a little bonnet with a big feather and a bow of red ribbon on it. A shawl was around her shoulders, but her teeth were already chattering in the shock of autumn chill.

"Miss Alison," Easterwood asked dryly, "do you have a fur robe?"

"Why, yes, I do, Captain, but it's packed in my trunk, and I shall be needing it, shan't I?"

He ordered one of the troopers to unstrap and open her trunk, waiting with elaborate patience there on the Palouse until she was wrapped in the robe, and was safely seated inside the ambulance. Knowlton had walked over beside Easterwood's horse. "Something you ought to know, Tom," he said quietly. "It may not mean anything, again it might. The telegraph line to Goldfield is dead this morning."

"If we find the break we'll splice your wire." He reached down to shake hands.

"Good luck," Knowlton said.

Easterwood turned to face the lieutenant. "Let's move out," he shouted, and turned to wave goodbye to Captain Knowlton. He galloped his horse forward through the gate, taking a hundred-yard lead across the flats. Behind him he could hear the muleskinner cracking his whip.

For an hour the little column moved steadily eastward, following the telegraph line across the level valley floor. The sun was well above the horizon when Easterwood ordered a halt to dismount the men and rest horses. As soon as they stopped, the girl was out the back door of the ambulance. She saw Easterwood leaning against a boulder smoking a small cigar, and walked over toward him. "Captain Easterwood, I was wondering if you have a spare saddle for one of the mules so I might ride outside."

"We carry no extra saddles, miss."

"It's lonely back there, and the ambulance side seats are so slippery I can barely stay upright."

Easterwood dropped his cigar and stamped it forcefully into the sand with one of his moccasins. He walked over to his horse, unrolled his gray blanket from behind the saddle, and carried it to the ambulance. Without a word of comment or explanation, he began spreading it over one of the long leather seats. When he stepped outside she was standing at the door, and he was so close to her he could hear her breathing and could smell the perfume she wore. Her yellow hair spilling from under her bonnet was full of sunlight.

His voice was edged with angry exasperation: "Will you get

back inside, miss. We have twenty-five miles to travel yet this
day."

As soon as the platoon crossed the flats they began following
the winding course of a small creek fringed with gray willows,
currant bushes, and wild cherries. The creek was broken occasionally with beaver dams in various stages of repair, and sometimes they could see dragpaths and mounds of chips in the grass
where the beavers had cut large bushes and pulled them down
to the stream. When they halted for nooning, the corporal assigned to commissary duties asked if water should be boiled for
coffee. Easterwood shook his head, and ordered the corporal to
issue a dried-beef ration. "As each trooper goes by, inform him
that he is to eat while watering his horse."

He took his share of the beef and walked down to the creek to
eat alone. Speckled trout were darting in the clear stream. He
filled his canteen, then watched the fish for a minute or so
before turning back to the trail. The girl was walking down
toward him. He met her halfway. "We'll be moving out in five
minutes," he said.

She looked directly into his face, and he was aware for the
first time of how blue her eyes were, a deep intense blue like the
October sky that morning. "Do you hate *everybody,* Captain
Easterwood?"

"No," he said, "not everybody."

He walked on, leaving her there, her blue eyes widening a
little. One of the men was bringing the Palouse up from the
watering place. Easterwood took the bridle, checked the saddle,
and then inspected each hoof carefully. He nodded to Lieutenant Bridges. "Form your column, Lieutenant."

As they marched on into the afternoon, the cedar-studded
sandstone ridge across the creek began growing higher, but on
their left the land flowed away, like an ocean after a storm, in
heavy rolling waves of browned grass. The sky was losing its
blueness under a wafting yellow scud, but the sun burned
through surprisingly hot after the chilly morning.

About midafternoon they halted again for water alongside a
thicket of willows. Easterwood ordered the water casks filled
and dead willow wood gathered and piled in the ambulance for
future cooking fires. "This is the last wood and water we'll see
this day," he told Bridges. "We're taking the pass through Med-

icine Range. Not enough grass up there for game to draw Indians."

Resuming march, he led the column away from the trail and the telegraph line. He had been watching the line carefully but thus far had seen no signs of a break; if the Indians had cut the wires they must have done it farther eastward. By late afternoon they were into a seldom-used pass across Medicine Range, following the bed of a dry creek. Grass, water, and trees had disappeared, and when they halted on the plateau they were on rough ground covered with dingy green sagebrush. There was not even a scrub bush for hitching mounts or mules.

Lieutenant Bridges was surprised when Easterwood ordered a halt for night bivouac; the young officer made no comment but his face showed his disapproval. Easterwood glanced at him briefly, his eyes going beyond him, studying the rugged unfriendly land around them. "Because it's the last place any cavalryman in his right mind would pick for a camp," he said. "No Indian would come up here unless he was looking for something special."

"I haven't seen Indian sign all day, sir."

"You didn't look hard enough, Mr. Bridges. At least two small parties were in signaling distance this morning."

Bridges opened his mouth, but Easterwood cut him off: "We'll have to race the dark with our cooking fires. Caution the men to use only dry willow wood to keep them smokeless as possible, and they must all be extinguished before sundown. Mounts to be picketed and hobbled securely. We'll fasten the mules to the ambulance wheels."

As soon as the coffee was hot and the salt pork crisp, they extinguished the fires. One heap of small coals was left alive for coffee in a narrow trench, and Easterwood and the lieutenant and the girl sat around it. Night had come suddenly. No stars showed through the thin overcast; the moon was barely discernible, yet it threw across the whole sky a pale light that was reflected to earth. Easterwood was watching the girl sipping coffee from a rust-rimmed quart cup.

"Captain Easterwood," she asked suddenly, "do you ever feel like singing?"

"I can't sing a note, miss."

"I like to sing," she said, "when I'm very happy or when I'm very sad and lonely. It's so quiet and still out here, I'd like to sing to break the loneliness."

Lieutenant Bridges spoke up gallantly: "I'd be pleased to hear you sing, Miss Alison."

She looked across the coals of the fire at Easterwood. "And the captain?"

"Sing if you like," he said.

She began singing an old Irish song:

> *"The gardener's son, as he stood by,*
> *Blossoms four did give to me;*
> *The pink, the rue, the violet blue,*
> *And the red, red rosy tree."*

As she sang she arose and walked slowly around the dying coals until she stood directly before Easterwood, and as she came to the end of the song her voice was like a whisper under the big milky sky. When she was finished, the lieutenant applauded, his handclaps sounding hollow and empty in the loneliness of the place.

She turned and smiled at Bridges. "Do you know 'My Love Is Like a Red, Red Rose,' Lieutenant?"

The young officer blushed and said that he knew the first lines, and she asked him to begin. "I'll join you in a duet," she said. Bridges had scarcely begun when the sound of wolves howling from far away broke across the stillness of the camp. Easterwood chuckled softly. The lieutenant stopped singing.

"Don't mind the captain," the girl said quickly. "Please continue, Lieutenant Bridges." She sat down beside Easterwood, the wind ruffling her yellow hair.

Stammering a little, the lieutenant began singing again, and the girl joined in softly. Some of the men had drifted up to stand as vague shadows in the background, listening. They were singing softly together when suddenly along the high range several miles to their east a bright flash of fire flared up, flickered and flared, and was gone.

As soon as Easterwood saw it, he felt the girl's fingers gripping suddenly into his forearm. "Just an Indian signal fire," he said, forcing reassurance into his voice. "Buffalo hunters, likely." But one of the troopers somewhere behind Bridges had spoken too, his voice drawling and disembodied from the darkness: "Like as not our names was writ in them flames, if you want my—"

Easterwood stood up on his long legs, his chin high, his hawk nose seeming to sniff the air. "Time for taps," he said. He ordered two of the men to prepare a place for the girl to sleep inside the ambulance, standing by while the soldiers removed the trunk and sacks of grain and let down the side seats. The four mules fastened to the ambulance wheels stood like dumb guards around the vehicle. "Good night, Miss Alison," he said, and walked down the slope to check the hobbles on his Palouse.

Easterwood lay flat on his back with his head against his saddle, his moccasined feet to the dead coals, staring at the shreds of clouds dimming the stars. His mind worried with the thought of the signal fire, then he dismissed it abruptly. One of the mules' chains rattled and was still. A chill wind moved soundlessly through the quiet camp. He rolled tighter in his blanket, but he could not sleep.

Perhaps it was the girl, Alison, he thought, that brought back the memories of Mellie. Mellie Sheffield. Mellie Sheffield Quill. He had dammed all those memories up somewhere back in his mind, but now they came racing again. Those last months of the war in Virginia. The old Sheffield plantation in the valley where the Union officers were quartered. And Mellie. The little dark-haired spitfire. Strange, how this yellow-haired girl reminded him of her . . . this yellow-haired girl he had to see safely through to Goldfield with her trunk of wedding clothes so she could marry Lee Bowdring, the man said to be backing Quill . . . Matt Quill . . . He remembered the first day he'd seen Quill, riding across the big lawn before Sheffield Manor there in the Virginia valley. Quill, with his long hair flying. Quill, the dashing cavalry leader, the Yankee *beau sabreur* with his picture in the New York weeklies.

Propping himself on one elbow, Easterwood pulled his saddlebag closer, rummaging far down into the bottom of it until his fingers touched a tiny metal box. He withdrew the box, knowing without seeing that there were green corrosive stains of time on the metal. He could not remember how long it had been since he had opened it. Working at the catch with his thumbnail, he pried the lid back. A small oval-shaped daguerreotype portrait lay on faded velvet. In the reflected moonlight he could barely see the face, but in memory he saw it clearly, a young woman smiling, the eyes challenging and daring, the lips full. He could hear her singing like the girl, Alison, "My Love Is Like a Red, Red Rose."

He wanted to fling the picture away from him, far down the slope, but instead snapped the case shut, tossing it back toward the open saddlebag. He missed, and the metal box clinked against a stone, but he let it lie there, drawing his blanket around his shoulders. Like the signal fire on the distant range, he could shut Mellie Quill out of his mind until another time.

He prepared now for sleep by sorting out the sounds around him—the occasional movements of the animals, the cough of one of the guards, the faraway cry of a wolf. He was drifting slowly into the sweetness of sleep when the big sound came suddenly, a rattling and wrenching of wood, a half-human grunting cry, and then the girl's high terrified scream.

Before the scream died, Easterwood was on his feet, flinging his blanket away, his carbine at ready. The black shadow of the ambulance reared at a crazy angle against the sky. By the time he came around to the end of the vehicle, Alison Stuart was already outside, a wraithlike figure in a white nightdress. She flung herself upon him, her arms tight around his neck, and her face pressed close against his cheek. "It's nothing but the mules, miss," he said awkwardly. "They must be restless." He had to force her arms from around his neck. She was shivering from cold and fear.

The sergeant-of-the-guard had come up on the run, and just behind him was Lieutenant Bridges. "One of the buggers crawled under the ambulance and got caught," the sergeant called out.

"We'll lengthen the tie ropes," Easterwood replied. The girl still held to his arm while he fumbled inside the ambulance for her buffalo robe. He flung the robe over her shoulders. "There's a little warmth left in that fire. Get over there while we take care of the mules." His voice was as stern as if he were giving a command to a troop.

Only by vigorous prodding from a stick was the sergeant able to free the stubborn mule from beneath the ambulance, and then the vehicle would have been overturned had Easterwood and the lieutenant not held it steady with their shoulders. Using trace chains for extensions, they paid out the ropes to give the animals more freedom of movement.

As soon as the job was done, Easterwood went back to his blanket. The girl was there, huddled in the robe. He could see her pale face, her eyes big and dark-looking in the strange night light.

"I've never known a man like you," she said softly.

"I'm sorry about the mules, miss," he began awkwardly. "They're unpredictable animals."

"And I'm sorry because you saw me afraid. You don't know what it means to be afraid, do you?"

"A man wouldn't live long out here, miss, if he didn't know the meaning of fear. And how to respect it."

She rose, tightening the buffalo robe around her, shaking her head slowly. "Yet you always seem to be sure of yourself, Captain."

He was going to defend himself, but instead said: "You'd better get back to bed. The mules shouldn't upset you again."

She turned, a slight, almost secretive smile on her lips, and started walking toward the ambulance; then she stopped, holding one foot uplifted and suppressing a cry of pain. For the first time he noticed that she was barefooted.

"If you were at all gallant, Captain Easterwood," she said cheerfully, "you would escort me properly to my quarters."

He moved forward, sweeping her up in his arms as he would a child. He could feel her lips breathing against his ear, and she was laughing almost soundlessly as he carried her across the rocky ground to the rear of the ambulance. He helped her inside, and said gently: "Good night."

"Good night, Captain Easterwood," she whispered.

One of the mules braying awakened Easterwood. The hazy sky was beginning to gray with morning. He rolled out of his blankets into air that was dry and quite cold; ice was filmed over the water in the cask beside last night's fire. He whistled up the commissary corporal and told him to get a smokeless fire going. Then he walked down the slope and with one boot toe nudged Lieutenant Bridges awake.

The young officer sat up quickly, his boyish face swollen from sleep. "Anything wrong, sir?"

"Have the men ready to march in half an hour," Easterwood

said. He turned and walked back to the ambulance, rapping his knuckles against its side until he heard the girl's voice.

Coffee was boiling by the time she came outside. Easterwood glanced up briefly in response to her "Good morning," then turned back to stare at her. She was wearing a short buckskin coat and a pair of men's mustard-brown Kentucky jeans, and as she came over to the fire to warm her hands she returned his stare boldly. "I'm going to ride one of the mules today," she announced.

Easterwood, rolling his blanket, was slow in making a reply. This seemed to annoy her, and she added forcefully: "It isn't at all civil to keep me cooped up in that uncomfortable old ambulance!"

"All right," he said mildly. "You can ride my Appaloosa this morning. We'll be going downhill on a rough trail. I can walk as fast as we'll move that ambulance."

They ate hurriedly in the cold and were started before the sun came up to burn away the haze. The trail was jagged and boulder-filled, gashed with deep gullies, and in one place became so precipitous they were forced to halt and lock the ambulance wheels together with ropes. On Easterwood's orders, Alison Stuart kept to the rear of the file, letting the Palouse pick his way down. The captain, on foot, stayed several paces ahead of the platoon, carefully searching the best route.

After eight hours, they had covered only ten miles, but they were out of the high country by then, in a grove of giant cottonwoods with luxuriant grass all around. Easterwood ordered a halt for nooning alongside a clear shallow creek bottomed with black and white pebbles.

He took his ration of hard bread and dried beef to the stream's edge, the lieutenant and the girl joining him there. "I'll be needing the Palouse this afternoon," he said. "We've got a lot of ground to cover before dark. And I don't think you'd better try mule riding."

She smiled. "After my jogging ride down the mountain, the inside of that old ambulance won't be so bad."

"I'm glad you feel that way." He noticed that she wasn't eating the meat. "Army fare is not very tasteful, is it, miss?"

"I suppose I'm just not hungry."

"We may have fresh buffalo for supper. If Lieutenant Bridges is a good shot."

"I'd be pleased to have a try, sir," the lieutenant said eagerly. "Are there herds in here?"

"Should be one somewhere up ahead. Take a look through your field glass off to the right of that rise."

Bridges focused his glass. "I see only one animal, sir."

"That's an old cayak. Herd should be somewhere about."

The girl asked to have a look through the glass. "He's old and grizzly and looks as if he would taste tougher than this army beef. Why do you call him a cayak?"

Easterwood's lips twisted in a slight grin. He explained that a cayak was an old bull that had been chased out of a herd by the young bucks and was never allowed to enter the group again. "If you see just one cayak, that means a herd is somewhere near. If you see several, they may be wandering around together for company away from any herd. Cayaks are not only outcasts of their own kind, they're also despised by men—who won't even waste a shot on them because their flesh is too tough to eat."

She held the field glass up again, peering at the dark speck on the lonely horizon. "How unfortunate," she said, turning her blue eyes half closed to Easterwood. "Did you ever know anyone, Captain, who reminded you of a cayak?"

Lieutenant Bridges laughed, caught himself, and then laughed again as Easterwood joined him. Alison's face did not change expression, and her blue eyes, opening wider, were as innocent as a child's.

"I've known several human cayaks, miss." Easterwood was still smiling, but after glancing at the sun he added quickly: "Better get the men moving, Lieutenant. We'll march in ten minutes."

Bridges leaned out over the water, filling his canteen, and then turned and walked rapidly downstream toward the shady spot where the troopers were resting. Easterwood stood up, stretching his long arms. "Excuse me, miss, I'd better go check my saddle."

"Just a minute, Captain." He saw that she was rising, and offered his hand. "I have something," she said, "which I'm certain must belong to you." She pulled a small metal box from one of the pockets of the brown jeans she was wearing. Easterwood recognized it immediately, the case containing Mellie

Quill's daguerreotype portrait. He stammered a reply: "I must have dropped it from my saddlebag."

"I found it last night and forgot to give it to you." As she handed the case to him, she gave him a cool sidewise glance: "An old friend, Captain?"

"Yes," he said, "a sort of memento of friendship."

"You were in love with her of course?"

"I couldn't say, miss."

"She married someone else, didn't she?"

"I don't believe the matter would interest you, Miss Alison." For a moment he faced her directly, then turned as if to walk toward his horse.

"But it does interest me, Captain," she replied sweetly. "I'm sure I know the lady."

He swung around on her, his face dark with sudden anger. "My personal affairs should not concern you, miss, any more than your personal affairs concern me."

"If I have bruised your feelings, I apologize." She smiled, almost contritely, but Easterwood's jaw tightened. He turned his back on her then, digging his moccasined feet into the sand as he moved away from her. Lieutenant Bridges was seated on his horse beside the ambulance. "Shall I give the order to mount, sir?" Bridges called.

"Mount!" Easterwood cried.

The platoon was mounted, but Lieutenant Bridges could not give the march order until the girl came up from the creek. While they were waiting, Easterwood edged his Palouse over beside the lieutenant. "Did you see the signal smokes this morning, Mister Bridges?"

"I saw one, sir. Along the farther range."

"You're learning, Mr. Bridges. There were at least three smokes. Sioux or Cheyenne in there. We'll know before tonight, I expect."

"Could it be a buffalo hunt, sir?"

"Could be."

That afternoon the column moved rapidly across the smooth grassy flow of the bottomland, heading straight for a butte at the end of Medicine Range. Around three o'clock Easterwood noticed the grass was cropped close, and there was a scattering of fresh buffalo dung. He told the lieutenant to take a Sharps rifle and move off beyond the out-riding sergeant on the left flank. "You might find some kind of a herd in this bunch grass. If you do, aim for a cow or a big calf. Keep within signaling distance of the flanker, and should you see Indians, come in fast. If and when I hear your fire, we'll halt and wait for you."

Less than an hour later, the sound of rifle fire brought the platoon to a halt. Three or four more shots followed in rapid succession, not all from the same rifle. The column was down in a grass-filled draw with a treeless slope to the left, shutting off visibility at about four hundred yards, and the flank-rider had disappeared.

For a minute, Easterwood sat motionless; then he turned and trotted his horse back to the ambulance. Alison Stuart had stepped outside when the ambulance halted, and she stood beside one of the rear wheels, looking questioningly at him. "Get back inside, miss," he said quietly. She made no move, but he was not watching her; he was half twisted in his saddle, listening to faint grass-muffled hoofbeats. A moment later, Lieutenant Bridges and the out-riding sergeant burst over the rim of the slope; they were coming at full gallop, the lieutenant waving and slapping his hat against his leg.

Easterwood shouted an order to the platoon: "Dismount and prepare to fight on foot!" He yelled at the muleskinner, and the trooper slid off his saddle and began unhitching the mules. The men had the ambulance turned over on its side before the lieutenant galloped up, his face drawn and white.

"How many?" Easterwood asked.

Bridges shook his head. "Not sure. More than us anyway." He was breathing hard.

About twenty Indians were coming down the slope, dancing their ponies sidewise. They seemed to be in no hurry, but were yelling and whooping. "Like a bunch of crazy birds," the muleskinner said.

Easterwood had grouped the sixteen troopers around and behind the ambulance. He noticed the girl close beside him then, and handed her his revolver. "Don't fire unless I fire first." He was fishing cartridges out of his belt, laying them in a row along the upturned side of the ambulance. "I'll take the Sharps, Mister Bridges," he said, reaching for the rifle.

"I got off one shot at this buffalo cow," the lieutenant was explaining. "Then the Indians came up out of nowhere."

"Oglala hunting party. Did they shoot at you?"

"I think so."

"You spoiled their hunt." Easterwood took a quick glance at Bridges; the young officer's face was still pale with sweat beads forming on his forehead and upper lip.

The Indians were angling in closer, spreading out as if planning to ring the ambulance. "If they swing too far to either flank, I'll give them a warning shot," Easterwood said, loud enough for all the men to hear him. One of the Indians took a lead over the others, darting in so close he could have been hit with a revolver shot. He was naked. A lariat bridle was knotted around the lower jaw of his mustang.

Easterwood stepped clear of the ambulance cover. *"Kola!* Friend of Lakota," he shouted. *"Ota-ku-ye!* Oglala brother!" He made the brother sign, touching two fingers to his lips and swinging his hand straight out from his mouth.

The young Indian gathered his horse, his dark face solemn, with not even an eyelid flicking; he sat there with his moccasins dangling, staring at Easterwood. His hunting party was drawn up in a semicircle behind him. They had stopped their chattering.

With a quick gesture, an upflung arm, the warrior leader danced his horse again, and the hunting party broke into motion, resuming their derisive whoops. They began racing their horses back and forth along the slope, and then suddenly they began firing.

They were too far away now for accuracy of aim, but Easterwood pushed the girl down behind the ambulance. He watched the nervous troopers, warning them quietly: "Hold your fire!"

In a moment the rattling gunfire stopped abruptly, the hunting party galloping away toward the east.

"Well, that's a relief," the lieutenant whispered hoarsely, and rubbed his sleeve across his forehead.

"Take a look on the ridge, Mr. Bridges," Easterwood said.

The entire rim of the leftward slope was covered with Indians, a long line strung out for half a mile. The center of the line moved forward slowly, then a group of four horsemen detached themselves and came rapidly down the slope. Easterwood's eyes narrowed to a squint as he watched them approach, their shadows long behind them in the late afternoon sunlight. One was a

chief with a warbonnet of eagle feathers trailing over the flanks
of his horse.

Once again Easterwood stepped around in front of the ambulance, the Sharps rifle raised in both hands high above his head.
He dropped the weapon lightly on the ground, walking forward
unarmed to meet the four Indians.

They had halted, and the chief dismounted. He was old, fat-
tening with age, and his legs bowed under him. But he held
himself erect and proud in the splendid finery of his warbonnet
with its long trail of coup feathers.

"It is good to look once again upon the face of my brother,
Spotted Wolf," Easterwood said.

Spotted Wolf came forward with an offering stick, a peeled
and painted wand ornamented with quill and beadwork. He
made the sign for brother, his dark leathery face wrinkling with
pleasure. "Spotted Wolf's heart is glad," he said, "to see his
white brother, Tall Man, come back in the country of the
Oglala."

"The young warriors of the Oglala have welcomed Tall Man
with arrows and fire-sticks. Why is this so?"

Spotted Wolf spread his hands. "This is Young Elk's doing.
He is young and hungry for power. He is bad for my young
men. When Tall Man's soldiers shoot buffalo, Young Elk become angry. All the young men are restless for the hunts, but
the buffalo are become as few as raindrops in the moons of
summer."

"It is so." Easterwood bowed his head. "Had it not been for
Tall Man's soldiers, Young Elk would have brought buffalo to
camp this day."

The chief shrugged. "There is meat of the antelope in plenty
among the lodges of Spotted Wolf's people. Tall Man and his
blue-coat soldiers will feast with the Oglalas before the large
stars of evening are in the sky."

Easterwood was looking along the line of Indians still drawn
up on the ridgetop. The late sunshine brightened the varicol-
ored dress of the warriors and the sleek coats of their mustangs.
Somewhere beyond the roll of the land would be Young Elk and
his hostile band of hunters.

"How far to the the camp of the Oglalas?" he asked.

"A good pony could race there without blowing spittle."

"Then Tall Man and his soldiers will make camp with the Oglalas."

Spotted Wolf's eyes lighted suddenly. He was looking beyond Easterwood to the ambulance. "It is strange," he said, "that Tall Man's bluecoats march with a woman and a wounded-soldier wagon."

Easterwood hesitated only the fraction of a second before replying: "It is Tall Man's woman who rides in the wounded-soldier wagon."

"He-he-he! So Tall Man has taken woman at last," The old chief laughed deep in his throat. "Come, let us ride as brothers to the lodges of my people."

The sun was setting when the little cavalry column, following the dusty trail of Spotted Wolf's warriors, first sighted the enormous ellipse of tipis that was the Sioux camp. The camp was spread along the shining waters of a creek, and smoke from a hundred cooking fires spun away in spirals into a grove of tall cottonwoods beyond. The Indians galloped in ahead, their quick short whoops mingling with the barking of many dogs.

Easterwood dropped back from his position with the chief to halt his troopers on a knoll a hundred yards from the nearest line of tipis. Along one side of the slope the grass was thick, shading into a deep green where it joined the stream. "We camp here," he said to the lieutenant.

Alison had come up behind them as they dismounted. "Surely you don't intend to stay here, Captain? Bring a white woman into a camp of Indians who wouldn't hesitate to scalp us all?"

Easterwood looked calmly down at her. "We'll be safer here as guests of Spotted Wolf than out there somewhere with Young Elk and his bucks on the prowl." He hesitated a moment. "I'm going to need your help, miss."

She stood with her hands on her hips, her trousered legs apart, her yellow hair tousled in the wind that had come with the twilight. "I wonder what Colonel Mathew Quill would say if he should hear of—"

He cut her off: "Colonel Quill likely will never hear from any of us, miss, if we leave this place before our horses are fresh enough to make a fast run for Goldfield." He turned to Bridges. "Lieutenant, see to your men. I'll want the sergeant to go with

me as soon as the horses are watered and picketed. Leave my
horse and two others saddled."

As the lieutenant walked away, Easterwood unfastened the
yellow scarf from around his neck and mopped the dust from
his face. "Miss Alison, had I known how mightily stirred up the
tribes are back here. I would have questioned the order to escort you to Goldfield. Colonel Quill must have known the danger, but being Quill he wouldn't have admitted there was danger."

Her face turned grave. "You said you needed my help. What
can I do?"

"For your safety and the safety of my men," he said bluntly,
"I'm asking you to pretend that you're my squaw." He added
quickly: "For the evening only."

Her blue eyes brightened with sudden merriment. *"Squaw,*
indeed? Have you lived with them so long you must use their
words?" She laughed, almost with relief. "You need not look so
embarrassed, Captain."

He slapped one of his gauntlets against his leg. "On the ride
in, Spotted Wolf invited me to supper in his lodge. I could not
refuse him, and I would not leave you here alone. I told him
you were my—"

"Squaw," she finished, her soft lips curving into a teasing
smile.

"Spotted Wolf knows white man customs, that their women
dine with them."

She seemed amused by his discomposure. "I promise you I'll
do my best to follow your wishes, Captain. And don't look at
me as if you thought having me for a squaw would be such an
ordeal."

He felt his face burning. *At least I've got her mind off the
danger,* he thought.

The sergeant was bringing the horses back from the creek.
"We'll ride up to Spotted Wolf's lodge as soon as you are ready,
miss."

Easterwood led the way through a patch of skunkbush and
sumac into the fringes of the Indian camp, the girl and the
sergeant close behind. As they approached the first ring of tipis
the dogs came swarming, and a frightened child scurried in
front of their horses, disappearing through the flap of the nearest lodge. The child's eyes peered out at them from the gloom.

On the left, inside a corral of rawhide strips strung around four trees, was a small horse herd. Two of the animals carried the U.S. brand, each with a small 12 C marking below. Easterwood remembered that detachments from the Twelfth Regiment were in the Goldfield area, probably now would be at the fort on the Yellowhorse. Quill's mounts. He turned his horse completely around the corral. No more cavalry horses were there, but a grounded saddle against one of the tree trunks bore a 12 B marking. Troop B. The leather looked fresh from burnishing.

He swung back toward the center of the camp until he saw Spotted Wolf's tall tipi painted in broad horizontal stripes of alternate black and white. On one side were several black crosses upon a white ground; on the other a wolf was emerging from a mysterious circular black hole. Spotted Wolf was waiting at the entrance beside the pole where his shield and coupstick hung.

The three riders dismounted, the sergeant taking the horses' reins while Easterwood and the girl approached the chief. Easterwood called out in a bantering tone: "I see few buffalo skins in the camp of the Oglalas. Can it be the buffalo are so few, or do the mountain Crows guard them too well?"

"Eyayo!" Spotted Wolf slapped his hands together. "The mountain Crows are too lazy to tie their own moccasins. Tall Man knows the buffalo become scarcer with each passing moon. He knows the mountain Crows are old women and could not keep Spotted Wolf's people from the hunts."

"That is so," replied Easterwood.

The old chief's eyes, fixed on the girl, were narrowing in their deep sockets. He folded his arms. "Tall Man's woman is like the morning," he said, smiling until his face was a network of wrinkles. "Her hair is the yellow of morning." Easterwood stole a quick glance at Alison. She met his look for a second, then turned away. "Among our people," Spotted Wolf continued, "is told the story of a woman with hair the yellow of morning." He looked at the girl and then at Easterwood's Appaloosa standing with ears erect. "In this story the man has many blue horses and oxen with horns of gold."

"I have one blue horse but no oxen with horns of gold," Easterwood said.

"Ha-ey-e-ya!" the old chief cried. "One blue horse and a woman with hair the yellow of morning."

From the open flap of the tipi the odor of fresh meat drifted, tantalizing in the cool evening air. "Ah-h, while we talk, Tall Man's bluecoat soldiers wait in hunger." He spoke loudly in Sioux, and a young boy brought out from the chief's tipi a freshly skinned antelope. It was soon fastened on the sergeant's horse, behind the saddle, and Easterwood signaled the soldier to carry it back to the cavalry camp.

Like all ceremonial Indian feasts, the one in Spotted Wolf's lodge was drawn out with endless ritual, the smoking of pipes, and symbolic language. Until the feasting was done, neither Easterwood nor the chief would bring up any subject which might embarrass the other. The two men and the girl sat cross-legged before the glowing coals of the cooking fire, eating roasted antelope from wooden bowls that had been scoured white in sand. The meat was sweet and juicy under its burned crust.

As the meal came to an end, Easterwood decided the time had come to speak of the cavalry mounts and the saddle he had seen in the corral at the edge of the camp. He raised himself to his haunches, rocking forward, and began: "Spotted Wolf has feasted his guests well. He has been good to Tall Man and his yellow-haired woman. But Tall Man is sad because of *wowakta,* a bad sign he saw in the camp of the Oglalas."

Across the fire, the chief's eyes narrowed. His tongue licked at the meat juices on his chin. His reply was cautious. "Tall Man does not speak in words Spotted Wolf can understand."

"In the camp of Spotted Wolf's people are horses of the Great Father's pony-soldiers." Easterwood's voice grew suddenly sterner: "Perhaps there are also fresh scalps." He stood up, and as he did so he helped the girl to her feet.

The chief remained seated working his lips over his teeth and gums. His eyes were fixed on the fire. "Spotted Wolf's heart is heavy with the words of his friend, Tall Man. There are no bluecoat soldier scalps in the lodges of the Oglala." He stood up, his bowed legs wide apart, then slashed the air with one hand. "This bad thing was done because of Killer-of-Horses. The soldier-chief Quill. He is at the fort on the Yellowhorse, only four sleeps toward the sun's rising place."

"I have heard of this," Easterwood interrupted.

"Not so many moons have passed since Killer-of-Horses and the Great Father's tall-hat men promise the Oglalas on piece of paper they go and leave sacred hunting grounds and Yellowhorse fort forever. But now they are everywhere again, like the *hoponkadans,* the gnats in the sore-eye moon. Killer-of-Horses has broken the white man's promise. He brings much trouble."

"The trouble will be greater," Easterwood said, "because of the soldier horses and saddles among the Oglala lodges."

The chief spread his hands. "My young men are angry. They are angry, remembering the horses taken and killed by Killer-of-Horses. Five sleeps ago they find pony-soldiers resting along big yellow river. So many horses they see, and the soldier watchers are sleepy and lazy. 'Look, there are many horses!' my young men cry. 'These are of the bad soldier-chief, Killer-of-Horses, who slew a thousand horses of the Oglalas. Let us take some of these horses. It is only fair that we take some of Killer-of-Horses' fine soldier ponies!' So my young men rode in swiftly like the wind. Maybe they shoot at one or two pony-soldiers, but they take no scalps. They want only horses this time."

Easterwood folded his arms. Through the smokehole in the tipi's top center he could see a sprinkle of stars in the night sky. "When the hunting is done and it is time to return to the reservation, what will Spotted Wolf's young men do with these soldier horses? Soon will come the deer-rutting moon and the Oglala must return as they promised the white agent. What will the white agent say when he sees the stolen horses?"

The old chief bowed his head slightly, and in the firelight the crisscross lines of his dark leathery face deepened as he replied sadly: "Spotted Wolf will keep his promise and return to the reservation in the first days of the deer-rutting moon. But only the old men and the women and children will follow Spotted Wolf. The young men will follow Young Elk, and they will fight the bluecoats in the fort on the Yellowhorse."

"Truly this will be a bad thing for the Oglalas," Easterwood said, and turned his back, indicating that the conversation was ended. He touched the girl's arms, walking with her to the entrance flap of the tipi, then turned and declared harshly: "Tonight Tall Man makes his camp beside the Oglalas. When the sun rises, the stolen horses of the pony-soldiers must be in Tall

Man's camp. He will take them back to Horse-Killer and try to stop this big trouble."

With Alison beside him, he stepped outside into the smoky air of the Sioux camp. In an open space beyond the first row of tipis, a huge fire was burning. Some women and girls were dancing there, formed in an ellipse facing one another, their elongated shadows moving against the screen of cottonwoods. Their faces were painted red and they wore many feathers in their hair. An old man was slowly shaking a tambourine, and the chanting of the women came faintly against the night breeze: *Eh-ah, ah-eh. Eh-eh, eh-eh, eh-eh.*

Suddenly from beside the chief's lodgepole a tall shadow emerged into the light of the campfire. Young Elk was standing there, challenging them with his eyes, his lips parted slightly. His face was vermilioned. His hair was freshly combed, his stiff topknot stood straight up, and a long braid of false hair was hanging to his knees. A looped necklace of beads covered his neck and chest. He had changed his old hunting moccasins for a pair of fine black ones.

Easterwood and the girl passed beyond the young warrior until their own shadows moved before them on the trampled buffalo grass. He could feel her fingers tight against his arm, and then she spoke in a whisper: "I don't trust any of them, Captain. The old chief may be your friend, but what can he do if Young Elk decides to challenge his power?"

"We're safer here until daylight."

She drew away from him, shaking her yellow hair. "You're a stubborn-hearted man, Captain Easterwood. Do you truly believe that a thousand savages will surrender those stolen cavalry horses to you and your handful of soldiers."

He shrugged, and his silence annoyed her. "Whether you know it or not, sir, you've turned Indian yourself!"

As they came up to their picketed horses, he took her arm to help her into the saddle, but she shook away from him and mounted alone. They rode down between the rows of darkened tipis, with packs of dogs barking at the horses' heels, the girl keeping a few paces ahead of him. When they came in sight of the cavalry camp, she widened the distance, racing her mount through the dew-wet sumac, her hair yellow in the starlight.

* * *

Easterwood came awake with the sergeant-of-the-guard calling his name. He sat up, shaking drowsiness away. Frost was on his blanket, and the air was sharp with cold.

"Early morning visitors, sir," the sergeant said.

Easterwood got into his moccasins and shirt and pulled his carbine from under the blanket. The dawn was a thick misty gray, but across the patch of skunkweed and sumac he could see the two stolen cavalry ponies. Both were saddled, and a young Indian boy was holding them. A tall warrior stood off to one side, motionless.

"The boy asked for the soldier-chief," the sergeant explained.

"Wake the lieutenant and the men," Easterwood replied, and started walking slowly down the grassy slope and through the wet brush. He was close enough now to recognize the warrior as Young Elk. The Indian boy said something in Sioux, and when Easterwood took the bridles, the boy turned and ran back toward the first line of tipis. Ignoring Young Elk's presence, Easterwood turned back to the cavalry camp; the troopers were already out of their blankets and a cooking fire was going.

Easterwood strode directly up to the ambulance, rapping on the side. The girl appeared almost immediately, her hair tousled. She had slept in her clothing, and was tugging at her rumpled shirt.

"You can ride outside with us today, miss," he said. "And one good cavalry mount to spare."

She had already noticed the returned horses. "So you were right as usual, Captain. My apologies for what I said last night." She brushed at her hair with her fingers. "I must look a sight."

He smiled at her and said softly: "Like the morning. Like the yellow of morning." He swung away from her, calling one of the troopers: "Double-check the saddles on these mounts, Corporal."

Ten minutes later the column was moving. Easterwood took one look back at the waking Sioux camp. The dogs were beginning to bark, and two children were racing one another around the patch of sumac. Young Elk had vanished.

All morning they followed an old military wagon road across an eroded badlands, but by afternoon they were in grassy country again, the trail following a small willow-bordered stream.

Easterwood kept four men well out on the flanks, and as usual he rode several yards ahead of the little column, setting a rapid pace. Alison Stuart rode alongside Lieutenant Bridges on one of the recovered cavalry mounts; the other horse was tied to the rear of the ambulance.

Late in the afternoon they entered the last rugged country between them and Goldfield, a series of short ridges and isolated moundlike formations, most of which were covered with thin grass, scattered pines, and outcroppings of rock. At one point the road ran between two of these gentle-sloped hills, and as Easterwood approached, he signaled the flankers to ride all the way to the summits. The two troopers on the left had scarcely started up the slope when a signal smoke flashed suddenly from the rocks above them. The smoke billowed for a moment, then was followed by two smaller puffs.

Easterwood had his revolver out, firing it in the air until the left flankers heard the reports. Signaling the two men to return to the column, he swung his horse around and galloped back toward Lieutenant Bridges. As he rode, he was watching the two troopers climbing the ridge on the right.

Bridges had brought the column to a full stop, and had his carbine out of its boot. "Ambush, Captain?" he asked.

"Might be." Easterwood was still watching the outriders on the right. "They've been on our tail all day."

"Young Elk?"

"Probably."

The two left flankers came trotting down to report. "See anything?" Easterwood called.

"No, sir," one of them replied. "Nothing but the smoke."

Easterwood jerked his hat off, spinning it over his head in a signal to the two men above them on the right. One of the troopers responded by riding rapidly back down the slope; the man's horse stumbled and slid in loose gravel, then came upright again. Easterwood slapped his Palouse forward to meet him. "All clear up there?" he asked.

"Yes, sir, up there it is. But a war party's on that north slope!"

Easterwood turned and shouted to the lieutenant: "Mister Bridges! March the column up this slope! All the way to the top. Double march time, if you can."

"What about the ambulance?" Bridges shouted back.

"If it'll roll, bring it!"

The going was rough in several places, but the mules got the ambulance up the rise. From the summit the thin line of the Yellowhorse River could be seen stretching up from the south toward Goldfield. Behind them, in the west, the sun was almost level with the horizon; there was no sign of life on the trail which they had come.

Easterwood placed the troopers along the crest in battle formation, facing the north slope from where the smoke signals had risen a few minutes ago. Then, with his field glass, he began studying the line of broken hills to the south. After a moment he slid the glass back into its case and turned to the lieutenant and the girl.

"We could stay here and fight," he said. "But I don't think we'd last beyond another daylight. Our best chance is to make a run for Goldfield."

"That many?" Bridges asked.

"Too many. What about it, Miss Alison?"

"How far is it to Goldfield?"

"With luck, maybe three hours. It'll be dark in one."

"Let's run for Goldfield," the girl said.

Bridges nodded toward the north slope. "What about the ones over there?"

Easterwood took a deep breath. "If I'm a good guesser, they're only a small scouting party. "That's why they signaled instead of attacking."

"They must be confident they've got us," the lieutenant said.

"You can't figure what's in an Indian's mind, Mister Bridges. Have your men drop all their gear except arms and ammunition. Cut loose the mules and put the skinner on that spare mount." Easterwood walked over to the girl's horse and checked the saddle girth carefully. Then he moved on to the Palouse. He left his small saddlebag attached, but dropped his blanket and poncho to the ground.

Before he could mount, the girl was at his side. "Must we leave my trunk here, Captain? It has my wedding things in it."

"I'm sorry, miss, but we can't run with the ambulance."

She looked crushed, her voice pleading: "After bringing it all the way from San Francisco, after spending a fortune on the most expensive laces and silks in California— At least, let me take my wedding dress."

"We've stayed too long already, miss."

He stood tall in front of her, shaking his head. Her mouth was open for a final protest, but he cut her off: "Perhaps Mr. Lee Bowdring will fetch your trunk for you tomorrow." He swept her up in his arms, carried her quickly over to her horse, and lifted her not too gently into the saddle.

Bridges already had the men mounted and ready. On a wave from Easterwood he shouted the forward command, and they swept down the hill in dust and flying gravel, heading for the wagon road. Easterwood kept to the rear. He looked back once; the mules had followed for a short distance, but they were already slowing to nibble at patches of grass.

As they entered the road, rifle fire rattled behind them from the north slope. A few Indians showed themselves, but there was no pursuit. Easterwood urged the Palouse forward until he could see the girl's yellow hair flying; she was midway up the column. She rode as if she were in a race, slapping her bridle violently. He let the Palouse run then until he was alongside her, gave her a reassuring smile, and pulled away until he was up with Lieutenant Bridges at the head of the column.

"Trot march, Lieutenant," he shouted. "We can't go like this for three hours."

With alternate galloping and trotting, and an occasional short walk, they covered four or five miles before darkness. They halted then on a low rise, dismounting but standing ready beside their horses. Far behind them they could see the dim shadows of the hills on each side of the short pass. A bright fire was beginning to burn on the southern hill.

Lieutenant Bridges fixed his field glass on the spot of orange flame. "They're burning the ambulance, sir."

Easterwood nodded. "That little celebration should keep them off our heels."

The girl came up out of the darkness. "Are you all right, miss?" he asked.

"I would like to have my wedding dress," she replied, looking away from him.

"That wedding finery wouldn't do you much good, Miss Alison, if you were back there now."

In another minute they were riding again, trotting and walking, trotting and walking, until at last the flickering lights of

Goldfield lay before them. They rode into the town slowly, horses and men weary from tension and spent muscles.

Goldfield was one long street of false-front saloons and supply stores catering to miners, soldiers, and occasional cowboys. It ran straight to the flat bank of the Yellowhorse, where the army's storehouses and barracks stood in neat military rows facing the river. The horses' hoofs stirred the dust in the street, and idlers along the wooden sidewalks stopped to stare in sudden curiosity at this troop appearing abruptly out of the night.

Piano music jangled from one of the buildings; yellow lanterns lighted the wooden sign above its open door:

TROOPERS REST

Adjoining it was Goldfield's largest hotel, a two-story frame with ascending wooden steps—the El Dorado.

Easterwood was suddenly aware that one of the horses had left the column; he saw the rider's yellow hair and knew it was the girl. He pulled the Palouse out of file and moved over beside her.

"I shall be leaving you here, Captain," she said, looking at the lighted hotel entrance.

"My orders are to escort you to army headquarters, miss."

"My father and Mr. Bowdring will be staying here at the El Dorado." They were at the hitching rail, and she was already dismounting. He walked with her up the steps. "You need not trouble yourself," she said, moving ahead of his offered arm.

A mustached clerk, seated in the entranceway, was reading a newspaper. He wore bright pink sleeve-holders; he stared for a moment at the girl's dust-covered shirt and trousers before getting to his feet. "Is Mr. Baird Stuart or Mr. Lee Bowdring here?" she demanded.

"They're both here, ma'am—why you must be Mr. Stuart's daughter, he was—"

"Will you call one of them?" Her manner had become icily formal.

"Mr. Bowdring is in the bar, I believe, ma'am, only be just a minute—" He disappeared quickly through the nearest curtained doorway, and reappeared less than a minute later with a large man dressed in a neat black suit and a starched white shirt

which looked as if it had just come from a laundry. Bowdring
was a handsome man, clean-shaven, and Easterwood noticed
that although his hands were soft he was muscular and powerful of build. The kiss he gave Alison Stuart was an audible one,
and he kept one of his arms possessively about her shoulders.
"We weren't expecting you until tomorrow," he said in a boom-
ing Texas voice. "Your father has already gone up to bed."

"My own father sleeping soundly and you gambling light-
heartedly, while I was almost getting scalped not ten miles from
here." She looked as if she were going to cry.

Bowdring smiled and patted her shoulder gently. "We had
full confidence in the United States Cavalry." He reached out to
shake Easterwood's hand. "It's a pleasure, Captain." He was
examining Easterwood's fringed shirt and worn moccasins as
critically as the hotel clerk had examined the girl's clothing.

"The name's Easterwood," he said, and felt Bowdring's soft-
skinned hand gripping his powerfully. .

"A most dreadful thing," Alison interrupted, "happened to
my trunk of wedding clothes." She turned to face Easterwood,
and he wondered if her blue eyes were blaming him. "My San
Francisco wedding dress—all my French silks and laces—oh,
Lee—"

"We had to ditch it," Easterwood said to Bowdring.
"Couldn't be helped." He put his hat on, stepping backward
toward the door.

"Never mind," Bowdring said soothingly to the girl.

The big Texan was still comforting her when Easterwood
slipped out through the curtains. As he went down the hotel
steps, he could not recall either the girl or Bowdring thanking
him. Perhaps Colonel Quill would receive later whatever ex-
pressions of gratitude the Stuarts and Bowdring might have to
offer the army.

He overtook Lieutenant Bridges and the men as they were
entering the post gate, and rode with them to the headquarters
building. Quill had already retired for the evening; the officer on
duty summoned a sergeant to assign quarters and direct the
men to the stables.

"We'll put you in with the professor, sir," the sergeant said to
Easterwood. "He's been expecting you."

"The professor?"

"Professor Greenslade. Third hut down officers' row, across the way."

Easterwood wondered mildly who Professor Greenslade might be, but he was too weary to ask questions. He took up his saddlebag and walked across the hardpacked strip of ground to the long flat-roofed log building that was officers' row. The door was closed, but through the tiny uncurtained window he could see a smoking oil lamp hanging from a rafter. He knocked, and heard a hoarse voice: "Come in!"

The door was stuck so that he had to force it with his knee. A round-faced, spectacled little man with a white goatee sat at a small unpainted table, facing him. What hair the man had was white, curling in ringlets over his ears and the back of his woolen shirt collar. He had a pile of oversized paper sheets in front of him.

"My name's Tom Easterwood. They said I was to bed here tonight."

"Yes, yes, come in, come in. I'm Professor Asahel Greenslade. I've been waiting for you." His voice was a hoarse whisper. He was on his feet, but had to look upward to see Easterwood's face. "They told me you were a tall one."

Easterwood dropped his saddlebag on the floor. "Which bunk is mine?"

"Take either one. I say, sir, you look like a man who's been running from something."

"I was." He frowned down at the professor. "Maybe I still am."

3

Easterwood was awake and dressing when reveille sounded from the parade. The night wind off the Yellowhorse had filled the tiny room with a damp chill, and the professor was rolled into a ball of blankets in the opposite bunk.

Deciding not to wake him, Easterwood slipped quietly across to the door in his moccasins. But he could not budge the door without force; the wood squeaked loudly and the professor came up out of the blankets, his eyes blinking while he fumbled for his spectacles.

"Sorry to disturb you, Professor."

"Not at all, Captain, not at all. We have a great many things to discuss this morning." His short fat legs covered with woolen underdrawers slid out of the covers to the floor.

"I'm afraid that what you have to say, sir, must wait until after I report to Colonel Quill." Easterwood jammed on his dusty hat, ducking his head to avoid bumping the top of the door framing.

"Yes, of course. Of course." Professor Greenslade sighed. "Military matters must come first. We shall talk later."

As Easterwood started toward Quill's headquarters, the trumpeter began blowing stable call. Through the river mists drifting across the parade he could see cavalrymen moving around the blacksmith and wagon repair shops; the familiar smell of horse was strong in the heavy air. The depot had been enlarged since he had last seen it. Below the permanent quarters was a new row of low wooden sheds where would be stored the supplies being gathered by Colonel Quill—arms, ammunition, food, clothing, and farrier equipage. And beyond these storage buildings long rows of new "A" tents, extending to the bend of the river, indicated recent increases in the troop strength of the command.

Returning the sentry's salute, Easterwood entered Quill's headquarters. He had no taste for this meeting; the sooner he could give his report and receive his new assignment the better. He wondered how long the colonel would keep him cooling his heels in the ante-room; that was a favorite trick of Quill's. But the colonel was not in, and the duty sergeant was not certain when he would be in. "He left a message for Major Johnson that if he was not back by eight o'clock, the major is to command at troop call."

"Do you know where the colonel is?"

"No, sir. But his orderly might know. He's sitting over there, sir."

Quill's orderly was dressed in a forage cap and a faded sack coat which bore corporal's chevrons on the sleeves. He was a man in his late thirties, with a lean dark-skinned face, long pointed ears, and a black down-curving mustache. His pale blue eyes were cold and expressionless. He had been cleaning his fingernails with a knife, and when he saw Easterwood looking at him he took his time before standing to attention.

Easterwood moved toward him. "You're Bratt Fanshawe!" He frowned at the chevrons.

"You seem surprised, Captain."

"Never expected to see you in uniform, that's all."

Fanshawe spread his long-fingered hands. "Times are bad everywhere, sir."

"For army scouts?"

"For *civilian* army scouts."

Easterwood dropped the informality; he didn't like the way the conversation was going. "I'd like to see the colonel. Right away. Do you know where he is?"

Fanshawe showed his white teeth in a humorless grin. "The colonel had an early caller. Mr. Lee Bowdring came by in his

carriage. I would guess the colonel is being treated to breakfast
at the El Dorado Hotel."

"Thanks, Fanshawe." Easterwood turned and went outside.
He walked around the post, waiting for mess call, puzzling over
Bratt Fanshawe's being in uniform. Fanshawe had been Quill's
favorite civilian scout since the colonel's first years in the West.
He had once been a professional gambler, and Easterwood recalled that women in the towns around army posts had always
seemed to have a weakness for the man. With the troopers,
Fanshawe had been almost as unpopular as Quill, but the men
in the field had learned to respect the scout's fearlessness, a
fearlessness that never edged into recklessness. Long ago, Easterwood had sized up Fanshawe as an amoral man with a
strange code of morality buried somewhere in him. Why he had
given up his enviable status as an independent civilian scout for
a noncommissioned officer's uniform was a mystery. Easterwood doubted that it would have happened in any command
other than Matt Quill's.

The trumpeter's call broke into his thoughts, and he walked
slowly on to breakfast in the log building used for officers' mess.
Ten men were seated at the single long table, Major Johnson,
three captains, and six lieutenants. One of the lieutenants was
Bridges, who seemed relieved to see him come in; Easterwood
took the vacant chair adjoining. From former campaigns, he
knew Major Johnson and one of the captains, a red-haired
Irishman named McGonigal, but the others were all strangers.

After the formalities of introduction, he ate in silence until
Bridges asked him if there were any orders concerning the platoon from Sun River.

"I haven't seen the colonel yet. But I'd advise you to get your
horses shod today. I'll see if I can arrange for a scout who
knows the country to accompany your outfit back to Sun River.
It might be touchy getting back through that bee's nest of
Sioux."

Bridges' boyish face colored slightly. "I'm sure I could make
it back, sir. But I could use a good scout of course."

After the breakfast ended and cigars were lighted, the officers
grew more talkative. By careful listening and by asking an occasional question, Easterwood soon learned that Colonel Quill
had returned during the past week from an inspection trip to
Fort Yellowhorse, that his living quarters there had been com-

pleted, and that his wife was already there. At present the fort
was garrisoned by two reduced companies who were occupied
in rebuilding the stockade and erecting temporary winter quarters. The three hundred cavalrymen in the Goldfield post were
expecting orders at any time to march to the fort. And there
were strong rumors that a reinforcing battalion would soon be
on its way up from Fort Laramie.

Easterwood was disappointed when Major Johnson arose,
ending the meal and the discussion. He would have liked to
hear what Quill's officers thought of the rebuilding of Fort Yellowhorse. But not one of them had expressed an opinion—an
indication that it was an unpopular subject.

As he came out of the mess room, Easterwood saw a fancy
carriage leaving the front of Quill's headquarters. The vehicle
wheeled sharply toward the gate, but he recognized the driver,
Lee Bowdring, wearing a large cattleman's hat. And beside him
in a bright blue dress was Alison Stuart, a feathered bonnet
perched precariously on her yellow hair.

They were gone in a flash, but the incident left Easterwood
with a feeling of sudden depression. He tried to shake it off.
Facing Quill, he thought, was enough to disquiet any man.

Quill kept him waiting only twenty minutes, and as soon as
Easterwood entered the small office he was carried back into
time and memory by the neat oak desk with its collection of
arrowheads, and the framed wall portraits of Abraham Lincoln
and Ulysses Grant that had followed Quill everywhere on the
frontier. The smells of chocolate and pomade were also familiar; Easterwood had long ago learned to associate them with
this man who was greeting him now with a tight smile and
extended hand.

They exchanged the usual meaningless pleasantries of men
meeting after long separation. "How is Mellie?" Easterwood
asked. Quill gave him a queer searching look before replying. "I
left her well. She's at the fort. Our new quarters have just been
finished."

Quill had crossed the forty-year mark, but he had changed
little in the past two years. His curly reddish hair was thinner,
his added stoutness made him appear shorter, and his clipped
mustache was too red under its obvious coat of dye.

"Sit down, Easterwood. I want to know about that trouble
with Spotted Wolf's band."

Easterwood sat down in the hickory chair facing Quill, won-dering how much the colonel had learned from Bowdring and the girl. "The trouble was of Young Elk's making, sir. Spotted Wolf will do what he can to take his people back to the reserva-tion."

"You seem to have acted rather hastily in sacrificing the am-bulance. No doubt you are aware that it costs the army one hundred and fifty dollars to replace an ambulance. Almost a month's pay for a captain."

Easterwood felt his anger rising, but he fought it down, press-ing his moccasins tight against the floor. "I considered the lives of the men and my civilian charge worth more than an ambu-lance, sir."

"Quite so, quite so. I might as well tell you I've already talked with Miss Alison Stuart. She was rather concerned by some of your actions and decisions during this escort." He smiled a tight humorless smile. "The young lady was quite dis-tressed over the loss of her trunk. Cost her a dollar a pound shipping charges from San Francisco. Not to mention the value of the contents."

Easterwood met Quill's eyes. "I was aware of all this, sir. But in the position we were in, there was no other decision I could make."

Quill leaned back, gazing at the wall beyond Easterwood for at least a minute in silence. "Very well." His voice was almost genial, then it changed to craftiness: "Now, what about this business of taking the platoon and Miss Stuart into the hostiles' village and making camp with them?"

Restraining an impatient oath, Easterwood came to his feet. In the tiny room he towered above the colonel sprawling behind the desk. "Again that was a decision I had to make, sir. The choice was between the demonstrated friendship of Spotted Wolf and the open enmity of Young Elk."

"In my opinion," Quill interrupted, "you had little to choose between, there. But you may explain."

Easterwood related the incident of the buffalo hunt, the armed demonstration by Young Elk's hunting party, and the friendly arrival of Spotted Wolf. He told of his visit to the chief's lodge, of his discovery of the stolen cavalry horses, and of his demand for their return.

"Spotted Wolf's braves stole those horses off my men last

week when I was en route to Fort Yellowhorse." Quill's voice rose to an angry shout: "You should have placed the old scoundrel under military arrest!" When Easterwood made no reply, the colonel continued: "You've gone soft on the savages, living up there amongst 'em on Frenchman's Creek. I'll wager you picked out a plump young squaw for a blanket mate, eh?"

Easterwood ignored these side remarks. "If my opinion is worth anything, sir, the horses were stolen by Young Elk's followers. Spotted Wolf returned them to me and they're back here in the stables now."

Quill was toying with one of the arrowheads on his desk. "As you see it, Captain, Young Elk is about to become the new leader of the Oglalas?"

"I'll put it bluntly. If Fort Yellowhorse is rebuilt and garrisoned, Young Elk will lead the Sioux to war."

The colonel's tongue licked at the edge of his dyed mustache. "He'll have his war then. The fort is practically rebuilt now. It'll be garrisoned before this week is out. And if the Oglalas are not back on the reservation by the first day of November I'll take the field against them."

Easterwood thrust his hands into the pockets of his fringed jacket. It was all out in the open now, the cards on the table. Quill, Bowdring, and probably Baird Stuart wanted this fight. Quill wanted it for glory, Bowdring and Stuart for the hunting grounds to be converted into cattle range.

Quill was rummaging in the top drawer of his desk. "Care for a chocolate, Captain?"

He shook his head. Quill sucked at the candy, and then said mildly: "I suppose you're wanting to know what your assignment is to be here."

"Yes, sir."

"First, I want it understood that I had nothing to do with the orders bringing you to this command. The whole thing was arranged by what passes for brains back east in the States." He licked at the chocolate on his lips. "Washington headquarters is so far away from practicality, its actions sometimes make a man feel like resigning and ducking out of the whole blasted mess."

Easterwood had heard Quill's opinion of high army administration before, and he waited in silence.

Quill continued: "I suppose you've talked with Professor Greenslade already?"

"Only briefly. He said something about my working with him
to gather weather data for the Signal Service. I've always
thought of this weather record-keeping as being sergeant's
work."

Quill motioned for him to sit down again. "Oh, but this is
different, Captain." There was sarcasm in his voice. He paused
to lick the last of the chocolate from his fingers. "Surely the
professor told you about his balloon?"

"No, sir." Easterwood tried to conceal his surprise with a
frown.

"Yes, sir, a balloon. Shipped all the way out here from Virginia. With three wagons of supplies. Of course I'm supposed to
man all this fancy equipment from my understrength battalion." Quill banged his desk suddenly with his fist. "A god-
damned balloon, Easterwood, when what I most desperately
need is a battery of four serviceable field guns. If I had four
little howitzers, just four little howitzers with twenty battery-
men, I could put down any uprising of the tribes on the whole
western frontier."

"I dare say you could, sir," Easterwood replied dryly. "But
we have the balloon. And what are we supposed to do with it?"

"Blow it up so far as I'm concerned." Quill laughed, ending
up in a nervous titter.

Easterwood leaned forward. "One question, sir. In regard to
this Signal Service assignment—exactly what is my status?"

"You have no status, sir. You have no command duties."
Quill grinned at him "And here's some news you can pass on to
the professor. The orders say these silly balloon observations
are to be carried out at my headquarters. As of tomorrow, my
headquarters are being transferred to Fort Yellowhorse. I'm
starting one of the squadrons early tomorrow, the other to follow as soon as sufficient winter quarters can be erected. March
orders will be going out to troop commanders this morning. I
shall be in command of course."

"I see." Easterwood rubbed his chin slowly with one knuckle.
"Is the balloon equipment to go to the fort?"

"Exactly. The march will require three days. It will be your
duty to get the balloon and its wagons out there with the column."

Easterwood wanted the question of authority settled; he remembered the months he spent in the Balloon Corps during the

Civil War when there was never any certainty as to whether civilian or military personnel was in command. The result had been utter confusion, which hindered operations and finally ended the usefulness of the corps. "Sir, are the balloon operations to be directed by Professor Greenslade or by me?"

Quill shrugged. He appeared to have lost all interest in the subject. "The orders don't state. But since you know nothing about this matter, I suppose you'll have to listen to Professor Greenslade. But you will have military authority."

Easterwood stood up. "There's one more thing, sir. The escort troop from Sun River. The lieutenant is a good officer but inexperienced. He'll need a seasoned scout for the return march."

"Don't concern yourself, Captain. The escort troop won't be going back. I'm attaching the platoon to my battalion, and if Omaha headquarters approves my request, the Sun River force will soon be joining me at Fort Yellowhorse."

"I see, sir."

Quill's vacant gaze had changed to a hard stare, his eyes moving from the captain's moccasins up to the beaded buckskin shirt and its faded shoulder straps. He said coldly: "Get yourself into proper uniform, Captain. You're not at Frenchman's Creek now. In this command, we wear sky-blue and mustard."

"Yes, sir." Easterwood stood at attention and saluted. Then he turned on his heel and moved rapidly across to the closed door. As his hand touched the catch, Quill's high voice suddenly filled the room: "Is it true, Captain, that you carry about with you a portrait of my wife?"

Easterwood felt his stomach draw into a knot as he turned to look in astonishment at the colonel. But he did not reply. Any reply would have been drowned out in the burst of high, almost hysterical laughter that came from Quill. Easterwood could still hear the laughter, even after he had closed the door behind him and walked out past the sergeant-major's desk into the bright October sunshine.

4

When Easterwood returned to the quarters he shared with Professor Greenslade he found the little man seated at the writing desk surrounded by a muddle of ruled-paper sheets. "Ah, there you are, Captain." The professor pushed his spectacles back on his forehead, looking like a fat, cheerful gnome. He pulled at his white goatee, transferring to it some of the ink from his fingers.

"So I'm back in the Balloon Corps," Easterwood said.

The professor smiled. "In a way, yes. But this time we use the balloons to benefit humanity, not to fight a war."

"Then why did you pick on a hardbitten old cavalryman?"

"Because the chief signal officer told me himself—when I was in Washington—that you were the only officer in the territory who had balloon experience. I trust the change in duties won't be too unpleasant for you, Captain."

Easterwood sat down on one of the bunks. The interview with Quill had left a dull bitterness in him, and he felt physically exhausted. "I'd like to know more about my duties and responsibilities, Professor."

Greenslade nodded sympathetically. "How long since you have been back in the States, Captain?"

Easterwood had to count the years off mentally. "Almost eight years. A long time."

"Then you wouldn't know much about the weather reports

and bulletins the Signal Service prepares for the more settled regions of the country." He began rummaging among the mountain of papers. "I have a memorandum which I was told to hand you explaining your part in the observation work out here—it should answer some of your questions." Easterwood took the yellow paper and began reading it:

> The duties now developed upon the service are, besides the instructions in military signaling and telegraphy to conduct the observation and report of storms. 159 stations of observation have been maintained at military posts during the past year, and the deductions made from the information reported by them has brought gratifying results. A careful analysis of the reports and a comparison with the weather changes afterward occurring within the time and district to which each has had reference, has given an average percentage of 86.16 as verified. An average of 90 per cent is believed to be attainable. The wide diffusion of the reports may be judged by the fact that they appear in almost all the daily newspapers of the country, and no great storm has swept over any considerable part of the U. S. without pre-announcement.

"It's all very interesting," Easterwood said, "and a revelation to a frontier cavalry officer who isn't too interested in the weather except when in the field where weather reports could not reach him. But just how does the balloon fit into all this?"

"Ah!" The professor nodded, his eyes sparkling. "We are going to try something new out here. It is my belief and the chief signal officer supports me in it, that if we can make observations in the very high air currents we may be able to predict weather more accurately over greater periods of time and space than we can with ground observation only."

"So we go up in the balloon. But why did you select this godforsaken wasteland out here for your observations? Why not back east?"

The professor nodded happily. "Because the prevailing air currents move from west to east. After making balloon observations in the Territory, we can telegraph Omaha a prediction of tomorrow's weather and perhaps Chicago a prediction of day after tomorrow's weather."

Eastwood smiled slightly at the enthusiasm of the little man.

"Nothing very military about all that, is there, Professor? I think I can understand why Colonel Quill hasn't been very cooperative with the Signal Service."

The professor thrust out his lips, frowning. "The colonel indeed, has been most uncooperative, but you and he are both wrong when you say there is nothing of military consequence in what we are doing. In warfare, weather is a most important element, and if we have the facilities to determine what the weather is going to be and the enemy does not, we have the advantage, do we not?"

"You have a point there, sir."

"And another thing—with our balloons we are learning much about aeronautics. The Balloon Corps in our recent Civil War was only the beginning of military aeronautics. Someday, possibly, wars may be fought in the air, Captain."

Easterwood grinned. "Possibly. But I prefer to do my soldiering no higher than a horse's back."

The professor had been pacing up and down behind the desk, emphasizing his words with gestures. He stopped suddenly and spread his plump hands. "Forgive me, Captain, for lecturing you like a schoolboy. Shall we go now and have a look at our equipment? It is still stored on the boat, you know. The colonel has not seen fit to have it unloaded."

Easterwood got up off the bunk. "I have some news for you, Professor. I just came from the colonel's office. We'll have to get the stuff unloaded today. Not only that, we're responsible for seeing that it is ready to transport overland to Fort Yellowhorse early tomorrow morning."

"But I understood we were to do our work here at Goldfield. Where is this fort?"

"Three days' march south. The colonel is moving his headquarters there."

"Ah, more delays, more delays." He shook his head sadly. "And how shall we get our supplies? Perhaps now you understand, Captain, why the Signal Service considered it necessary to obtain an experienced officer for this work?"

"I believe I do, sir." Easterwood put on his hat, remembering as he felt the dusty crown Quill's orders to obtain a regulation uniform. "Sky blue and mustard," he mumbled.

"What did you say, Captain?"

"Nothing important. Let's go inspect the balloon. You know, it's been ten years since I've even seen one."

As they walked down the slope from the parade, the muddy Yellowhorse lay before them, shining like fluid gold under the bright light of the noon sun. Although the military supply post was at the highest point of navigation, the river's sources lay many miles southward, the stream gradually narrowing and shallowing until it passed the fort named for it, and then split into several feeder branches which drained the heart of the sacred hunting grounds of the Sioux.

"That river would put weak coffee to shame by its color," Greenslade remarked. They were approaching the embankment where the steamer *Starlight* was moored. Along the loading platform lay stacks of buffalo hides covered with myriads of flies, the stench almost overpowering.

They went aboard, the professor leading the way to the three balloon wagons. They were partially covered with canvas, and were securely lashed and blocked against the deck. Easterwood rolled one flap of canvas back and read the fresh paint lettering on the first wagon's side SIGNAL SERVICE. FORT WHIPPLE, VIRGINIA. "The gas generator wagon, isn't it? This takes me back. Where were you stationed during the war, Professor?"

"They sent me west as a civilian aeronaut to Cairo, Illinois, in '62. The cooperation I received there was about the same as I've received here. I could never persuade the quartermaster to requisition sufficient iron filings and sulphuric acid to generate gas, so I never got off the ground."

Easterwood laughed. "The same old story. If it wouldn't shoot, the commanders had no use for it. We had our troubles along the Potomac, too. Somebody rigged up a balloon boat, but everytime we'd go down river to make observations, the weather would cloud up and rain. One day, when the sun finally came out and we made an ascent, the Confederate batteries opened up with everything they had on us. We spotted their placements, all right, but they damn near scared us to death. We let all the gas out coming down, and when we moved to a quieter sector, we couldn't go up again. Somebody had forgot to load on acid." He rolled the canvas back over the wagon. "Do these three wagons include all the equipment?"

"Everything. The balloon envelope is brand new Wamsutta muslin, better than the India silk we used in the old days. A rattan basket for two men, good supply of cordage and rigging, pulleys, ballast bags, extra valves and shutters."

"How about gas-generating materials?"

"That's our weak spot. Only eight barrels of iron filings and twenty carboys of sulphuric acid."

"As I remember, enough for about two inflations."

"Yes, maybe two weeks of observations, if we're lucky and have no storms. The quartermaster's contract boats will be bringing filings and acid up regularly from St. Louis, but what good will they be to us if we're three days' overland from Goldfield?"

Easterwood shook his head. "I can't answer that one." He gazed out at the muddy river. "Our immediate problem is to move these wagons off the boat, rustle up a dozen mules, and persuade the adjutant to assign us some men."

"You are sure you could not persuade Colonel Quill to change his mind and let us stay here to do our work?"

"Anything I might say, Professor, would only reinforce the colonel's desire to move us to the fort. Possibly as a civilian you might have some influence."

"But you are dubious."

"Yes, sir."

From the post above them came the short merry call of the trumpeter, sounding noon mess. "Let's go and put some army rations under our belts, and then you can see the colonel."

Quill was present at the midday mess. He nodded to Easterwood and greeted Professor Greenslade with such unusual affableness that the professor made the mistake of immediately asking him why he and Captain Easterwood could not remain at Goldfield to make the balloon ascensions. Quill's reaction was instantaneous: "As a civilian employed by the army, sir, you should learn first of all not to question decisions made by the military command."

Patiently Greenslade explained the problem of generating gas, the necessity for continual replacement of heavy barrels of iron filings and containers of acid.

"The Signal Service should have considered such problems when they planned this foolish experiment," said Quill. "The army is engaged in fighting a war of survival out here, sir, and cannot be concerned with informing farmers back east what their weather is going to be. Your orders assigned you to my headquarters, and after today my headquarters will be Fort Yellowhorse." He picked up his knife and fork, indicating that the subject was closed.

That afternoon was a busy one for Easterwood. He persuaded the adjutant to assign him the services of Lieutenant Bridges' platoon for purposes of moving the three balloon wagons ashore, greasing the axles, and putting them into condition for the overland march. Mules being in good supply, he found no difficulty in obtaining twelve from the quartermaster to be used in pulling the wagons, but his request for six troopers to serve as muledrivers was turned down when the adjutant consulted Quill. The colonel granted him only two men, which meant that he and the professor would have to share the driving of one of the wagons. Easterwood also managed to find time late in the day to pick up a new officer's coat, and a pair of boots. After his familiar old buckskin jacket and moccasins, the new uniform seemed tight and uncomfortable.

There was no time for fitting the coat, and as soon as the storekeeper had sewed on the shoulder straps Easterwood hurried over to headquarters where the sergeant-major had a stack of papers waiting for him. By the time he had filled out his last estimate form and signed the last requisition statement, the post was busily preparing for retreat ceremonies.

As he had no command to form, he decided to go into town for the evening, He walked down to his quarters, and found the professor already there, noisily washing his face over a tin basin. Greenslade picked up a towel and rubbed his face until it was pink. "So everything is ready to march," he said, regarding Easterwood with one open eye. "Even a new soldier suit, eh?"

"Sky blue and mustard," Easterwood replied. "Are you a drinking man, Professor?"

Greenslade's little white goatee wagged slyly. "I must confess I partake of strong spirits on occasion, Captain."

"Then I'd be gratified to have you as companion for the evening, sir. In the glorious little town of Goldfield."

5

After walking up one side and down the other of Goldfield's only street, Easterwood chose the Troopers' Rest. "The food in the Hotel El Dorado might be better," he told the professor, "but I think we'll enjoy the company more in the Troopers' Rest."

As they entered the open double doors, warm air blew the smells of men and whiskey and cooking food into their faces. Oil lamps suspended from the ceiling glowed yellow through a haze of tobacco smoke. The place was only half filled with miners, teamsters, cowboys, and buffalo hunters; the soldiers from the post would be coming in later.

From somewhere in the rear a piano was playing in slow waltz time. Three or four waitresses were moving among the tables; they wore faded red circus-girl skirts and tights that looked as if the wearers had been melted and poured into them.

"Sin and corruption," said the professor, peering over the rims of his spectacles.

Easterwood led the way to the bar. "Set up a bottle of bourbon. Two glasses."

They drank and looked about the long room. A scrawny little man wearing a dirty apron came hurrying up from the gambling tables in the rear. "By God," he cried, thrusting out a stringy hand. "Tom Easterwood!"

"How've you been, Domino, you old rawhide." Easterwood slapped the little man on the back. "Professor Asahel Greenslade, Domino Ruark. Domino is my oldest and truest friend, a scoundrel nevertheless. One of the best scouts the army ever had, but he married a pretty little half-breed and she settled him down to running this honkytonk."

The professor, who had been watching one of the waitress girls, said: "I daresay this is much more delightful employment than pursuing the savage red man."

"In some ways," Domino replied, studying the professor's face. "You must be the gentleman just arrived on the *Starlight?*"

"The professor is an aeronaut," Easterwood explained. He poured a drink from the bottle for Domino. "He and I are going to fly a balloon for Colonel Quill's army."

"You don't say!" Domino downed the drink in one gulp. "I saw one of them things in Saint Louie back in '72. You wouldn't catch me floatin' around up there with the clouds, nosirree, bob. And if you ask old Domino, a balloon ain't a-goin' to do you boys much good if Horse-Killer Quill don't clear out of that fort and leave the tribes' huntin' grounds alone."

Easterwood nodded agreement.

"Yessirree," the former scout continued, "before snow flies they's goin' to be war dances in all the lodges between the Missouri and the Platte—if Quill don't get out of Yellowhorse."

The professor was peering sharply at Domino. "I was assured in Washington," he said, "that the Indians were all pacified in this Territory."

"They *was,*" Domino replied. "But they ain't now."

While they were sitting down at one of the tables near the end of the bar, two men entered the Troopers' Rest. The pair hesitated for a moment in the entrance, blinking in the light. Both wore dirty gray woolen shirts and trousers and their beards were several days old. They were big men, heavy of bone and flesh, their skins burned to a reddish brown from the sun, their faces, hands, and clothing stained with dust and perspiration.

One of them hitched his belt and came walking like a muscular cat toward the bar; he saw Domino Ruark then, and moved over to the table where the three men sat. "Hiya, Domino, you dried-up little muskrat."

Domino kept his seat. "Buffalo Charlie. I thought you and

your brother was workin' with the wood train down to the
fort."

Buffalo Charlie pinched his nose with two fingers and pre-
tended that he smelled a foul odor. "Pete and me, we quit. They
wanted to pay us with promises, besides that damn major down
there don't allow no whiskey drinkin' on the post."

"Thirst must've nigh killed you, Buffalo," said Domino.
"Last time you come in town to live off me and the Troopers'
Rest you drunk sixty-five dollars worth of whiskey while you
was eatin' sixteen dollars worth of grub. And still ain't paid
up."

Buffalo Charlie grinned, his large yellow teeth showing
through his stubble of beard. "You'll git your pay, Domino. Old
Charlie always squares up." He turned to beckon to his brother.
"Hey, Pete, over here." They sat down at the adjoining table.
When one of the waiter girls came up, Buffalo put his arm
about her waist, squeezing until she protested with a sharp out-
cry. "Ho, ho, ain't used to real men, are you, dovey? Bring us a
bottle of Injun whiskey."

Domino Ruark ignored the pair and began reminiscing with
Easterwood about old times, while Greenslade sipped at his
bourbon and watched the unfamiliar activities around him. The
piano player was pounding out a fast-time version of "Dixie,"
and some Texas cowboys across the room leaped up to dance
wildly with one of the girls, swinging her back and forth among
them.

While he talked, slow and rambling, Domino's blue eyes were
always alert, watching the boisterous action and noting every
newcomer entering the door. His eyes narrowed suddenly, and
he drawled: "Here comes a fellow you know, Easterwood. Bratt
Fanshawe."

Fanshawe was in a dress uniform which fitted him perfectly.
His moustache was waxed to fine sharp points. He stopped at
the bar, alone, staring at his narrow dark face in the tarnished
mirror, his long fingers drumming on the wooden bar top.

"He always was a dude," Domino said. "He still wears them
silver Mexican spurs he took off a dead Kiowa when we was
down there in Indian Territory with Quill."

"I spoke to him this morning," replied Easterwood. "What
puzzles me is Fanshawe being in uniform. When I knew him he
despised the men in the ranks."

Buffalo Charlie, who had been listening to the conversation, shifted his chair closer, a big grin breaking his face. "Ho, ho. So you don't know why Bratt Fanshawe is wearin' a blue suit, Captain? Then you must be the only man in the army don't know."

Domino scowled at the big man. "The story I heard was that Quill said he wouldn't be usin' no more civilian scouts. If a man wanted to scout for his army, he said, he'd have to wear a army outfit."

"Ho, ho!" Buffalo Charlie wiped the back of his hand across his mouth. "Fanshawe could've moved to another command, couldn't he? He didn't have to stay with Horse-Killer Quill, did he?"

Easterwood turned his head for the first time and looked squarely at Buffalo. "Suppose we ask Fanshawe why he joined up?"

Still grinning, the big man slapped his hand down hard on the table in front of Easterwood. "That's a good one, Captain. You don't think that lady-killer would tell *you*, do you?"

"Did he tell you?"

"Nah, he didn't tell nobody. But just you ask any soldier in Quill's command. I been down to the fort, Captain, I know. And every son-of-a-bitch down there knows the colonel's lady can hardly wait till Fanshawe comes back to give her some more lovin'!"

Domino coughed over his whiskey. Greenslade was staring curiously at Buffalo Charlie. Easterwood pushed his chair back slowly from the table. "Buffalo," he said coldly, "you just talked out of turn."

Buffalo Charlie rolled his head from side to side. "Maybe you thought Bratt Fanshawe put on a suit for love of his colonel. But everybody else knows it's the colonel's lady he couldn't stay away from."

Easterwood was on his feet; he could feel the whiskey running through his veins and an angry recklessness was in him that he had not known for many months. All the frustrations of the day had left his nerves raw, and now Buffalo Charlie's slur upon Mellie Quill was like a knife thrust into tender flesh.

Sensing Easterwood's anger, Buffalo came up at a half crouch, his heavy-set legs spread wide. The grin had gone from his face. "She ain't worth it, Captain!"

Easterwood's right arm swung in a straight punch, but Buffalo Charlie was quick and the blow only grazed his head. The big man sprang forward like a wildcat, his long powerful arms encircling Easterwood, the momentum carrying them against the table which collapsed with a splintering crash. Easterwood tried to roll with the fall, but Buffalo had him pinned, squeezing his ribs until he could barely breathe. Then with a sudden movement Buffalo slapped one of his hands against Easterwood's chin, forcing his head back.

Through a blur of pain, Easterwood could see the oil lamps in the ceiling; they seemed to be swinging in circles. For a moment, as in a spinning kaleidoscope, he saw the pale startled face of Professor Greenslade, then Domino Ruark, and Pete, Buffalo Charlie's brother. The Troopers' Rest was in a dead silence. He could hear the heavy breathing of his assailant, could smell the stale sweat and whiskey stench of the man.

For just a second, then, he felt Buffalo's legs relaxing as he put all his effort into the arm thrust. Easterwood brought his knees up suddenly, and Buffalo was off balance long enough for him to roll free and come to his feet.

The two men faced each other now across the shambles of the smashed table, ringed in by the crowd that individually began breaking the silence, partisans encouraging one or the other of them to battle. Easterwood realized he had underestimated Buffalo Charlie. The man's bulk belied his quickness of movement and his cunning, yet he was a dirty fighter and Easterwood guessed that he was no boxer. With his boot toe, Easterwood kicked a piece of the broken table to one side, at the same time moving in quickly. Buffalo was watching him from eyes that had gone bloodshot, his body rolling from side to side on his thick legs. As he came in range, Easterwood feinted with his right and landed a solid blow against the side of Buffalo's mouth. He howled, spitting blood, and sprang forward bull-like, his head low, both arms flailing. Side-stepping, Easterwood shot a solid right to the belly, following it up with a blow that rocked Buffalo backward into the other table. Buffalo hit the floor on his buttocks, his back against the upturned table top.

Unbuttoning his new coat, Easterwood started to slip out of it, but his eye caught a sudden movement from the right.

"Hold it, Pete," Domino Ruark said calmly. Domino had

brought a revolver out from under his apron, and Pete dropped back, glowering at Easterwood.

As he slid out of the tight coat, Easterwood saw Bratt Fanshawe looking at him. The corporal was the only customer still standing at the bar, his cold blue eyes disdainful of the scene, his lips contemptuous below the waxed mustache. Easterwood swore under his breath, angry with himself, his physical hatred against Buffalo Charlie ebbing away.

Buffalo Charlie, meanwhile, had risen on one knee, his eyes squinting malevolently at the tall man in front of him. Blood trickled from one corner of his mouth into his beard stubble. Easterwood moved closer, waiting for him to rise. Buffalo growled out an oath, and a second later he sprang upward.

One of the waitress girls was screaming. Domino Ruark's high voice was barking out a warning. Then Easterwood saw the whiskey bottle, flashing for an instant in sparkling reflections from the ceiling lamps. He dodged, but too late. The Troopers' Rest exploded into fireworks and stars and then he was spinning in a whirlpool of blue smoke and sound that took him down and down and down.

6

It was dark when Easterwood awoke, but he could hear sounds of muffled voices, occasional loud outcries, and the rattle of bit and trace chains. For a moment he thought he was in one of the back rooms of the Troopers' Rest, but when his fingers touched the familiar army blanket and he smelled the river, he knew that he was somewhere on the post.

He raised his head. A throbbing ache ran down into his spine, and he remembered the clenched bottle in Buffalo Charlie's hand. His fingers reached for the tender swelling on the back of his skull. Somebody had cleaned and dressed the wound.

As he swung his legs over the side of the bunk, he swayed slightly from dizziness. He was getting too old, he thought, for brawling in honkytonks like a drunken trooper, brawling over the colonel's lady, at that. Mellie and Fanshawe. Fanshawe the lady-killer with the long narrow saturnine face and the perpetual sneer of indifference. Easterwood's tongue felt thick and there was a bitter taste in his mouth. It was cold in the room and his teeth began chattering.

The voices from outside were shouts and commands, sounding from far down the parade. This was the morning of the march out for Fort Yellowhorse. He shook his head to clear the pain and dizziness, and began fumbling for his uniform. Somebody else was moving across the room. He heard a rasping noise, a light flared, and in a moment the oil lamp was burning. Professor Greenslade was standing under it in his long underwear, his head turned to one side, his sleep-swollen eyes peering sympathetically at Easterwood.

"The blackhearted scoundrel struck you with a bottle," he said indignantly.

"How'd I get here?"

"Your good friend Mr. Domino Ruark assisted in moving you here. I insisted on having a surgeon."

"Not the post surgeon?"

"Mr. Ruark thought that would be unwise. He dressed the wound himself."

Easterwood began pulling on his clothes. "I'm sorry for the trouble I caused you. I acted a fool."

"You defended yourself manfully, Captain, until your assailant took foul advantage of you. The reprobate is in the custody of Goldfield's marshal. I assume you will make a charge against him this morning."

Easterwood brushed at a dusty spot on his new coat. "I bear no grudge against Buffalo Charlie. By the time he wakes up, you and I will be on our way to Fort Yellowhorse. And I'd advise you, sir, to get into some clothes before the colonel's trumpeter blows boots-and-saddles."

Greenslade frowned. He looked more like a gnome than ever, standing there in his baggy underwear. "But you're in no condition for duty, Captain. You're pale as a ghost, man."

Easterwood squeezed into his boots. They felt tight after his old moccasins. "I'll be all right when I get moving." He stood up, fighting off the aching dizziness, and buttoned his coat. "You'll find me down by the stables. We'll get coffee later."

He went out into the cold dawn, breathing the damp river air. He could smell the horses and dust and hay, and felt much better, walking toward the twinkling lanterns and the familiar confusion of voices and commands that was a cavalry post at morning, preparing for a long march.

By the time the sun was up, orange-red in a bank of ragged clouds, the noisy commands and bustling activity had brought together a wagon train and two troops of cavalry. The train extended in a line along the length of the parade—a dozen corn wagons, wagons piled high with tent rolls and mess chests, supply wagons packed with boxes of ham, bacon, flour, beans, coffee, crushed sugar, vinegar, sperm candles, soap, molasses, dried peaches, desiccated vegetables, tea, and hard bread. There were two heavy ammunition wagons, a blacksmith wagon, an ambulance, and, bringing up the rear, the three balloon wagons.

Easterwood ordered the two troopers assigned to him as drivers to take over the two balloon supply wagons, and after he had hitched his saddled Appaloosa to the rear of the generator wagon he and the professor mounted the high overhanging seat. The generator wagon was the most vulnerable piece of equipment: extra care would be required in driving it across the rough trail to Fort Yellowhorse.

Greenslade sat with a woolen scarf drawn tight around his neck and over his ears, watching the sergeants galloping back and forth along the train. "A most impressive piece of organization," he said. "We seem to be equipped for a very long journey."

"Only a three days' march," Easterwood replied. "But judging from the supply wagons, we're going to stay a while."

The two cavalry companies were wheeling into formation on the parade, and to Easterwood's practiced eye it was evident that both were at full strength, forming a squadron of at least one hundred and fifty men. These were Quill's show troops, Troop A being mounted on chestnuts, Troop B on bays, and the horses' coats shone like satin in the first rays of the sun. Breath from their nostrils squirted in jets of steam against the frosty air.

He saw Quill, wearing a white sun helmet and a blue cape, taking his position in front of headquarters facing the squadron. The sergeants began barking commands; reports to the captains followed in rapid succession. Quill returned the final salute, and wheeled his horse.

Three mounted civilians were riding slowly toward the colonel from the post gate. Alison Stuart was in the center of the group, her yellow hair flowing under a tiny blue hat. She was wearing a leather jacket with a furred collar, and black velveteen trousers. On her left was Lee Bowdring. On the other side was her father, Baird Stuart, in a white linen duster. Easterwood had met Stuart some years before. The rancher's hair and beard had been long and black then; they were snow-white now, and he sat his horse like a king on parade.

Along the side of the train, the wagonmaster came at a rapid trot. Behind him was Lieutenant Bridges, leading the platoon from Sun River. "Move your wagons in closer, sir?" the wagonmaster called respectfully.

"Good morning, Captain." Lieutenant Bridges gave Easterwood a quick salute, his teeth flashing in a grin. "It seems we're marching together again. My platoon is assigned to flank the wagons."

"Then you'll eat alkali dust all day," Easterwood replied. He nodded toward the head of the column. "Our pretty little yellow-haired charge seems to have deserted us for the colonel's company."

Bridges grinned again. "I'd say that was mighty poor judgment on her part," he said.

The trumpeters began blaring ready calls, and Bridges ordered his men into position beside their mounts. Up ahead, officers were moving toward the front; guidons were raised. Commands echoed through the ranks. On the call to mount, the troopers as one man rose into their saddles. Quill's high voice came faintly down the parade. A drum began beating, and a small brass band in front of headquarters broke into "The Girl I Left Behind Me."

As there were no wives on the supply base, only a scattered group of post workmen and a few men in forage uniforms watched them march out. There were no fluttering handkerchiefs or tears of farewell; no one applauded or cheered.

In spite of this unceremonious departure, Easterwood felt his emotions stirred by the march out. He had ridden out of posts and forts hundreds of times like this, but each time was like the first time. A tingling thrill of pride ran through him when he heard the reverberating hoofbeats, the familiar farewell music, the creaking of saddle leather, the rattle and clinking of metalwork and chains. At no other time was he so conscious of the smells of leather and horse, of dust and sweated wool. Once a march was underway he rarely noticed the guidons, but at the start he was always aware of the swallow-tailed pennants fluttering proudly in early morning sunlight.

This morning he was unhorsed, sitting on a high wooden seat behind four mules, his head throbbing from a barroom brawl, serving under a colonel he despised. Yet he felt the same sense of dignity and pride in his chosen calling that he had always felt

on marching forth into the unknown that lay beyond the far
horizons. A man could endure much, he thought, to gain the
rare moments of keen satisfaction this hard life provided.

They marched for an hour under the climbing sun, following
the telegraph line that cut straight away from the river, the
cavalry column alternating from gallop to canter to walk, keeping well ahead of the wagons.

During the early part of the afternoon the column marched
through a succession of rugged hills, entering then a long ravine
that was the bed of a dry creek leading into Arrowhead Valley.
From his knowledge of this part of the Territory, Easterwood
guessed that Quill was planning to make his night bivouac
along one of the clear streams near Arrowhead Pass.

The evening meal was late that day, for Quill always dined in
style even when in the field. A canvas shelter, a folding mess
table, campstools, and tripods to support washbasins, all had to
be assembled in front of his command tent.

Quill, the two troop captains, a lieutenant serving as adjutant, the Stuarts, Bowdring, Greenslade, and Easterwood
formed the dining party at the table. Quill and Bowdring did
most of the talking during the meal. But after they had finished
eating, and cigars were passed around to the men, Baird Stuart
joined in the talk.

Easterwood sat drawn back in the shadows, watching the
girl's face in the flickering lights from the campfire. She seemed
lost in some sort of reverie, and obviously was paying no attention either to her father or the pointless stories which Lee Bowdring interjected at convenient moments. Easterwood wondered
what he saw in Bowdring. A man who seemed sure and confident of his power, a man who was handsome, a man who
dressed well?

Although the campstool was uncomfortable, he sat there silent and motionless, fascinated by the girl's face in the firelight.
He was startled when he heard the trumpeter sounding taps; the
time had passed like a fleeting dream.

He stood beside the canvas fly, waiting for Professor Greenslade who was still talking with Baird Stuart and Bowdring.
After exchanging their good-night farewells, the officers began

moving off to their tents, and then before Easterwood realized it, the girl was standing beside him in the shadow of the canvas.

"Good night, miss," he stammered.

"Captain Easterwood," she said, "you haven't spoken a word to me all evening. You remind me of one of your cayak buffaloes, self-exiled from the herd."

Greenslade came shuffling across the sand. "Ah, there you are, Captain—and Miss Stuart. Good night to you, Miss Stuart."

"Good night, Professor," she said, and leaned closer to Easterwood so that he could see her eyes dancing. She whispered: "Pleasant dreams, Captain Easterwood."

After the slight shower, the wind blowing from the pines across the creek smelled rich and resinous. Easterwood stood for a long time in front of the tent flap, listening to the faraway breeze in the pines and watching the bivouac fires twinkling against the purple night.

7

A few hours later Easterwood stepped out of his tent into a morning that was surprisingly balmy for mid-October. The wind still blew strong from the south; the dawn sky was metallic, almost colorless, the air murky with dust and smoke. As he stood fastening his cartridge belt, he looked out across the awakening cavalry camp, watching the men crawling out of blankets and canvas shelters into a clutter of field gear. Uniforms were rumpled, hair unkempt. All the spit-and-polish of a cavalry outfit, he thought, vanishes during the first night bivouac. But he had never ceased being amazed by the rapidity with which the slovenliness of reveille could be brought into marching order—cooking fires scattered, debris buried, gear assembled, the slouching men transformed to attentive troopers.

Already officers were shouting orders: "Get in your herd, sergeant!" Saddle blankets were swinging in signals for the guards to come in. From the grazing area down by the creek, guards were driving in some of the horses; they came at a gallop, manes and tails streaming in the wind. These were mounts of the bay troop, and when their riders ran out with bridles to meet and check them, the spirited lead horses settled on their haunches, plowing into the sand.

Easterwood walked over to the balloon wagons, and was pleased to find the two drivers already there with the mules and his Appaloosa. While he worked with them at fastening the harness, the smells of coffee and bacon drifted by on the warm air.

At seven o'clock the column was in motion, streaming dust and sand back over the wagons in the rear. As soon as they were through Arrowhead Pass, Quill placed small squads at short intervals on both flanks, three hundred yards out. Beyond the squads rode single troopers riding as lookouts. Fanshawe and his platoon kept almost half a mile to the front, spreading out and climbing the crest of every rise to carefully scan the country.

But there was no sign of Indians, no smokes, no evidence of their previous passage. The morning was without incident, and by early afternoon they were into the pine-covered ridges that marked the division between the wasteland and the rich grasslands of the cattle ranchers. It was here that the rain caught them, the winds shifting abruptly from south to west, and bringing first a long gray roll of clouds with wind that roared in the tall pines, lashing the branches. The sky grew inky black, cutting visibility to a few yards, relieved only by bright quivering flashes of lightning.

The column halted between two ridges, the orders coming back to unstrap ponchos. These were scarcely settled on the men's shoulders and march resumed, when the rain struck. It was almost tropical in its intensity, men and horses bowing heads before sheets of water which ran in streams from the animals' manes and tails.

Easterwood sat hunched on the high seat of the generator wagon. The brim of his old field hat wilted under the downpour which beat against his face and leaked under the collar of his poncho. The trail had grown slippery, and on the slopes the mules slipped and stumbled. The wagon lurched and bumped against water-loosened stones, and he had trouble holding the wet lines. Within a few moments the dry washes alongside the trail filled with water, swirling and rushing along in yellow foaming torrents. He glanced at Greenslade; the little professor had pulled the top of his oilskin over his head so that only his white goatee was visible.

After half an hour the squall passed over, the gray clouds breaking away to reveal patches of deep blue above the tall lodgepole pines. The trees' green needles sparkled in the light, the drenched branches occasionally releasing a shower of water on the troopers riding below.

As the column crawled out of the pine country, the ranch lands rolled far away before them to the southern horizon, with patches of sage in the foreground and then an unending stretch of gray-green grass. After the storm, the air was cool and fresh, cleansed of its burden of dust, fragrant now with its smell of rain-washed sage.

"Even in my Pennsylvania," said the professor, removing his oilskin, "I have never seen a sky of such intense azure. Or a valley so rich and limitless."

"The Sioux have a name for this place," Easterwood replied, "a word that means Beautiful Country."

"One can understand why they might be of a mind to fight for it."

"They gave up everything on this side of the Yellowhorse, and the ranchers moved in. South of the river are the sacred hunting grounds, which the treaty left to the tribes. When I was first stationed out here, only a few years ago, you could shut your eyes, shoot wild, and hit some kind of game. Now the buffalo are all gone, north and into Canada. The Indians believed the hunting grounds to be sacred; they believe the buffalo will come back someday—if the ranchers stay out."

"A pity," Greenslade said, "that a land so beautiful must be a cause of strife."

Easterwood pointed off to the right. "There's the first ranch house, back in that draw."

In the remaining hours of the afternoon they passed several other ranches. Most of the houses were long, solid, barracks-like structures of solid logs, with rock chimneys at each end. The windows were small, sometimes unglazed apertures like loopholes in a fort.

Less than an hour of daylight remained when the column began curling down a crooked trail, the balloon wagons jolting and swaying at the rough turns. In the valley ahead was a splash of green trees and grass, with a sprawling whitewashed ranch house almost hidden among willows and towering cottonwoods. Nearby were a smokehouse, a log barn, and a row of hayricks, and off to one side was a rectangular corral fenced with poles. Scattered herds of cattle grazed in swales where the bunch grass grew thickest, and along the stream that had cut a gash out of the earth where it curved around a low sandstone butte on the west. A pair of eagles floated in the clear blue above the butte.

"Stuart's Ranch," Easterwood said.

Asahel Greenslade shaded his eyes. "Is that a white picket fence I see running along the front of the house?"

"It is, and every board was freighted overland from Goldfield. That machine you see by the barn is a hay mower, also freighted overland. I've heard it said the Stuarts have the only piano in the ranch country, as well as carpets and paintings from the family castle in Scotland. Old Baird Stuart is the baronial type."

"Cattle brought him all this?"

"Gold and cattle. He made the first gold strike in the Territory, but he got tired of prospecting and digging. He went down to Texas and bought up a herd of Longhorns. Drove them overland to supply the miners with beef. He's made it pay better than gold."

"Yet he still wants more land."

"The barons always want more land."

The cavalry troop was to bivouac beyond the ranch house on a lush strip of grass along the stream. After crossing a log bridge that was the entrance to Stuart's Ranch, the column marched up the drive toward the house, and turned off sharply between a pair of gigantic cottonwoods. As Easterwood tugged hard on the lines to turn the mules, he saw Alison Stuart standing beside her horse near the side veranda. Quill, Bowdring, and Baird Stuart were still mounted, watching the wagons pass.

Dinner was served in the largest room in the ranch house, a show place with animal skins and gilt-framed paintings on the walls and thick carpets on the floor. Suspended from the heavy cedar crossbeams, elaborately designed oil lamps lighted the linen-covered dining table, which Easterwood guessed had been imported from abroad.

Baird Stuart, dressed in a black suit, sat in a high-backed chair at the head, his white beard jutting out as he smiled down the table upon his guests. His eyes, Easterwood noted, were of the same startling blueness as his daughter's. She sat on the old man's left, and next to her, in order, were Lee Bowdring, Asahel Greenslade, and the two troop captains. On the opposite side were Quill, Easterwood, and a man whom the visitors had just met, Steve Faulkner, the ranch foreman.

"As soon as Colonel Quill's scouts showed in here this afternoon," Faulkner was saying, "I told my boys to slaughter a steer. I knew Mr. Stuart would be craving some of his own beef."

Later, while dessert was being served, a sergeant entered the outer hall, standing at the door until he caught Quill's eye. The colonel beckoned him to come forward. "A message for you, sir."

Quill frowned as he took the sheet of paper, holding it away from him in the light until he had finished reading it. "Sergeant, I want the telegrapher to put through this order to the commanding officer at Fort Yellowhorse: 'Keep fort on continual alert. Double strength of all guards. My command of one squadron will arrive there tomorrow.'" He ordered the sergeant to repeat the words, and then dismissed him.

Meanwhile, Baird Stuart's keen blue eyes had remained fixed expectantly on Quill's face. "Nothing is amiss at the fort, I trust, Colonel?"

Quill set his jaw and then smiled his tight humorless smile. "On the contrary, everything is going well, very well indeed. A large band of Sioux made a demonstration before the fort late this afternoon. They went into camp at the base of Skeletons' Rock in full view of the stockade."

Easterwood shifted his glance to Bowdring. For a fleeting moment there was a knowing, crafty look on the Texan's face. "So they went south, instead of east to the reservation?"

"You will recall, Mr. Bowdring," said Quill, "my prediction that I would be forced to drive the hostiles back on the reservation." The colonel reached for his wineglass, gulping at the liquid.

The ranch foreman turned to Easterwood, his brow wrinkled. "You army people wouldn't be expecting trouble, would you, Captain?"

"If there's any trouble brewing," Easterwood replied dryly, "the army will meet it—more than halfway." Out the corner of his eye he saw Quill's head jerk around, the color rising in the colonel's already ruddy face. But Quill said nothing; he merely drained his glass.

Baird Stuart was offering Quill more wine from the decanter.

"Takes the chill off the evening, doesn't it, Colonel? I was just thinking—there's only one thing prevents this pleasant repast from being complete. The colonel's lady, Mistress Mellie, a charming woman. Too bad she couldn't be present."

Quill swallowed another gulp of wine. "Yes," he said, "that would make everything complete, if Mellie were here—" He turned his head toward Easterwood, the tip of his tongue moving over the wet surfaces of his dyed mustache. He added softly: "Don't you agree, Captain Easterwood?"

Easterwood fought down the tight sickness in his stomach and nodded politely, ignoring the perversity of Quill's remark. "Yes, sir." But he could not restrain himself from reading the faces of the others: Professor Greenslade glancing in embarrassment at the cedar beams above his head; Lee Bowdring's amused, almost contemptuous stare; Alison Stuart blushing as she put one hand to her throat, her blue eyes turning away from him.

Only Baird Stuart remained unconcerned; probably he had not heard Quill's side remark. He pushed his high-backed chair away from the table. "Gentlemen, I must beg to be excused for a few minutes to discuss some urgent business matters with Steve Faulkner. My daughter will be pleased, I'm sure, to divert you with some piano music until I can rejoin you."

The room became a hubbub of movement and voices, the men standing awkwardly about the room, while Alison with quick birdlike movements searched through her collection of music. Gradually the guests moved closer to the piano, one or two sitting gingerly on the edges of chairs, the others remaining standing. Easterwood found himself beside a door, and at the first opportunity stepped out into the broad open hallway that ran through the center of the ranch house.

He walked softly across the creaking boards to the back steps and down to a graveled path, the frosty night air chilling the dampness of his body. Through the frilly branches of a giant willow the stars glittered unnaturally large, and he could hear a stream purling beside the gravel. He followed the path for twenty or thirty yards until it stopped beside a half-finished rock wall where a wooden bench faced to overlook a spring.

For several minutes he sat in the darkness, looking at the reflected stars in the pool made by the spring, listening to the faint piano music, incongruous in the immensity of the wild land and the starry sky.

After a while the music stopped; he heard voices, outside, probably in the open passageway of the house, and footsteps moving away toward the cavalry camp. Then someone came walking lightly down the gravel. Easterwood sat rigid on the bench, his eyes fixed on the pathway, knowing that it was the girl even before he saw her. She was wearing a dark coat over her white dress.

She was humming gently as she passed him, the rustle of her dress loud in the silent frosty night, and he caught the faint scent of her perfume. She stood looking at the star reflections in the dark pool, drawing the coat tighter around her throat.

Without turning, she said: "Why don't you speak, Captain? I know you are there."

"I have nothing to say, miss."

She whirled on him then, facing him, her head thrust forward slightly, hands on hips. "Do you dislike me, Captain Easterwood?"

"Why, no, miss."

"You're angry for what I told the colonel, aren't you?"

He stood up, the fine gravel gritting under his boots. "I'm not angry," he said, "only puzzled."

"What do you truly think of me, Captain?"

Easterwood came forward in one long stride and caught her by the shoulders. "I admire you very much, Miss Alison. I think you'll make an extraordinarily lovely bride." He was suddenly conscious of the soft flesh of her arms through the coat. He tightened his grip abruptly, and kissed her hard upon the lips, with her yellow hair falling against his forehead and her cheek cool against his.

She drew away slowly, and he could see her breath on the frosty air. "You had no right to that."

"Perhaps not," he said bitterly. "But it was what you expected. Or did you come out here to talk of cattle and land?"

He could see her eyes for a moment in the starlight, a hurt look deep in them. "I'm sorry for what I told the colonel," she said. "When I heard his remark to you tonight, I could have died with shame. He'll rake that into you every chance he gets, like a spur."

"I suppose a cayak should expect rough treatment."

She moved in close to him, meeting his lips. "You're no cayak," she said softly, and turned and ran away from him up the gravel path.

Long after she had vanished in the blue shadows, Easterwood stood there motionless beside the pool. After a while he took a small cigar from his pocket, lighted it, and started walking in long slow strides toward the cavalry camp.

8

At breakfast the next morning Alison carefully avoided speaking to Easterwood, and the one time he managed to meet her eyes she glanced away shyly. Before he could find an opportunity to ask her a direct question, Colonel Quill announced for the benefit of the officers that he was purchasing one hundred of Stuart's prize range steers for the fort's commissary. Because of the Indian threats he had decided to move the cattle under protection of the cavalry, the herd to be driven by Stuart's cowboys immediately behind the wagon train.

From subsequent remarks by Baird Stuart it appeared the bargain had been sealed the night before, the old cattleman promising that his cowboys would not only deliver the herd but would stay long enough to construct a pole corral adjoining the fort. Stuart himself was planning to accompany the drive and supervise construction of the corral.

The column was delayed in marching by several hours while the cowboys rounded up the steers and then ran them through a chute for Quill's inspection. Easterwood, mounted on his Appaloosa, watched these proceedings during the first part of the morning. Then he rode back to the cavalry camp to see after the condition of the balloon wagons and the mules. He found the camp in a state of complete relaxation, every officer and man aware that the fort lay less than ten miles away, and taking advantage of the unexpected easing of pressure for a hurried march. Most of the troopers were lounging in the bright sun; a few were bathing or washing their shirts in the clear-running stream.

Around eleven o'clock orders went out to fill canteens and pack saddle pouches. As soon as the herders started the bawling cattle down from the corral, the command of "Saddle up, men!" began echoing across the green flats of the camp.

Easterwood and Professor Greenslade were ready in their places on the high driver's seat of the generator wagon when Quill, Baird Stuart, Bowdring, and Alison rode down from the ranch house.

Baird Stuart galloped back down the line of rolling wagons, his long hair and beard flying in the wind. Easterwood watched the old man shake hands with Bowdring, then lean from the saddle to kiss his daughter goodbye.

The trees cut them off from Easterwood's view then, and he was too busy guiding the mules through the cottonwoods and across the log bridge to look back again until the train was out upon the trail, headed south. By this time, Bowdring and Alison had returned to the veranda of the ranch house, where they stood waving; the ranch foreman was trotting his horse up toward the corrals.

For the first hour the column moved steadily southward, but as they approached the Yellowhorse bottoms the trail grew rougher, slowing the wagons. Off to the left was an unusual formation known as Skeletons' Rock, a lone promontory of clay and sandstone towering two hundred feet above the flat country. It was almost perpendicular on three sides, one of which formed the south bank of the Yellowhorse River.

Greenslade remarked on the oddity of the flat-topped elevation, and suggested it might be a good site for balloon launchings. "How far does it lie from the fort?" he asked.

"Not more than half a mile," Eastwood replied, "but the river runs in rapids at its base. To get to the summit from the fort, we'd have to cross at the ford a couple miles upstream, circle the Rock, and climb from the far side. The Rock slopes off on the east, and there's a natural sort of trail to the top. A horseman can get up there without difficulty, but we'd have our hands full with wagons. Trail too narrow and too steep."

Before the professor could express his disappointment, the

generator wagon dropped with a sudden shuddering jar into a
washout in the trail. Easterwood seesawed the lines and pulled
the mules to a halt. He leaned over to look at the front wheel,
and swore in disgust at what he saw.

"Damaged spokes and a loose rim," he said, and slapped the
mules forward again, turning the wagon off to one side of the
trail. The cattle were coming up close behind, and he signaled
the point riders to slow the herd.

Handing the lines to Greenslade, he dropped down to give
the wheel a closer examination. It might take them to the river,
he thought, but if it broke up in the ford they would risk losing
the generator. "We'll need a blacksmith," he called to Greenslade. He went back to the rear of the wagon, unhitched and
mounted the Palouse, and rode quickly forward along the line
of wagons.

The face of the land had changed quickly, grass giving way
before sagebrush, the dull yellow soil bare in spots and slicing
away in cutbanks and coulees. Fanshawe and the scouts were
strung far out on the right along a low escarpment of sandstone;
because of the rugged footing they were having difficulty keeping pace with the column.

At the head of the march column, the first troop was already
turning away from the Rock, which seemed to tower higher in
its nearness. The outriders on the left were moving into a screen
of high brown grass that billowed like wild wheat under the
wind.

Before Easterwood could reach the blacksmith wagon the
column halted, and he saw Quill and the trumpeter riding back
down the files. A guidon carrier was signaling Fanshawe to
come in from the ridge. Easterwood continued forward to the
blacksmith wagon, dismounted, and waited for Quill to come
up.

"What's the delay back there, Captain?" Quill called.

"Broken wheel on one of the balloon wagons, sir."

"Get the blacksmith on it right away. We'll dismount and
rest horses for ten minutes."

While the commands to dismount echoed along the column,
Fanshawe came in on the gallop at the head of the scouts. He
pulled up alongside Quill, saluting.

"Any sign out there, Fanshawe?"

"No, sir. Not a thing." Fanshawe looked straight at the colonel, but his eyes seemed focused on some remote object beyond infinity; the cold expression on his face did not change.

"Get up ahead and scout the river approaches thoroughly. The hostiles are camped on this side of the river on that sand flat below the Rock. Some of the young bucks may be waiting for us at the ford."

"Yes, sir." Fanshawe saluted lazily, but moved away at a brisk canter.

By this time, the blacksmith sergeant had rolled a spare wheel out the end of his wagon. Easterwood put the sergeant's tools in his saddlebag, and then helped the man up behind his saddle. They held the wheel between them, and started slowly back down the trail.

"You have nine more minutes," Quill called after them.

Back at the generator wagon they had to work in choking dust churned up by the herd of restless cattle, but they finished the job with a few seconds to spare. When the forward command came down from the head of the column, Easterwood pulled the generator wagon back into line, and they moved away smoothly.

The trail crooked slightly, slanting toward the river ahead. Skeletons' Rock now loomed to the sky on their left; a narrow band of tall willows screened the ridge on the right. The wind had stopped in the lee of the Rock, and the high browned grass below was motionless except where the outriders were beating their way through. The sounds of creaking wagons and rolling wheels, and the slow beat of hoofs were intensified by the stillness.

For a few moments, Easterwood and Professor Greenslade, upon their high perch atop the generator wagon, were the only members of the column who could see the west ridge clearly above the thick growth of willows.

It was Easterwood who saw the first one, as sudden as a drumbeat, a Sioux on a black-and-white mount framed against the sky. Except for the jerky wave of a blanket, the horse and rider were motionless. Then for half a mile along the ridge at least fifty others thrust into view, poised there facing the column on the trail. Easterwood's first thought was that only a few minutes earlier Bratt Fanshawe had scouted that ridge, and had reported no sign of Indians.

His boots dropped hard against the footboards, and he was

up tightening the lines, his mouth wide as the sound came out: "Ho-o-o-o!" Sergeant Connors, commanding the flanking platoon, swung his head around facing him, and Easterwood stabbed an arm toward the ridge.

The wagons jarred to a halt, dust from the cattle herd boiling up over the rear, the shouts of the cowboys as loud as the excited cavalry commands up ahead. In the dead air, the war cries of the Sioux broke incredibly sharp. "Hit the ground, Professor," Easterwood cried. "Get down fast and hold the mules by the bridles!" He fastened the lines and leaped down, carbine in one hand. Through the willows he could see the first wave of Indians, halfway down the ridge. Many of the attackers had rifles, and they were brandishing them like lances.

Easterwood ordered Sergeant Connors to dismount the rear platoon of flankers. With carbines advanced, the troopers aligned themselves in loose fighting order in front of the balloon wagons.

Now the first wave of attackers was slowing, their long black hair flapping in the wind. The leader on the black-and-white pony was turning them away from the massed squadron of cavalry up forward, the line swerving and spinning out to form a file pointed at the column's rear. They were so close now that Easterwood could see the bunches of feathers and bits of red flannel on their bows and rifle barrels. And from the ridge beyond, another wave of Sioux came rolling down.

Easterwood watched the warrior on the black-and-white pony pointing for the cattle herd; he was naked from the waist up, with streaks of yellow ocher daubed on his leathery trunk. But he was not Young Elk. Easterwood ordered carbines brought to ready; the locks crackled in a chorus. The mules were beginning to stamp and jerk in their harness.

Now the Indians were breaking the steady forward motions of their ponies, zigzagging and dancing the mounts from side to side. They were singing their war songs. A rifle cracked, the bullet screaming through the willows. An arrow whistled out of nowhere, hitting one of the canvas-covered wagons with a noise like a man coughing.

"Order your men to fire at will," Easterwood said to Sergeant Connors. After a quick glance at Greenslade, who was red-faced from exertion but was still controlling the excited mules, he brought his carbine up. He watched the warrior on the

black-and-white mount until he could see the battle markings
on the Indian's face. He squeezed the trigger and the Sioux was
gone out of his sights. Jerking his head up, he saw the black-
and-white pony veering toward the cattle herd, the rider still
mounted but slumped forward, fingers twisted in the animal's
mane.

The firing was suddenly deafening. One of the mules on the
first balloon wagon was down on the trail, squealing and thrash-
ing, and the driver was having trouble holding the others.

At this moment Baird Stuart came galloping down from the
head of the column, pistol in hand, shouting to the herd riders.
Even if they could have heard his orders, the cowboys could
have done little to execute them. The first wave of attackers was
swarming in among them, the Sioux yelling and whooping, and
waving blankets and buffalo hides. Several animals broke loose
from the boiling cloud of yellow dust, racing away into the high
grass on the left of the trail.

With a burst of profanity, Stuart spurred his horse forward
into the melee, firing his pistol. A moment later, a horse broke
loose from the tangle, the rider screaming. He was one of
Stuart's cowboys, with an arrow all the way through from side
to side under his ribs. He had dropped his bridle to grip his
saddle horn with both hands, his head hanging forward. He was
hanging on, screaming, wobbling with the motion of his terrified horse.

An Indian darted in upon the man suddenly, striking him
with a heavy bow across the back of the neck. Before Easterwood could reload, the warrior had got his coup and was
gone.

The second wave of attackers was already upon them now,
Young Elk in the lead, zigzagging in toward the cattle. Young
Elk's naked body glistened with paint; he was flattened out
against his pony. He lashed his mount with the end of a rawhide rope. Suddenly he rose, legs braced, the fire of his repeating rifle raking the mules in front of the generator wagon.
Swerving his pony skillfully, he headed for the stampeding
herd. Easterwood had time for only one wild shot, but as he
came up he saw that the pony was hit and going down, Young
Elk springing over its head, landing on his feet and disappearing
into the high brush on the other side of the trail.

Disaster struck then, from the direction of Skeletons' Rock.

As if by prearrangement, the first wave of attackers had turned back, racing along the wagon train, firing lead and arrows into the horses and mules.

By this time, Quill had his nearest troop remounted and galloping back single file to relieve the hard-pressed rear. But they were too late. The train was a bedlam of shouting incoherent drivers, of screaming struggling animals. Two supply wagons were overturned, another was wrecked against a cottonwood.

The cattle herd was gone, stampeded through the high grass, and most of the cowboys were dismounted, standing in the settling dust around Baird Stuart. The old man's hat was gone, his beard streaked with yellow dust and spittle. As he shook his fist in the direction of the disappearing Sioux, puffs of blue smoke arose in the high grass, changing quickly into a blazing mass of fire that swept in a protective curtain behind the fleeing Indians and the stolen cattle.

Easterwood's Appaloosa had escaped unharmed, but only one of the mules hitched to the generator wagon was still standing. Asahel Greenslade was on the ground, one leg caught under a dead mule. With the help of a trooper, Easterwood got the leg free, but the professor winced when he tried to stand.

"We'd better get you up into the ambulance," Easterwood said.

Greenslade looked along the disorganized train. "There'll be others needing the ambulance a sight more than I, Captain. Just help me up to the seat."

Casualties, however, were lower than Easterwood expected. From where he stood he could see only two men out of action, the dead cowboy and one trooper. It was the horses and mules that had suffered the brunt of the attack. The men in the disorganized wagon train had only to look about them to know that the Sioux had achieved a measure of revenge over Horse-Killer Quill for his slaughter of their war ponies two years before.

After assisting Professor Greenslade to the top of the generator wagon, Easterwood reloaded his empty carbine and set about the grim task of ending the miseries of two of the wounded mules. A third was already dead.

The other balloon wagons had fared better. Only one animal had to be destroyed, but three others had received flesh wounds which left them temporarily unfit for draft duty.

All along the train, the sounds of occasional carbine fire told the story of other crippled animals being put to death.

Colonel Quill, meanwhile, had rallied B Troop at the end of the train and had sent out one platoon around the end of the grass fire with orders to overtake and harass the rear of the Indians until he could form A Troop for pursuit and attack.

While A Troop was forming, Bratt Fanshawe and his patrol came up at a gallop from the front where they had been scouting the river approaches. When he saw Fanshawe, Quill's face flushed with anger. He spurred his horse forward to meet the scout, his lips beginning to tremble with rage.

His voice was high, almost hysterical, as he addressed Sergeant Connors who was standing by with his wagon flankers. "Sergeant, disarm that man!"

Connors was startled; his mouth opened; he was uncertain of Quill's meaning until the colonel pointed directly at Fanshawe: "Disarm that man, I say, and put him under guard. Strip his chevrons. He is demoted to private. Deliberate carelessness in scouting will not be tolerated in this command." Quill sucked in his breath, exhausted from the tirade. "Where is Captain Easterwood?" he demanded.

Easterwood stepped forward from the rear of the generator wagon. "Here, sir."

"Captain Easterwood, mount up and take command of the wagon train. This man is under arrest. He is your prisoner. I want him placed in the guardhouse as soon as the train reaches the fort. He'll be court-martialed later."

Fanshawe's mouth twisting downward was the only change of expression on his face as he handed over his carbine and bandolier to Sergeant Connors. His cold blue eyes studied Quill unwaveringly.

The colonel swung his horse around, shouting an angry order to one of the troop captains. He turned back to Easterwood. "I am leading the squadron in immediate pursuit of the hostiles. As you can see, Captain, losses among our draft animals make it impossible to move all the wagons. You will leave behind only such wagons as are least likely to be pillaged by any marauding bands in the vicinity."

Easterwood had untied the Appaloosa and was climbing into the saddle. "Yes, sir," he said.

Quill had withdrawn a notebook from his pocket and was

scribbling on one of the sheets with a stub pencil. "This is an order to Major Robinson, commanding at Fort Yellowhorse. He is to mount C and D Troops and join me in the field." Quill's eyes narrowed. "I intend to finish what was started here this afternoon, Captain. Once and for all."

"I'll second those words, Colonel!" Baird Stuart, remounted on a lean gray pony, had come up beside them. "With your permission, my boys and I will ride with your men. We have a score to settle ourselves."

Quill nodded, a vacant stare on his face. He handed Easterwood the written order, whirled his horse, and rode toward the squadron formed along the trail. The colonel, Easterwood thought, had been jabbed to the quick by Young Elk's insult— the slaughtering of the wagon train's draft animals.

Quill's gauntleted hand was up to signal the forward command, his voice shrilling: "By twos!"

Before the first platoon was away, Easterwood set about the task of bringing order out of the chaos of the wagon train. He sent a sergeant along the line to make a count of the serviceable draft animals, and then went to attend the wounded. He found seven men with deep flesh penetrations and leg wounds; a half dozen others were less severely injured from bullets or arrows.

As Quill had taken the surgeon with him, Easterwood assigned troopers to devise temporary bandages and slings. He ordered the seven nonambulatory patients wrapped in saddle blankets, four to be placed in the ambulance, the other three in supply wagons.

The next half hour was spent in selecting wagons to be left behind. He cut loose all but one of the corn wagons and doubled up supplies in the commissary wagons, putting the drivers to work at shifting sacks of Rio green coffee, rice, beans, and slabs of salt pork.

To Professor Greenslade's dismay, he decided to leave one of the balloon wagons. They both agreed that the heavy vehicle carrying the barrels of iron filings and the crated carboys of sulphuric acid should be left behind. The lighter wagon with the balloon envelope and its equipment, and the big generator wagon would be driven in to the fort.

By the time the train was reorganized and ready to move, the sun was well down toward midafternoon. Easterwood went forward, taking Sergeant Connors and Bratt Fanshawe with him,

and gave the command to march out. As soon as the wagons
were rolling, he rode back down the trail, cautioning the drivers
to keep closed up until they reached the river.

Within a few minutes he could see the Yellowhorse, fringed
with thickets of willows and choke-cherry bushes. A perfect
screen for an ambush. He turned to Fanshawe, who rode silent
and straight in his saddle. "What do you make of it, Fanshawe?"

"I don't smell a thing," Fanshawe said.

"You scouted the ford. Any sign?"

"A few hoofprints in the mud. Hours old. But I made one
mistake today, Captain, and I'm not saying what's in there
now."

Easterwood looked sharply at Fanshawe. "We all make mis-
takes. Forget it." He wasn't sure whether the scout was being
surly or was feeling sorry for himself. "Let's move in there. At a
gallop."

As they swept through the trees into the muddy entrance to
the river crossing, Fort Yellowhorse came into view on its knoll
half a mile away. A flag flapped lazily in the late afternoon sun
above a fort that was almost a replica of the one that Easterwood had seen the Indians burn and wreck two years earlier.
After the treaty signing and the departure of the last troopers,
Sioux and Cheyenne warriors had moved in with torches. Now
a line of fresh yellow earth circled the new stockade where a
deep trench had been dug to set the posts. Brown roofs of in-
completed winter barracks showed above the stockade. Against
its background of cedars and box elders, Fort Yellowhorse
looked solid and impregnable.

A few minutes later the first wagon was into the ford, the
mules thrusting their muzzles deep into the swirling waters that
were yellow as the land was yellow. Because of the animals'
thirsts, the crossing was a slow one.

Easterwood rode on until he was halfway up the winding trail
to the fort's gates. There he could see the Sioux camp on the
sand flats along the north bank, just below the small rapids at
the east end of Skeletons' Rock. A quick glance through his
field glass told him the tipi village was empty except for women,
children, and old men. All the braves were somewhere on the
other side of the Rock.

He had heard no firing, but the fighting could be too far away by this time for the sound to carry. Perhaps the Indians had outrun Quill; perhaps they were awaiting him somewhere in ambush.

The wagons were coming up the slope now, the wheels crunching against the graveled road. He waited until Sergeant Connors and Fanshawe came up, then spurred his Palouse forward. A shout sounded from the corner bastion; a lookout sentinel at the parapet was silhouetted against the washed blue sky of late afternoon.

9

The main gate of Fort Yellowhorse swung open as Easterwood came up to the stockade. He returned the guard's salute and trotted the Palouse on past the guardhouse to the parade. Troopers in forage uniforms were moving about, some going to the nearest loopholes to watch the approaching wagon train.

In front of the pine-log quarters at the south end, groups of women in sunbonnets were gathering with an air of expectancy. They watched him as he rode past the flagpole and approached the headquarters building. Everything was new, the air heavy with fresh-cut wood odors of logs and sawed boards and shingles.

He saw a woman step outside the largest of the quarters in officers' row, facing him. Her hair was coal black, knotted at the back and worn in short bangs over her forehead. She was not wearing a hat, but carried a parasol in one hand, a folding fan in the other. The cut of her blue jacket simulated the style of a military blouse, but her tan bustled skirt was ultra-femine with its flaring petticoat hem.

She took one hesitant step along the planked walk, and he knew her for Mellie Quill. She was looking at him over her shoulder, her dark eyes full of wonder, continuing forward again as if out for a stroll along a country lane, her hips moving with that provocative grace he had never forgotten.

Easterwood wondered if she knew him under his yellow dust coating. His eyes squinted against the low sun, never leaving her until his horse halted before the headquarters hitching rack. But she gave no sign of recognition, and he restrained himself from any gesture of greeting.

He dismounted, tossing the Appaloosa's reins to a trooper who had come forward from the whitewashed steps. The headquarters sentry gave him a sharp salute. He hesitated briefly before the door, stamping some of the river mud from his boots.

He went on inside. A sallow-skinned, elderly sergeant-major was standing behind an ancient field desk, facing him, his slack mouth forming a silent question.

"Major Robinson?" Easterwood pulled off his gauntlets and drew Quill's penciled order from inside his shirt.

"In there, sir." The sergeant-major's voice was low; he made a listless gesture toward the closed door of the commander's office.

Easterwood walked on to the door and pushed it open; the sour-sweet smell of fresh-cut cedar was stronger in the dead air. The late sun was shining directly through the single window of the inner room, leaving the huge desk in contrasting shadow. The desk was of cedar slabs, constructed as a part of the building, and Easterwood looked twice before he realized there was a man behind it, slumped low in a whirligig chair, his head sunk against his chest.

"Major Robinson!" The man stirred slightly, and Easterwood walked across the solid flooring, deliberately jingling a spur. He moved around the desk and as he came up to the officer he caught the rank smell of whiskey. He shook the major's shoulders, and the man came awake suddenly, his head thrown back, his eyes blinking. "Major Robinson?"

"Major Sylvanus Robinson at your service, sir." He spoke each word deliberately, his bloodshot eyes widening and then coming to a focus on Easterwood. With one hand, he pushed back his mop of dark hair. He frowned and asked: "Who are you, sir?"

"Easterwood. Captain Easterwood." He handed Robinson the order from Quill; the major glared warily at the folded paper in his hand. "What's this?" he asked.

"Orders from Colonel Quill, sir."

Robinson's lips moved silently, his facial muscles tightening.

He pushed the paper to the end of the cedar desk nearer the sunlit window, then unfolded it and read the penciled scrawl. As he read, the color drained from the major's face. He glanced up nervously at Easterwood: "Join his command north of the Rock? What does he mean, Captain? What's going on out there?"

Easterwood told him of the Sioux attack and of Quill's hasty pursuit. "The colonel said he was going to finish what was started this afternoon. For good and all."

Robinson grunted. "Bully for old Horse-Killer," he said. "When he telegraphed that he was moving his command here, we all guessed what was coming." He fumbled at the bottom drawer of the desk. "But, by God, I didn't expect it to happen so soon. I need a drink. You, Captain?" He brought a half-empty quart bottle up from behind the desk.

Easterwood smiled at him. "You know what, Major? Just three days ago a wood-train freighter from down here told me the reason he quit Yellowhorse was because the major wouldn't allow whiskey drinking on the post."

Robinson's shoulders squared suddenly, his face reddening until he saw the grin spreading on Easterwood's face. "Whiskey is for officers and gentlemen, Captain." He poured some of the liquor into a glass and pushed it across the desk to Easterwood. "But it wasn't lack of whiskey that made your wood-train man leave Fort Yellowhorse. Perhaps the colonel didn't inform you that Omaha headquarters refused to allot him any more money to pay civilian laborers."

"That's news to me."

"The colonel rarely confides his news to his officers." Robinson poured himself a drink, raising the glass high. "To the colonel's success in pacifying the hostiles." He swallowed the liquor in one gulp, and then frowned down again at the scrap of note-paper on the desk top. " 'Immediate action,' he says." The major swung the cane-bottomed whirligig chair and looked out at the leveling sun. "Maybe two hours of daylight left. A half-strength squadron's got no business brushing about in those willow thickets north of the Rock, with half the Sioux nation buzzing around like bees out there. But an order's an order, Captain, and an order from Quill is a double order." He shrugged, exaggerating the movement of his shoulders. He stood up then, fortified by the alcohol, adjusting his neat, trim-fitting uniform. "Jonas!" he called.

"Yes, sir." The sergeant-major's face appeared in the door-way colorless of flesh and expression.

"Instruct the orderly to forage a pot of hot black coffee for the captain and me. When you've done that, find Lieutenant Marsh and inform him that both troops have marching orders. Boots and saddles. On the double, Jonas!"

The sergeant's face had become even more pallid as he lis-tened to the major; the hollows in his cheeks seemed to deepen.

There was fear in this place, Easterwood thought, in Sergeant Jonas' soul and body, behind Major Robinson's whiskey bra-vado.

After the sergeant had gone, Robinson said: "That man re-minds me of a wraith, Captain. The army should have retired him after Appomattox." He added, half to himself: "And Sylva-nus Robinson, too. Jonas and Robinson, as fine a pair of garri-son troopers as ever wore the blue." He swung his chair around, facing a hand-drawn map of the country surrounding Fort Yel-lowhorse. Easterwood watched the major's long forefinger trace a line around a stippled circle that marked Skeletons' Rock.

From outside came the sudden excited notes of the trumpets sounding boots and saddles. "Your man Jonas can move fast when he wants to," Easterwood said.

"A scared man usually moves fast." Robinson picked up a quill pen and began writing on a sheet of ruled paper. A mo-ment later footsteps banged on the floor of the outer room. "Major Robinson!"

"In here, Lieutenant."

A young officer walked hesitantly into the commander's of-fice; he was breathing hard. "May I have a word with you, sir?"

"Captain Easterwood. Lieutenant Marsh, my adjutant."

The lieutenant shook hands hurriedly with Easterwood, and turned to Robinson. "I just learned that Fanshawe is here, sir."

"No! Well, that puts a different color on the march order. Bratt Fanshawe can guide us through anything."

Marsh's eyes blinked rapidly. "But he's in the guardhouse, sir."

"Fanshawe a prisoner?" Robinson turned toward Eas-terwood. "I suppose that explains why he isn't with the colonel. What about this, Captain?"

"The Sioux attack came from a ridge less than fifteen minutes after Fanshawe scouted it," Easterwood said. "When it was over, the colonel blew his boiler. He had to blame somebody."

Robinson whistled softly. "And after all the years that pair has been together. Fanshawe should be due one mistake. I'd be a fool to march out with my green garrison soldiers and leave the best scout in the Territory sitting here in the guardhouse. You're releasing your prisoner to me, Captain Easterwood."

"You're in command," Easterwood said.

"I'll take the responsibility. Mr. Marsh, order the prisoner Fanshawe released and assigned to scout duty with C Troop."

"Yes, sir!" Marsh turned to go. "The men should be ready to march in ten more minutes, sir."

The lieutenant had scarcely departed when they heard lighter footsteps in the outer office. Easterwood supposed it was the sergeant-major bringing the coffee, and he did not turn his head until he heard the soft feminine voice behind him: "May I interrupt you for a moment, Major?"

Easterwood and Robinson both stood up. "Tom Easterwood!" she cried, and stood there in the entrance, twirling her closed parasol, smiling her familiar enigmatic smile.

"You know each other?" The major's eyebrows were raised in surprise.

"You're looking well, Mellie," Easterwood said, moving across the room. Her gloved fingers felt small and warm in his hand.

"Tom, I am so pleased to see you again. We had heard you might be joining the command, but I had not expected you to arrive until Mathew returned to the fort." She had not lost her rich Virginia drawl, he thought. It was the same voice, the honeyed voice that had whispered in his ear on nights so long ago.

Easterwood glanced at Robinson, and the major said: "I should have sent you word, Mellie. Colonel Quill is pursuing a Sioux war party somewhere north of the Rock. I'm marching the garrison troop out to join him."

Her red lips formed a round pout; Easterwood remembered that little gesture, too. "But who will command the fort in your absence, Major?"

"Captain Easterwood will take command as soon as I ride through the gate. You will be in good hands."

She smiled at Easterwood. "I'm sure of that." They could hear the loud shouts of the sergeants outside on the parade, assembling the troops. "And you must take care of yourself, Sylvanus."

"I'll be in good hands also," the major replied briskly. "Bratt Fanshawe is scouting for me."

"Bratt—Corporal Fanshawe is *here?*"

At this moment, Sergeant Jonas knocked on the door facing. "Your coffee, sir."

"In here," Robinson replied quickly. "Mellie, will you have coffee?"

"It isn't Mathew's way to go off on an Indian chase without Bratt Fanshawe," she said, ignoring the major's invitation. Easterwood was watching her face, but he remembered he had never been able to read this woman's thoughts by searching her pretty countenance.

"Dear Mellie," Robinson interrupted patiently, "in five more minutes I must take leave of Fort Yellowhorse. The captain and I have several important matters to discuss. Will you excuse us?"

Again she rounded her lips in a pout, spun her parasol, and bent her knees slightly in a mock curtsey. "I'll have some questions to ask Tom Easterwood later," she said, and marched out through the open door.

The smell of coffee curled up in steam from the tin cups. "When that woman makes her lips that way," Robinson said, "I always want to kiss her." His smile vanished, like a mask quickly removed. "But we haven't much time, Captain. How many men did you bring in?"

"The wagon drivers and a few wounded. Forty or more."

"I'll leave you a platoon, convalescents and ineffectuals such as my sergeant-major. The surgeon will stay, too old for field duty."

"There are no civilians?"

"Two or three males, of no account. The best of them left when the pay stopped. Dozen or so troopers' wives and a few women in haybag row."

"Single women on this post?"

Robinson shrugged. "The colonel's way of keeping the wood-cutters down here on a low-paid job. We had to shut off the

whiskey when the men got to carousing all night and wouldn't
put in a day's work."

The room became suddenly quiet. The sounds of the forming
troops had died away, and both men knew the time had come
for the major to go; his men were waiting out there on the
parade in the light of the dying day. A clock ticked somewhere
in the outer room.

Robinson had lost his brittle bravado. He reached in the desk
drawer, upended his almost empty bottle, and drained it. Easterwood noticed the man's fingers trembling, and looked away.

"Fort Yellowhorse is yours, Captain." The major slapped a
pair of elaborately fringed gauntlets slowly against his high riding boots, killing the last possible moment.

"Good luck," Easterwood said.

Robinson squared his shoulders, took his broad-brimmed
campaign hat from the wall rack, and started toward the door.

Standing in the headquarters entrance, Easterwood watched
the troop prepare to march. Sylvanus Robinson was conferring
with Bratt Fanshawe and his adjutant, Lieutenant Marsh. Fanshawe still wore his dust-stained uniform, and as he slouched in
the saddle his appearance was in direct contrast to the neat
major who sat his mount stiffly, the very model of a garrison
officer.

After a moment, Fanshawe and the lieutenant took their
places at the head of the troop, and Robinson, elbows erect,
shouted the march commands. The troop wheeled, marching
out by twos past the guardhouse and through the open gate of
the stockade.

Several women had gathered near the flagpole, waving their
handkerchiefs at the departing troopers. Easterwood looked
down the plank sidewalk that ran in front of officers' row. Mellie was standing on the top step of the commander's quarters,
one hand at her throat. He wondered what she was thinking,
whom she was watching among that departing company. He
thought of Buffalo Charlie's remarks that other evening in the
Troopers' Rest; he could see the big man's yellow teeth bared in
laughter, mouthing the words that had brought on the fight. He
wished now for some similar violent physical action, for some
release from the tension building in him.

As the rear troopers marched through the gate, he turned

and walked back into the orderly room. For the first time he
noticed a table against the side wall, beside a small fireplace,
with a telegraph signaling box and a key.

"Can you work the telegraph, Sergeant?"

Jonas swallowed nervously before he spoke. "Yes, sir, but the
line has been dead since early afternoon."

"Try it again, try to rouse the Goldfield station."

He knew it was useless, but he waited while Jonas fiddled
nervously with the key. "All right, try again an hour from
now."

When he turned he almost stumbled over a gunny sack lying
before the sergeant's desk. "What's this?" he asked sharply.

"The mail sack, sir. They brought it on the wagons. I was just
going to sort it out."

Easterwood went on into the office and stood looking down
at the cedar desk. He could still see Sylvanus Robinson there,
fortifying his lack of courage with whiskey. The sunlight in the
single-windowed room was fading.

He noticed for the first time the old lumpy haircloth sofa
pushed against the side wall; he remembered it as Quill's personal property, transported from post to post across the west.
Quill had read somewhere that Napoleon Bonaparte reclined on
a sofa while planning his military campaigns; he had immediately acquired one from some trail-town emporium in Kansas.

Easterwood's lip twisted in a slight smile; then he walked
around the desk, kicking over Robinson's empty whiskey bottle.
He put the bottle in one of the desk drawers, and sat down in
the cane-bottomed chair.

He had never cared for command responsibility, had never
sought it, always preferring the subordinate role, with freedom
of action whenever possible. He had often told himself that he
would have been worth more to the army as an anonymous
trooper than as an officer. He thought now of the irony of command being thrust upon him in a fort manned by wagon drivers, invalids, and women.

Jonas interrupted his thoughts by appearing in the door with
a lighted taper. "Excuse me, sir, I'll be lighting the lamps."

"When do you usually go off duty, Sergeant?"

"After retreat, sir. I suppose there'll be no formation today,
sir?"

"There will be a formation as usual, Sergeant. Send the orderly for First-Sergeant Connors. I want Connors here right away."

"The orderly went with the major, sir." The lamp wick began smoking, and Jonas turned it up quickly. He blew out the taper.

"Then you will serve double duty as my orderly. You'll probably find Sergeant Connors with the wagons."

"Yes, sir." He moved away silently. The lamplight had little effect upon the room; the setting sun reflected a rose-colored glow against the wall facing the desk.

As soon as Connors reported, Easterwood informed him that he was to serve as his acting adjutant until such time as a commissioned officer arrived at the fort. The big Irishman blushed, shuffling his boots nervously on the floor; he said he would do his duty as best he knew how.

"You have about twenty minutes to get the wagon drivers assembled for retreat. Dismounted formation of course." He handed the sergeant a sheet of paper. "These are my orders for the next twelve hours. There's a six-man day guard on now, left by the major. Before you dismiss the men, you will assign a night guard and such details as are necessary to complete the unloading of the wagons. Take a tattoo roll call at nine o'clock, after which the guard will be doubled to twelve men. Taps at nine-thirty. You will read these orders to the men at retreat. That is all, Connors."

At the first call of the bugle, Easterwood took a dress saber from the wall behind him and walked out to the parade. He saw Connors marching the men up from the soldiers' quarters at the south end of the fort; they were a nondescript lot, some wearing caps, others hats, and as there had been no time for sprucing their uniforms they looked more like a fatigue detail than the dress formation they were supposed to be. Only the handful of fort personnel in one file was properly uniformed, and they looked out of place in their indigo-blue forage caps. The last rays of the sun caught their brass buttons, and then they marched into the shadows facing Easterwood.

Sergeant Connors took his station in front of center; a moment later the trumpeter was sounding retreat. With the last note, the flag came fluttering down, and the sergeant began barking out orders. He turned smartly to Easterwood, saluted, and reported.

"Troop dismissed," Easterwood said. He looked toward the commanders' quarters; a lamp was burning in one window, but he saw no other evidence of Mellie Quill's presence.

"Captain—ah—Eastwood?"

He swung around. An elderly civilian in a black sack suit, a man with long gray sideburns, came forward with one hand extended. "Surgeon Campbell, sir. Jamie Campbell."

"The name is Easterwood, Surgeon."

"Yes, of course, Captain *Easter* wood. I would have made my presence known to you before now, sir, but I've been a bit busy with the wounded men and only just now heard the news of the major's departure." He had a slight Scotch burr, and sharp little blue eyes that looked out from under a worried brow.

"How is Professor Greenslade?"

"Ah, that stouthearted little man would be up and hobbling about right now if I'd let him. Good bones, that man. But he seems to have got a kind of bilious fever, from the pain and shock I'd guess."

"Nothing broken, then?"

"Not a thing. I loaded him full of paregoric and hot water. Keep him on half-diet for a week and he'll be sound as a new hickory nut."

"How about the others?"

The surgeon pulled a folded army form from his vest. "I have the report all ready for you. The colonel always was one for promptness in these matters of record."

Easterwood took the report. "Won't you come into the office, Surgeon?"

Campbell shook his head. "Haven't had my tea and toddy, sir. Must be getting along."

Easterwood bade him good night and re-entered the headquarters orderly room. Jonas was hunched over his desk, carefully inking in his last entries of the day. "You know how short we are for men, Sergeant," Easterwood said. "You'll have to bring in some blankets and bed down here for the night."

"Yes, sir," Jonas replied quickly, but he didn't look pleased about the order.

Easterwood went on into the office and sat down, staring distastefully at the empty desk top. There was nothing to do now but wait. He unfolded the surgeon's report of casualties, reading the first names and the terse, detached descriptions:

Private Joseph Martin, Co. B, killed.
Sergeant Orion McKee, Co. B, left leg, slight.
Corporal Daniel E. Nolan, Co. A, left leg.
Private George Baird, Co. A, thorax, right side,
  penetrating, dangerous.
Private Michael Welch, Co. B, right poplitic
  region, slight.
Private Thomas Andrews, Co. A, right thigh,
  severe.

He folded the paper and stared blankly at the wall. He opened the desk drawers, and found a book in the top one, *The Story of the Great March*. A marker lay in it, and he read: "It was a proud day for the soldiers of Sherman's army."

He wondered if Major Sylvanus Robinson had been with Sherman on that proud day. He wondered where Major Sylvanus Robinson was now. It was almost dark outside, and he guessed that Robinson would be somewhere beyond Skeletons' Rock. He swung around in the chair, frowning at the hand-drawn wall map.

In the outer room, he heard footsteps and voices; the sergeant's chair creaked and then everything was still. Unnaturally still. And then he heard the firing. It was from far away and would have been barely distinguishable against other sounds, but it was rapid firing, and continued without a break.

Easterwood came up out of the chair and was through the door in three long strides. Jonas was standing in front of his desk, his face ghastly pale under the oil lamp.

"Try the telegraph once more," Easterwood said. "If anybody asks for me, I'll be on the north bastion."

He crossed the parade, half running, and when he climbed the ladder to the bastion, he found Sergeant Connors already there, leaning against the parapet and staring across the river through a field glass. A guard had come out of the sentry box, and was standing uncertainly beside a small swivel gun.

"See anything, Connors?"

Connors turned around, surprised to find him there. "Not a thing, sir. The action seems to be somewhere beyond the Rock." The firing was not so rapid now, continuing in scattered volleys.

Easterwood took the offered glass, scanning the river ford

and all the approaches to the rock formation. The dusk was
thickening, the earth unreal in the half-light that precedes darkness. When he focused the glass on the Indian camp he could
detect scarcely any movement, only an occasional prowling dog
and a group of old men sitting cross-legged before a tipi.

"I don't like the sound of it," Easterwood said, "the spaced
volleys."

Connors shook his head slowly. "Nor I, sir. A surround,
likely enough."

"And not a damned thing we can do." He watched the night
darkening the land, creeping up from the river toward the summit of the Rock. The red and tan coloring of the formation
remained for a few moments in soft illumination from sky reflections, then grayed out until it became a blank wall. Somewhere beyond that wall were Quill and Robinson and the men
of their commands. And farther beyond them was Stuart's
Ranch, only ten miles into the grass country. He fought back a
fretting thought of Alison, who would be there now with Lee
Bowdring, and the soft night falling. And then like a cold shock
came the realization that the ranch was virtually undefended,
most of the cowboys being with Baird Stuart. The ranch house
was built like a fort, but how long could a handful of men hold
off a band of warriors, drunk on victory?

"Connors," he said then, "keep a sharp eye on that Indian
camp. If you see any action, sound the alert. And keep your
ears tuned to that firing. I'm going to make a quick inspection
of the fort."

Easterwood made a hasty circuit of the stockade, and was
satisfied with the solid strength of the heavy poles set deep in
the earth. Quill had followed the plans of the old fort, his one
addition being a narrow enclosed runway at the south end, connecting the fort proper with the cavalry stables and corral. The
old fort's stables had been separated from the main stockade, a
hundred yards farther down the slope.

He found two men on duty as stable guards. In addition to all
the wagon mules, about twenty cavalry mounts had been left by
Robinson. The guards wouldn't last two minutes against a night
raiding party, he thought; the men would be dead and all the
animals stampeded through the lower gate before an alarm
could be sounded.

He hurried back through the runway, passed the commissary storehouse and the quartermaster storehouse, where men were unloading the last of the supply wagons. He crossed over to haybag row where oil lamps glowed yellow in the tiny windows. This line of buildings had been hastily constructed of unbarked pine logs, the roofs made of poles and brush overlaid with earth a foot thick. At the end of the street was a half-completed ice-house; strips of sod and raw yellow earth from its excavation were heaped to one side.

On the way back, he paused a moment in front of the weather-boarded hospital to wash his hands in the water barrel —kept there as a fire precaution—and dismissed the thought of looking in on Asahel Greenslade. He listened carefully above the normal sounds of the fort, but could hear no further sounds of firing from the direction of the Rock.

Cutting across the parade that was dark now under the first pale stars of night, he re-entered headquarters. Sergeant Jonas came alert.

"You'll find Sergeant Connors on the north bastion," Easterwood said. "Tell him I want all the animals moved up from the stables into a rope corral inside the main stockade. And the corral gate is to be staked and spiked shut permanently."

As soon as Jonas was gone, Easterwood sat down wearily on the waiting bench beside the door. He remembered suddenly that only twenty-four hours earlier he had been seated on another bench, watching Alison Stuart coming down the starlit path from the ranch house. Though it seemed now like a long-ago dream, he remembered every detail of the scene, the light crunching of the gravel, her yellow hair, her voice, the touch of her hand, the coolness of her cheek, and the warmth of her lips.

"Tom! I didn't expect to find you here."

Mellie Quill was standing in the doorway, a gray cloak around her shoulders. Her dark liquid eyes blinked against the light from the room. He watched the familiar parting of her full lips as she spoke: "I came over to pick up the mail. Sergeant Jonas said it would be ready."

Easterwood looked helplessly around the stark room. "I suppose you know where the mail is kept."

She laughed, low and almost husky. "Behind the desk in that old cartridge box."

He went over and picked up a bundle of papers and magazines and letters, all neatly tied with string. She was looking at him, her head tilted slightly to one side.

"Tom Easterwood," she asked with mock sternness, "have you had your supper?"

He looked at her quickly, a comic expression of surprise on his face. "Good Lord, I knew I'd forgotten something," he said, and laughed.

"That's the first time I've heard you laugh in ten years, Tom Easterwood." She smiled at him. "I have some tea on the stove, and it'll only take a minute to warm up some supper."

"No—"

"Yes. As the colonel's lady, I'll put it as an order. And remember, I have some questions I want answered, some questions you and Major Robinson avoided this afternoon."

She was still beautiful, he thought, and persuasive. "If you order it," he said, "I must obey. Besides, I'd like some tea."

She laughed, and he liked the sound of it.

10

Mellie led the way through a tiny storm vestibule into her living room. To Easterwood it was like a swift entrance into another world, a feminine world of curtained windows, lace-decorated furniture, rug-covered floors, and pictures on the walls.

"How do you do it, Mellie?"

"Do what, Tom?" She turned her head, her cheeks glowing from the crisp night air.

"All this." He indicated the room with his hands. "By some kind of magic you can change any army post quarters into a world of your own. If I couldn't smell the fresh-cut cedar and pine, I'd swear I was back in Sheffield Manor, Virginia."

She unwound her neck scarf and handed it to him, smiling; he caught the spicy odor of her perfume. "Perhaps I live too much in the past, Tom." She frowned prettily, and added: "I'll see if the tea is warm enough. Sit down by the fire and be cozy."

When she went out through a green calico curtain at the back of the room, he crossed over to the stone-and-adobe fireplace. The fire had almost burned itself out in a bed of orange coals. He poked them up and added a fresh log; the sparks flew up in a mad crackling that reminded him unpleasantly of the gunfire from the Rock earlier in the evening. He pushed the memory aside, and stood with his back to the flames.

He was certain that this living room, though far from spa-

cious, was larger than any other on the post. There was a large
center table, three or four comfortable chairs, a book rack and
writing desk. The sofa facing the fireplace was a converted army
cot covered with a mattress and a buffalo hide decorated on the
flesh side with bright colors. Around the walls were still-life
prints of flowers and fruit, and a large framed painting of Sheffield Manor. He walked over and looked at it; the artist, he
guessed, must have been an amateur. Some of the lines were out
of perspective so that the big yellow house looked flat against its
background of trees.

He heard the whispering sound of her skirt. "Does it remind
you of anything?" she asked. He turned. She was holding a tray
with a wine bottle and two glasses.

"It's Sheffield Manor, to anybody who's ever been there," he
said.

"You'd never guess where it came from. How do you like it,
as a painting?"

He turned his head to one side, squinting at the green and
yellow colors. "Well, I don't know—"

She laughed. "I'll tell you before you say something you
might regret. I painted it myself."

"Oh—"

"When we were stationed in Arizona, there was a young
lieutenant on Mathew's staff who liked to paint. I borrowed his
paintbox, and I did it from memory. He was going to give me
lessons, but Mathew had him transferred." Her mouth drew up
suddenly in the familiar pout. "He reminded me a great deal of
you, Tom, the young lieutenant—"

"Why did he remind you of me?"

"He was tall and lean and stubborn, and a little bit sad, I
guess." Her face colored slightly, and the wine bottle rocked on
the tray.

Easterwood took the tray, steadying it. "How long have you
been serving tea from wine bottles?"

The smile came back to her lips, teasing. "The tea was
overboiled. I thought sherry would do as well."

"Even better," he said.

"I'm warming over some supper for you. But there's time for
a drink, for old time's sake."

They sat at opposite ends of the sofa-cot, facing the fire, with
the wine bottle on an ottoman made from a cartridge box. The

new log crackled, and again he thought of the firing from beyond the Rock.

She leaned back against a cushion, tasting the wine with the tip of her tongue. "Why so solemn-faced, Tom? Do you realize this is the first time we've been together alone—since Virginia?"

"That was another time, another world, and two other people. Neither of us is the same, Mellie."

"Oh, I wouldn't be so sure of that." She sneezed, and giggled softly. "Wine always makes me sneeze." She drained her glass. "Pour me another one, Tom."

She took the second glass and curled up languidly, like a cat, against the pillow. She looked at him over the rim of her glass. She hadn't changed as much as he would have guessed. Living with Quill for ten years, he would have thought . . . but by God, she was hardly past thirty, full-fleshed of bosom and thigh, her eyes as liquid and dark and deep and full of mystery as ever . . . he'd seen western army posts shrivel and dry the juice from many an officer's wife in less than ten years . . . but Mellie . . . suddenly he felt the ache he had suffered and shut away more times than he could count these last ten years.

She was up on her feet, her dress whispering, touching his lips gently with a finger tip. "Solemn-face. I'll bring your supper before it burns. Maybe that will cheer you up."

The spicy smell of her was all around him, after she had gone. He poured himself more wine, and wandered over to the writing desk. A new book lay open where she had been reading. *Our Mutual Friend,* by Charles Dickens. Beside it was the mail where she had dropped it, mostly *Harper's Weeklies* two or three months old. On top of the book shelf was a pipe rack and a tin of cut black government tobacco, the only evidence in the room of Mathew Quill's existence. The pipes were dusty.

He could feel his jaw tightening as memories of the afternoon whirled with memories of ten years ago, memories that began the first day he'd seen Quill riding across the big lawn before Sheffield Manor, there in the Virginia valley. From that moment, Mellie was lost to him. Quill with his long hair flying, the dashing cavalry leader, the Yankee *beau sabreur* with his picture in *Harper's Weekly.*

His teeth bit against the edge of the wine glass, and then he heard her skirts rustling. He turned quickly and they almost collided. She sucked in her breath, her red lips parting. She held

the covered dish aside, handing him a napkin; at the same time
she leaned forward and tasted the wine from his glass, her dark
eyes smiling, never leaving his.

"Tom, I'm happy, so happy I'm dizzy."

"Wine makes people dizzy," he said, and took the food dish
and put it down on the ottoman beside the sherry bottle.

He sat down on the edge of the buffalo hide, and then she was
there beside him, busying herself at stacking pillows behind
him. In the yellow lamplight her skin was pink and golden. She
reached out one hand to lift the cover from the dish; a wide-
banded gold ring glittered on one finger.

Easterwood took her hand before she reached the cover. "I
remember this ring," he said, and twisted it gently until it slid
off in his hand. He held it up against the lamplight, and read the
initials cut on the inside: "M. S. Q."

"It's the only beautiful thing I have," she said.

"This ring broke a young cavalry officer's heart once, on a
spring morning in Virginia."

She moved against him, and the spiced perfume was heavier
than the smell of wine. "Oh, I was cruel to you that morning. If
you had only taken me over your knee and spanked me. Instead
you just walked out of the house and got on your horse and
rode away. Stubborn and proud, you were, Tom Easterwood."

She put one hand up to his cheek, and then his arms were
around her, the crisp material of her dress crackling in his ear
like the log on the hearth, and the gunfire. Just the edges of
their lips were touching, barely touching. *Jezebel, O Jezebel
. . .* he had called her that once, after Quill had come to Sheffield Manor and set up his headquarters there. *Jezebel . . . So
let the gods do to me . . .*

From somewhere a bugle sounded, the clear and mellow bugle blowing first call for tattoo. Easterwood broke away from
her; he still held the napkin she had given him, crumpled in one
hand. "Good Lord," he said, "it's nine o'clock!"

"Don't go, Tom! Don't go yet, not now."

He said nothing, but got up and walked over to the window
facing the parade. He pushed the curtains back; the glass was
fogged with moisture, and little beads of water had run down to
the wooden frames. The temperature outside must have
dropped suddenly, he thought, and with the napkin he wiped
the glass clear until he could see the men gathering on the

parade in blue moonlight. The lanterns looked out of place in the clear light. "Did you hear the firing, about dusk?" he asked. "Robinson and the colonel should have been back by now."

When he turned she was gone. He blinked at the fire, and wondered how the wine bottle could have become almost emptied in so short a time.

He felt a little drunk, leaning back on the pillows, watching the fire die. The windowpanes rattled, and he knew a wind was rising. The wind brought an intermittent sound of a flute being played somewhere in the troopers' barracks, a mournful, lonesome note. He moved restlessly, and decided to call and tell her he would have to be going back to headquarters.

He heard the swish of the green curtains behind him, but no other sound, and he wondered if she had gone out of the room again. He saw her feet, then, bare on the rug before the couch. She had changed to a flowing *robe de chambre* that draped to her naked feet. She held one full-sleeved arm before her, moving like a sleepwalker between him and the fire to the yellow lamp on the table. She turned the lamp wick down, and he smelled the oil smoke before she was back, a vague flowing shadow in the slow dancing light of the fire.

She was humming softly when she sat beside him, her mouth moving closer to his ear, her throaty voice singing almost in a whisper: "My Love Is Like a Red, Red, Rose." Alison had sung that song, too, he thought, and tried to remember the other voice, the other face, but a spiciness was in the shadowy room and he turned to meet her mouth. She drew back so that again only the edges of their lips touched.

"Mellie," he said, "I'd better go. They may be looking for me at headquarters."

She sighed, stretching in his arms, and then her lips moist and open were on his. Her body moved so that the robe fell partially away; she wore nothing else, and his hands felt the silkiness of her thighs.

Taps was like a wailing on the rising night wind. Easterwood picked up the buffalo hide from where it had fallen on the rug, and draped it over Mellie. She lay on the couch, her eyes closed, breathing softly. But he knew she was not asleep.

He buttoned his jacket and walked over to the window. Blue moonlight streamed over the parade where the trumpeter was sounding the last note of the bugle call. In front of headquarters, Sergeant Connors was mounting the late guard, the men standing at attention before him for inspection.

Easterwood found his hat on the table, and then, feeling like a thief, he turned and went out through the green calico curtains at the rear. The back door had a hook latch; when he opened it the brilliance of the moonlight startled him. A sentry was walking slowly along the stockade. He stepped back inside, noticing a washstand with a tin washbowl and a pail of water. He poured some water in the bowl, dipping his face and rinsing his mouth. He rubbed his wet skin hard with a towel.

When he looked outside again the sentry had passed and was walking toward the north corner of the stockade. He closed the door gently after him, and moved quickly along in the shadows of the building. The frosty air stung his face and cleared his lungs. He suddenly remembered that he had not eaten the food Mellie had brought in the covered dish.

As there was no rear entrance to headquarters, he cut between the buildings. The frosted earth and grass crumbled beneath his boots as if he were treading on coarse sand. By the time he reached the plank sidewalk, Connors and the relief guard were moving off toward the main gate.

He stamped his feet on the narrow porch and walked into the headquarters entrance room. Sergeant Jonas was curled up in blankets on the floor by the telegraph stand, his mouth open in sleep. The oil lamps still burned, the wicks turned low.

If there had been any news from Quill, he was sure Jonas would have been awake, waiting for him. He went on into the office, turned out both lamps and dropped on the horse-hair sofa.

When he closed his eyes formless faces and figures spun confusedly across the screen of his vision, lighted vaguely by firelight and moonlight. He threw one arm across his eyes, but the fantasies moved and changed. Mostly they were Mellie, smiling and pouting prettily. Suddenly the dark eyes would change to blue and were full of fire and anger, and then in a blaze of moonlight he would see Alison's yellow hair, moving away from him, her voice laughing. And in the shadows, the face of Lee Bowdring changing abruptly to Bratt Fanshawe's. He came cold awake, remembering that Mellie had not mentioned Fanshawe's name at any time during the evening.

In the outer room a clock ticked, ticked, ticked. His mind worried with the thought of Quill and Robinson, remembering the earlier gunfire. Tick, tick, tick. Quill must have thought it safer to bivouac for the night, and march for the fort by daylight. Tick, tick, tick. But Connors had guessed from the volleys that it must have been a surround. Tick, tick, tick.

Whether he had passed from consciousness to sleep, he did not know, but he heard voices calling his name and boots shaking the floor. The office was still in darkness, with only a dim light coming through the door from Jonas' low-burning lamp. He was up, pushing the sleep away with one hand hard across his face.

"Captain Easterwood!" He recognized Connors' silhouette in the door.

"All right, all right. The troops come in?" His voice sounded unnatural, unlike his own, his tongue thick and numb.

He walked across the floor, looking beyond Connors into the lighted room. On the bench beside the entrance a man was sitting hunched over, his shoulders shivering uncontrollably. Easterwood came awake fast. Someone in the outer room turned the lamp up then, and he saw the man's face clearly. It was Bratt Fanshawe; he looked like a man who had been to hell and back. He was covered with mud and grime, even his mustache was dirty.

Connors stepped aside, and Easterwood went across to the scout, gripping him by the shoulder. "You all right, Fanshawe?" The scout's face was scratched, and there were narrow streaks of dried blood on the long-fingered hands that were gripping his knees. "I'll be all right." His teeth chattered. "I'm freezing."

"Jonas! Get a blaze going in that fireplace."

Jonas, who had been hovering nearby, rubbing his white hands nervously together, scurried over to the fireplace behind the telegraph stand. In a moment he had the fire started.

Easterwood touched Fanshawe's elbow. The scout drew away from him, but stood up and walked to the fire, crouching in front of it, his hands held over the rising flames. Easterwood propped himself against the edge of the telegraph stand. "What happened?" he asked.

"I don't know everything that happened." He added a "sir" belatedly. With the fire in front of him, Fanshawe's teeth had stopped chattering.

"Tell me what you know." Easterwood cut back the harshness in his voice. Whatever it was hadn't been pretty, and Fanshawe's day had been rough enough even before he went out with Major Robinson. "Anybody come back with you?"

"Yes, sir."

"How many?"

Fanshawe's lean face swung around toward him. "I don't know. Not many. The sergeant brought me straight here from the gate."

Connors moved over from the sergeant-major's desk. "Twenty-one men including the corporal, sir. They brought in four horses."

"What about Major Robinson?"

"I'd say he was dead, sir." Fanshawe leaned forward a little. Steam was beginning to rise from his wet trousers.

Easterwood told Connors to bring two chairs. He motioned Fanshawe to sit down, and he took the other chair, facing the scout. "Start at the beginning."

Fanshawe picked up a sliver of wood from the hearth and as he talked began scraping mud from the silver Mexican spurs he wore on his boots. "Everything went all right until we got around on the north side of the Rock. Just before we hit the shallow coulees in there, the major halted the squadron and I went ahead to scout."

"Alone?"

"Yes, sir. The major ordered it that way." Fanshawe turned his chair slightly so the heat would strike his back. "I hadn't gone two hundred yards before I picked up Indian sign, plenty. It was beginning to get dusky about then, but I could smell 'em, and picked up a call or two—whistle signals. Then I saw two Cheyenne hunched down in one of the coulees."

"Cheyennes?"

"I didn't see any others, but you know as well as I, sir, there wouldn't have been just two. I figure a Cheyenne war party has come in from the Sandhills to take a hand in Young Elk's game. They always join the Sioux when the stakes are worth playing for."

Easterwood nodded. "Go ahead."

"I didn't know it then, but they were packed in there, Cheyenne and Sioux both, laying for Colonel Quill's squadron. If they heard me, they must've thought I was one of them. I got

out of there as fast as I could and gave the hard facts to the
major. He was still trying to make up his mind what to do when
the firing broke out. The colonel had marched right into a bee's
nest, and I guess the major figured his duty was to draw some of
the sting off on his side. The only trouble was, when the major
took us in, Colonel Quill ran out, right up that trail on the east
side to the top of Skeletons' Rock."

Easterwood's boots came down hard on the floor, and he
strode quickly to the headquarters entrance. From the narrow
porch he could see small fires glimmering on top of the dark
shape of the Rock. He came back into the lamplight, frowning
heavily. "Connors, why was I not informed of this? Surely you
saw those campfires on the Rock?"

Connors' round face reddened furiously. "I first noticed them
just after tattoo, sir. I came here immediately to notify the captain, sir, but Sergeant Jonas said you were not in. I made a
search about the fort, sir, but—"

"Never mind." Easterwood saw Fanshawe's pale blue eyes
fixed on him, expressionless as usual, and he did not care to
dwell on the reasons why Connors had been unable to find him
after nine o'clock. He glanced at the ticking clock on the wall.
It was just after two o'clock in the morning.

"After placing the extra guards," Connors continued, "I
came back here. But the sergeant told me the captain was
sleepin,' sir, and I thought it best—"

"Forget about it, Connors."

Fanshawe had got all the mud scraped from his silver spurs.
The spurs he had taken from the dead Kiowa, Easterwood
thought, down in Indian Territory. He was polishing them now
with his handkerchief. Easterwood wondered if it was partly the
scout's passion for neatness that made him attractive to women.
"Where did you last see Major Robinson?"

"I was with him when he took the first troop in. I tried to
warn him to go cautious, but he rode into them thickety coulees
sitting like a ramrod in his saddle—like he was on parade. They
came at us from three sides just as it was beginning to turn
dusk. He bugled up the other troop and we made a stand."
Fanshawe leaned back and squinted at the polish on his spurs.
"We couldn't see them and I guess they couldn't see us too well.
But the Indians are getting smart, Captain, they've learned
things. They didn't bother too much with the carbine men, they

went for the horseholders. I reckon every damn horseholder in that first troop was a marked man. They got it with arrows and lead and war clubs and even knives. The horses were all gone, stampeded out, before we knew what their play was. We couldn't of rode out of there if we wanted to. The last time I saw the major, he ordered the men to charge through on foot and join up with Colonel Quill. He was waving his saber and leading the charge, last I saw of him. Dark was coming down fast by then."

"Did the men follow?"

Fanshawe stared at him coldly. "We did the best we could. A man can't do much charging through a coulee full of brush. Everybody got scattered out and separated and lost. It was hell out there in the dark, sir, not knowing friend from enemy. A handful of us got together in a little hollow, and we signaled in a few others. We picked up some more on the way back."

"Did you leave any wounded?"

"Not to our knowledge, sir. Four or five wounded rode in on the horses we recovered."

Easterwood stood up and faced the fire that was now blazing high. "All right, Fanshawe. You'd best go by the hospital and have those scratches cleaned up. Get some coffee and find a bed."

"Thank you, sir." The scout rose and started to go.

Connors moved in closer. "Beggin' your pardon, sir, but Trooper Fanshawe was in the guardhouse, sir."

"We can't spare a man to the guardhouse right now, Sergeant. If I need Trooper Fanshawe I can find him."

"Yes, sir."

"And Connors—see if you can dig up a flash lantern in the storehouse and meet me on the north bastion as soon as you can."

By the time Easterwood reached the bastion, the fires on top of the Rock were dying to small pinpoints against the sky. He leaned against the parapet, feeling the frost bite through his clothing, remembering that wood for fires was scarce up there on that flat-topped summit. Quill had done it up properly this time . . . and poor old Robinson . . . seventy-five mounted men went out, and twenty returned with four horses. He looked down at the river flowing like a cold sheet of metal under the moonlight, and he cursed quietly until the guard came out of the sentry box and stared curiously at him.

A few minutes later Connors came up the ladder, swinging a flash lantern. "An old one, sir, and smoked up, but it should throw a beam they can see."

"All right, set it up here on the parapet. You know code?"

"No, sir, I don't," he replied apologetically.

Easterwood took the lantern, turning it to face the Rock, leaving the flash on steady. He waited for several minutes, but there was no change in the campfires, no sign of response. He signaled dot-dash, dot-dash, dot-dash, intermittently, peering intently at the tiny winking fires, but there was still no reply.

"It may be worse than we thought, Connors."

"The men who could see us are all likely asleep, sir."

"You may be right. Likely the pickets would all be on the slope side, guarding the pass." He turned to the sentry. "Trooper, keep your eyes on those fires. If you see anything that looks like a signal, get the word to headquarters, double quick."

"Yes, sir."

"And pass that order along to your relief." He added, to Connors: "Unless we hear from the colonel, we'll wait until daylight for further signaling. Get some sleep, Sergeant, but be back here before daylight."

"Thank you, sir."

Easterwood went down the ladder and then crossed the moonlit parade to the hospital. He found Surgeon Campbell in the narrow hallway, drying his hands on a towel. The old man looked tired.

"Any bad ones, Surgeon?"

"Two or three won't be ready for mounted duty for at least a month, sir, but they're healthy boys and ought to mend proper." Campbell rubbed one of his long sideburns thoughtfully with a forefinger. "A devilish business, sir. Can you hold out any hope for the others?"

"Some may have got through to the colonel's squadron. If I had enough men to risk, I'd take a search party out now. As it is, I doubt if we could defend the fort for long under a strong attack."

"As bad as that, sir."

"We may know how bad when dawn breaks."

Campbell stared down at the floor. "I know. Indians seem to

prefer dying at sunrise. I learned that years ago when I was a contract-surgeon in Texas."

"We'll worry about it when it comes." Easterwood touched the old man's shoulder lightly. "Good night."

Before returning to headquarters he made a circuit of the stockade, warning all the guards to be on the alert and to report any suspicious movements immediately. He found the headquarters door closed, and when he opened it a blast of hot dry air struck him in the face. Sergeant Jonas had kept the fireplace blaze going and had fallen asleep in his tangle of blankets on the floor.

After the brisk night air, the room was oppressive. He went over to the fireplace, scattered the logs with a poker, and then went outside and sat down on the single entrance step. The moon had drifted lower, throwing heavy shadows along the lines of buildings. In the silence, his thoughts began churning; he knew he could not sleep again before dawn.

From somewhere along the south line of buildings then, he caught a slight movement, a shadow merging with moon shadow. The movement was stealthy, a skilled stealthiness, so that he barely saw the human figure slide across a narrow block of moonlight. He knew only that at the farther end of officers' row some one had moved behind the buildings in the direction of the stockade.

Easterwood stood up and walked slowly along the sidewalk planking, then turned sharp right into the shadow of the headquarters building. He had crossed this strip of frosty ground once before this night, returning from Mellie Quill's back door.

When he reached the end of the building, he crouched against the corner wall, facing south along the rear line of officers' row. A pacing guard, unaware of Easterwood's presence, moved past him along the stockade thirty feet away, halting mechanically at every loophole to peer outside the fort.

A minute passed and then he saw the skulking figure again, approaching in long strides, almost obscured in the black shadow behind the officers' quarters. Easterwood was certain that if he had not been deliberately looking for him, he would not have been aware of the man's presence.

At Mellie Quill's back door the figure paused, and Easterwood heard a faint scratching noise, repeated once or twice. The man pressed close to the door, then drew back quickly as it opened a few inches. A moment later he was gone, melting into the blackness of the house and the mysterious night.

11

Half an hour before dawn, Easterwood waked Sergeant Jonas and sent him with an order to the trumpeter to sound reveille immediately. By the time the platoons were formed on the parade, the moon was beginning to fade out in a slate-gray sky.

As soon as the rolls were called and reported, Easterwood ordered Private Fanshawe to fall out and advance to front and center. The scout marched forward, halting at attention. "At ease, Fanshawe." The scout relaxed slightly, staring calmly at Easterwood. His face was pale in the gray light, but he looked spruce and refreshed in contrast to his bedraggled appearance of a few hours before. "You know how to send code, do you not, Fanshawe?"

"I've done some sending with mirror signals, sir."

"How about flags?"

"I can send with flags, but not so fast as with a mirror."

"There doesn't seem to be a heliostat in the fort. It'll have to be flags."

"Yes, sir."

"Fall out and wait in headquarters." Easterwood turned back to the formation, and began explaining to the men as briefly as possible the situation which confronted the fort. He informed them that Colonel Quill's squadron appeared to be trapped on top of the Rock, and that an Indian attack possibly would be made against the stockade at sunrise. After ordering them to count off for loophole positions, he dismissed them to quarters to ready firearms. "Assembly call in five minutes. All men who presently lack arms report to the commissary for issue. On the double!"

He called Sergeant Connors forward. "When the platoons reassemble, inspect arms and inform the men that breakfast call will be sounded only when we are certain there is to be no immediate attack."

Connors saluted briskly. "Yes, sir."

"Even if we're lucky to escape attack this morning, Connors, morale is going to be low in this fort. If there is no attack, have troop call sounded as soon as the men have breakfasted. Inspect weapons and uniforms rigidly. All men with dirty uniforms are to have them laundered before retreat call. Keep every man busy every minute of this day. If there are not enough regular duties to keep them busy, assign details to police the grounds as if a major-general were coming for post inspection."

"Yes, sir."

Easterwood returned Connors' salute and hurried back to headquarters. Fanshawe was sprawled on the entrance bench, staring vacantly at the floor. Jonas was making entries in his morning report. A jointed signal-staff and a roll of red, white, and black signal flags lay across the sergeant's desk. "Bring the four-foot white flag," Easterwood called sharply to the sergeant. "And don't forget a writing board."

When they climbed to the top of the north bastion, the eastern sky was brighter, with light pulsing upward from the horizon in streaks of pale yellow and pink reflected on the Rock. Easterwood turned his field glass on the Indian village along the sand flat, vague in mists across the river. Dogs were beginning to bark down there, but he saw no evidence of the usual ceremonies that precede a battle. As the mists slowly dissolved, he noticed that a new circle of tipis had been erected beyond the first village. He handed the field glass to Fanshawe. "Look beyod that little sand spit."

"Cheyenne tipis," Fanshawe said.

"Domino Ruark used to say a man could read what Plains Indians were planning to do by the arrangement of their camps. How do you read that one?"

Fanshawe squinted through the glass, moving it slowly back

and forth. "Open at both ends. I wouldn't say it was pitched for battle."

"One good sign anyhow." Easterwood took the glass, shifting it along the near side of the river. No Indians appeared to be on the south bank. He saw only the fort's small sawmill and its water turbine about four hundred yards out. He focused the glass on the summit of the Rock.

"Maybe they don't figure we could ever get that far, to their village," Fanshawe said dryly. He was peering over the log parapet at the river. "They got us by the short hairs, Captain."

Easterwood didn't reply. The smell of the Yellowhorse came up with the morning breeze, the smell of mud. Bright sun reflections were on the heights now; a gnarled pine came into clear focus, then one of the fires, dying in the breaking dawn. He saw a horse, shadowy against a boulder, and finally a man, or what appeared to be a man, propped in blankets against a dead tree trunk.

"The colonel had a telegraph sergeant with him," Easterwood said. "Do you know if he carried any other signaling equipment?"

"His orderly usually packed a heliostat mirror."

Easterwood glanced to the east. "We'll soon know if they have it." The sun was over the horizon rim, already brilliant in a cloudless sky.

The three waited patiently, watching the Rock for signs of movement. Fanshawe finished fastening the flag to the signal staff, and Jonas propped a flat board against the parapet for a makeshift recording table. Inside the fort, the loopholes were manned. Down on the sand flat, the Indian women were building their morning cooking fires, the blue smokes drifting upward to replace the dissipated mists. Children came out to play in the early sunshine; the dogs kept up their incessant barking.

From high on the Rock, the first signal flashes came suddenly like streaks of white fire. Long, short, long, short, long, short. "All right, Fanshawe, there it is. The colonel's mirror." Easterwood fixed his field glass on a rocky point; he picked the signaler up immediately, a young trooper with a bandage strapped over one ear. He shifted the glass to the right and Quill's stocky figure jumped into view. The colonel had a glass fixed on him.

Fanshawe brought the white flag up, bracing the staff against the breeze.

"Back up and move over to your right," Easterwood said. "You'll need more room." Fanshawe shifted his position. "Damn it, sir," he cried, "I've forgot the first signal." He glared angrily at Easterwood.

"Give him a two-two, two-two, three—and he'll go ahead with his message."

Fanshawe brought the flag down sharply, four times to his left and then one time again straight to his front.

The flashes came again in quick reply—short, long, short, short, short. "He wants us to wait up," Easterwood said. "When he starts sending again, I'll read the letters off, Jonas."

In a few moments, he was reading a cryptic query: HOW MANY TROOPS C AND D RETURNED TO FORT? QUILL.

"Tell him, TWENTY MEN, FOUR HORSES," Easterwood ordered. He had to help Fanshawe with some of the letters, and then Quill's signaler ordered a repeat.

"He thinks we made a mistake in the numbers," Easterwood said quietly. "Repeat the message, Fanshawe."

This time there was a long pause from the Rock, and Easterwood guessed this was an indication of the shock of surprise the information had brought to Quill. He peered through his glass until he could see Quill, bent over with a notebook resting on one upraised knee. When the flashes began once more, they spelled out a rambling explanation from Quill of what had happened at dusk the previous day, of how he had been surprised by superior forces and for defensive reasons had turned up the narrow trail to the heights of the Rock. The Rock, Quill asserted, was a perfect defense position, but as long as the Indians held the pass below, it was also a trap, and he had insufficient reserve strength to attempt a breakout.

During the withdrawal, Quill added, several of Major Robinson's men had broken through and joined his squadron. He concluded with a long sentence: IF MAJOR ROBINSON HAD NOT RETREATED IN DISORDER VICTORY WOULD HAVE BEEN CERTAIN. As Easterwood read off the final letters, Fanshawe spat over the edge of the parapet.

"Ask him if he knows the fate of Major Robinson," Easterwood ordered.

Fanshawe sent the message, whipping the flags savagely against the breeze.

The answer came back: NO. And the flashes continued: SURVIVING TROOPERS OF ROBINSON'S COMMAND SAY FANSHAWE WAS SCOUTING. IS THIS TRUE?

"Tell him YES," Easterwood said.

The heliostat flashed back: WHY?

"Tell him, MAJOR ROBINSON'S ORDERS."

But Quill was not satisfied with the reply, demanding to know why Easterwood had disobeyed orders by releasing a prisoner from custody.

"He knows the answer to that one," Easterwood said sharply. "Query for further orders."

Quill made no reply for two or three minutes, then asked if Easterwood had made any attempt to inform Goldfield by telegraph or by messenger of the desperate situation at Yellowhorse.

Easterwood replied: EXACT SITUATION UNKNOWN TO ME BEFORE THIS HOUR. TELEGRAPH DEAD SINCE LAST EVENING, AND A SINGLE MOUNTED MESSENGER COULD NOT CROSS YELLOWHORSE ALIVE BY DAYLIGHT.

Quill's heliostat blinked back: MY ORDERS ARE: SEND THREE MESSENGERS TO GOLDFIELD ON BEST MOUNTS AVAILABLE AT DIFFERENT TIMES AND BY DIFFERENT ROUTES AT EARLIEST PRACTICAL MOMENT, REQUESTING AID IN FORCE. The message continued with a recital of the trapped squadron's shortages of ammunition, food, and water. Eight men were wounded, two severely. Six others of A and B Troops had been cut off in the withdrawal and were presumed dead. Quill ended his long period of signaling by requesting Easterwood to repeat back the order concerning the messengers.

As soon as Fanshawe flagged the repeat, the mirror flashed dot, dot, dot, dash, dot, dash, and spelled out Q U I L L.

Easterwood blew his breath out in a long voluminous sigh. "Rest your flag, Fanshawe. They're through signaling for a while." He went over and picked up the message record sheets from Jonas' board, and then glanced down at the Indian camp. The Sioux and Cheyennes were enjoying their breakfasts. Except for a half dozen mounted braves who were either returning from or going forward to the point where they held Quill's troops besieged, there was no sign of imminent hostile action.

He left Sergeant Jonas to watch for further call signals, ordered Fanshawe to go and find himself a hasty breakfast, and then hurried down the bastion steps. At the foot of the ladder he was surprised to find Asahel Greenslade on crutches, talking with Sergeant Connors.

"Good morning, Professor. You're looking as spry as a jackrabbit."

Greenslade's goatee bobbed as he nodded cheerfully. "I must say you appear a bit more confident than I would have expected, Captain. Considering all the rumors that are going about this morning."

"What rumors?"

"I suppose, sir," Sergeant Connors interrupted hastily, "the professor must have heard from some of the men about the precautions we're taking."

"I see. Well, you may start your men to breakfast in small details, Connors. But keep a sharp lookout." He turned back to Greenslade. "I was just going to snatch a bite of bacon before we start waving that flag again. I'd trade a solid gold nugget for a mirror device. We could send twice as fast."

Greenslade's eyebrows shot up. "Have you looked through our balloon supplies, Captain?"

"No. There can't be—"

"The best and newest model heliograph in the Signal Service. One of the British type recommended by General Sherman when he came back from his trip to Europe."

Easterwood grinned sheepishly. "I should have thought of the balloon supplies. While I'm digging out the heliograph, you hobble over to Surgeon Jamie Campbell's quarters. Campbell's invited us to breakfast. He has a lady cook from haybag row, a good cook, he says. I'll join you as soon as I get that heliograph set up for sending."

Easterwood found the two balloon wagons pulled over to one side of the commissary building. With the help of one of the guards, he moved the supply boxes from around the balloon envelope until he found a large one marked in charcoal: FIELD SIGNALS. He pried back the pine boards with a hand axe. The heliograph, consisting of a mirror signal equipped with control rods and screws, was wrapped in oilskin. Beside it was a folded tripod. And to his surprise, the box also contained a supply of colored signal lights, candle bombs, and a copper signal mortar.

A few minutes later, he had the heliograph mounted for action on the bastion, and after showing Sergeant Jonas how to flash a "wait" signal, he hurried back down the ladder, and crossed the parade to Surgeon Campbell's quarters.

Campbell lived adjoining the hospital in a square one-room log hutment chinked with clay and roofed with slabs. When Easterwood entered, the surgeon and Greenslade were seated at a box table in one corner, sipping tea. From behind a curtain of unbleached cotton in the opposite corner, sounds indicated the presence of a cook at work in some sort of make-shift kitchen. "Bring tea for the captain," Campbell shouted, and before Easterwood could sit down on the backless hickory stool waiting for him, a tall angular woman appeared from behind the curtain with a steaming cup.

She was of a type Easterwood had seen in frontier trail towns and on army posts from Kansas to California—not homely but not attractive—the sort of woman most usually referred to as "she has seen better days," though in all probability she had not. She gave Easterwood a searching, suspicious glance, and set the cup and saucer ungently upon the rough table top in front of him.

"Thank you, Rosie," the surgeon said, "you may serve breakfast now."

She nodded, mumbling to herself, and went back into the corner kitchen. Easterwood could smell bacon frying, and he was suddenly ravenous. He had eaten nothing for twenty-four hours. He looked around the room, dimly lit by only two small windows.

Campbell had tacked strips of unbleached cotton over the rafters to form a ceiling of sorts; a mud wasp was buzzing angrily, trapped behind the cloth somewhere on one of the ridgepoles. Above the small open fireplace, a rough mantel shelf was crowded with bottles of all sizes and colors; they contained insects, snakes, and other reptiles. And on the wall above the box table, a shelf of medical books was suspended from the rafters by strips of the unbleached cotton which the surgeon seemed to use for all purposes.

"A cozy little cottage," Easterwood said. "From the bottles, I'd guess you were interested in natural history."

"Natural history and Indian ethnology are my recreations, sir." Campbell looked tired after his night of interrupted sleep;

the flesh around his eyes was swollen and the veins in his cheeks were purplish and distended.

"I suppose you've spent some time in the West."

"About a quarter of a century," Campbell replied. "Served in every western department."

Greenslade interrupted: "The surgeon was just telling me he came out here during the Mormon troubles in the fifties. He's seen field duty in six major campaigns against the Indians."

The cook brought the food on long tin platters—bacon, fried trout, prunes, and hot biscuits. For the next several minutes there was little talk. Greenslade finished first, grumbling about being on a half-diet. He pushed back his chair and sighed. "Maybe I am a wee bit out of turn bringing the matter up, Captain, but I'd somewhat like to know our condition. The surgeon, when he was telling me of his experiences, expressed an opinion that our circumstances are about as desperate as any he has ever been involved in."

Easterwood glanced sideways at the cotton curtain concealing the kitchen and the cook. "Desperate maybe, but not hopeless," he said quietly. "The fort is well stocked with supplies and ammunition. Short of men, true. Morale, uncertain. You two gentlemen are in a sense officers and it is your duty to assist me in quelling wild rumors and in putting on a show of confidence before the men."

Campbell brushed one of his long gray sideburns gently with a forefinger. "And what is Colonel Quill's situation, sir?"

"Not good. Water short, probably half the canteens empty by now, and no water supply on the Rock. Food about gone, maybe a few hard crackers in some haversacks. Ammunition low. But his casualties have been light, and he believes he can hold his position as long as his troopers can endure without food and water."

"As a surgeon, sir, I must tell you that cannot be for long."

Easterwood nodded slowly. "Now I shall ask a question of you, Surgeon. You have observed the tribes more years by far than I have. When do you believe they will attack the fort?"

Campbell smiled slightly. "I can't answer your question, of course. No white man can say for certain what or where or when an Indian will do anything. An Indian's actions are determined by too many factors—his superstitions, his religion, often the weather or some other phenomenon of nature. Any one of these factors could bring about an attack, possibly a withdrawal, though I would discount the latter. Is there a possibility of outside help reaching us anytime soon?"

"Not soon enough," Easterwood said. "The colonel has ordered me to send three messengers separately to Goldfield. This I shall do, immediately after nightfall. But help could not reach us for at least three, maybe four days. I'm afraid we don't have that much time." He was looking at Greenslade; the professor's face was grave.

A knock sounded on the door then, and Campbell cried: "Open it and come in."

Sergeant Connors' round red face peered into the half-darkened room. "Cap'n Easterwood, sir?"

"What's up, Connors? More signals from the colonel?"

"No, sir, it's about the fort's water wagon, sir. The quartermaster corporal in charge tells me it has to be filled today, or we'll go short."

Easterwood whirled around, facing Campbell. "Good Lord, Surgeon, isn't there a well inside the stockade?"

Campbell shook his head slowly. "We've been using the big spring down by the river, Captain. I believe the colonel planned to dig a well later."

Easterwood's hawk nose came up as if he were sniffing the air, his mouth tightening. "All right, Connors," he said quietly, "send your quartermaster corporal with an order to assemble a mounted platoon of twelve men. He is to have the platoon and his wagon at the main gate, ready for marching in a quarter hour. Next, I want you to pass this order to every man and woman on this post: Water is to be used sparingly henceforth and only for cooking and drinking."

"Yes, sir." Connors withdrew respectfully, closing the door after him.

Easterwood turned to Campbell, thanking him for the late breakfast. He picked up his hat from the floor. "Is the spring down by that little sawmill, Surgeon?"

"Just this side of it."

"A long three hundred yards, and uphill all the way back."

"Good luck to you, Captain," Greenslade said.

"We'll need it." He turned and started for the door.

* * *

From the bastion, Easterwood studied the Indian camp through his field glass. It looked peaceable under the late morning sun, the variegated pictographs on the tipis and the buckskin dresses of the women forming a mass of colors—sagegreen, soft orange-brown, ocher-red—and the yellow river and the strip of tawny sand. Some of the warriors were washing and currying their ponies. One young buck was shoeing the hoofs of a spotted mustang with pieces of buffalo skin, tying them on with rawhide strips. Another was proudly leading a recently captured U.S. Cavalry mount through the lodges.

Easterwood turned to Jonas, who was leaning against the parapet beside him. "Can you handle the swivel gun, Sergeant?"

"Yes, sir. I've had gunnery training, sir."

"I want you to sight it on the Indian camp. The sentry here will act as second gunner to help you load and fire, if necessary. Most of the time while I'm out there, I'll be in plain view. If I throw up my arm to you, or if you see the Indians making any show of crossing the river, fire off a round."

"The gun is shorter range than the river, sir."

"I don't expect you to hit anything. Just fire it off in that general direction."

"Yes, sir."

Fanshawe was squatting beside the heliograph tripod, his eyes on Easterwood, cold and uninterested.

"All right, Fanshawe. Let's go."

At the main gate the platoon was waiting, drawn up beside the green water wagon; a trooper was holding Easterwood's Palouse and another mount for Fanshawe. Connors and the quartermaster corporal stood at attention as Easterwood came up. "As you were," he said. "Fanshawe and I will lead out at a quick pace. Corporal, keep your wagon rolling smartly. The platoon will march in files on either side. Prepare to mount!"

They were well out of the gate and heading down the slope before the Indians down on the flat reacted to their sudden appearance. The women began scurrying toward the tipis, corralling their playing children on the way. The warriors stopped currying their ponies; some mounted and began riding back and forth. One blanketed old man refused to be disturbed; he was seated in the sunshine on a log far out on the sandspit. Through

his glass, Easterwood could see that he was fishing with a wil-
low-wand trap.

As they marched down the slope, the empty water wagon
bounced loosely over the rough trail. Easterwood glanced back
once at the bastion; Jonas and the sentry had the swivel gun in
position and were watching the river alertly.

They moved down to the spring, following the trail around it
and then dropping sharply to the level of the sawmill. Here,
where a turbine had been set into a man-made waterfall, the
wagon had to be backed in for loading through a canvas hose.

While the quartermaster corporal was getting his wagon set
properly, Easterwood ordered one of the troopers to string the
hose. With Fanshawe, he then rode out for a closer look at the
Indian camp. The old man on the sand spit had stopped dipping
his fish trap; he seemed to be squinting across the river as if
puzzled by the actions around the sawmill. Behind him a dozen
warriors were racing their ponies along the hardpacked sand,
waving and pointing excitedly. More were coming up from the
lodges, some mounted, some on foot. Easterwood slid his glass
along the line, searching for Young Elk. He hoped Young Elk
was occupied up on the Skeletons' Rock trail.

Fanshawe said: "It'll only take one wild 'un to start 'em
swimming the river."

Easterwood pulled the Palouse to the right and galloped up
the rise and around the spring where he could look down upon
the wagon; the water was already running through the hose into
the wooden tank. "How much longer, Corporal?"

The quartermaster corporal had one ear against the tank,
listening to the water churning inside. Easterwood had to call
louder. The corporal looked up. "Ten, maybe fifteen minutes,
sir."

For the next few minutes, Easterwood kept the Palouse moving in a half circle. At least fifty braves were mounted now;
some of them were beginning to whoop and call in derision
across the river. One warrior raced his pony a few feet into the
shallows, the water splashing high and silver in the sun. But
when the river deepened and slowed his mount he turned and
went back, the others laughing at him.

All at once something moved, jerkily, and as Easterwood
brought up his glass, he saw the old man on the sand spit falling

against the log, as if he had stumbled. A rifle cracked, the noise resounding against the flat face of the Rock.

Easterwood whirled on the wagon escort, but none of the men had a weapon at ready. He saw it then, the puff of smoke from a jutting ledge high on the Rock, followed by a shrill triumphant cry.

"By God, what a shot!" Fanshawe shouted. His pale eyes gleamed for just a second. "That was from a Henry buffalo rifle. The colonel's adjutant always carries one."

Easterwood was watching the Indians. One mounted brave was dashing his pony out along the sandspit. The Henry rifle fired again but this time the target was moving. The Indian halted, and leaned forward, clinging to his horse's mane, looking down at the old man lying against the log. Then he turned quickly, shaking his fist toward the Rock.

From across the river, Easterwood heard the brave's long keening cry. Fanshawe swung his head around. "We better start moving, Captain."

Easterwood was already spurring the Palouse back toward the spring. "Get that wagon rolling! Form files, carbines at ready!"

Before the wagon had moved a dozen yards, the enraged Indians were swimming their horses in the river. The quartermaster corporal lashed his mules furiously with his whip; even with a half-empty tank, the animals were struggling against the steep grade.

"They'll catch us halfway," Fanshawe warned, "unless we run for it."

Easterwood measured the distances. The current had swept the Indians downstream, but the leaders were already coming in to the south bank, their rifles held high. He waited a few seconds, and then jabbed his right hand skyward and down toward Sergeant Jonas on the bastion. The sergeant waved back, vanished from the parapet, and a few seconds later a shell was screaming from the swivel gun, exploding in a blast accentuated by echoes from the Rock.

"Keep it rolling," Easterwood shouted to the wagon driver. The Indians had hesitated before the artillery explosion, halting now on the riverbank. Some of their horses were floundering in the mud.

Before the warriors could rally again, the water wagon was

inside the fort. But after the gate was closed they moved in
closer to the stockade, racing their horses in a spreading circle.
Easterwood watched them from the gate loophole, but they
never came in close enough for rifle fire to be effective. After
half an hour of riding and whooping, they withdrew, trotting off
toward the shallow ford to recross the river.

As he turned away from the loophole, Easterwood saw Mellie Quill coming across the parade. She was carrying a tiny
parasol and wore a mustard-yellow cavalry circular around her
shoulders. As she came closer, he could see the smile on her full
lips. Her face was unworried, her dark liquid eyes almost
merry. She looked as if she had just awakened from a long and
dreamless sleep.

She twirled her parasol and he saw beyond her, then, a group
of women gathered around the entrance to headquarters. As she
came closer, he removed his hat and said: "Good morning."

"Good morning, Tom." Her eyes flicked briefly to Fanshawe.

"Morning, ma'am," Fanshawe said. He was standing to the
left and slightly behind Easterwood. His voice had turned nasal,
with no feeling in it.

"I suppose you've heard that the colonel is all right?" As
Easterwood asked her the question, he could not resist a glance
back toward Fanshawe; the scout's eyes met his for a second,
narrowing slightly as if to conceal the hostility in them.

Mellie laughed gently. "Matt is like the proverbial cat. Nine
lives and always lands on his feet."

"I would guess from that female delegation," Easterwood
said, indicating the women collected in front of headquarters,
"that some wives are not so confident of their husbands' run of
luck."

She looked at him coolly, adjusting the yellow circular with
her free hand. "They're not married to Matt Quill," she replied,
almost in a whisper.

"What do those women expect me to do about their men?"
he asked harshly.

"They wish only to know the names of the wounded and
missing."

"I'll see that they get them." He put his hat back on, and
started again toward the north bastion.

She called after him: "Tom." He turned back. She was spinning the parasol. "It's almost noon. Will you have dinner with me?"

"I'm sorry," he said. "There won't be time."

"Supper then?"

"If possible, after retreat. I'll be honored, Mellie"

"I'll hold you to your promise," she said.

He cut across the parade toward the bastion, Fanshawe following close behind. Before they started up the ladder, the scout spoke suddenly: "I've been wondering, sir, about the messengers Colonel Quill ordered sent to Goldfield. If you aim to carry out that order, sir, I'd like to volunteer."

Easterwood looked at him sharply. "The colonel's orders will be carried out, of course."

"I wish to volunteer as one of the messengers, sir."

Without reply, Easterwood turned back to the ladder. He remembered hearing Fanshawe, as a civilian scout, boast more times than once that he had never volunteered for any duty and never would.

"Not bragging, sir," Fanshawe persisted, his voice whining slightly, "but I'll bet my luck against any man's in this command, I can get through to Goldfield before him."

Easterwood wondered at the eagerness in the scout's plea. It was out of character. He was silent a moment, and then replied quickly: "I daresay Colonel Quill would disapprove of such an assignment. You're a prisoner, Fanshawe."

During the next half hour, while they were sending and receiving signals, the scout remained silent, his face sullen. But he worked the heliograph efficiently, sending so rapidly at times that the receiver on the Rock had to signal "repeat last message" and "send slower" on several occasions.

Easterwood's first message to Quill was a blistering comment on the rifle fire from the Rock. He pointed out that the useless killing of the old Indian fisherman had jeopardized unnecessarily the lives of the cavalrymen attempting to obtain water for the fort. Quill's reply was that any Indian coming into rifle range of his besieged squadron would be fired upon regardless of consequences. The colonel ended his message with a terse report that his men were down to their last water rations, and would prefer to see the people in the fort engage themselves at killing Indians rather than in obtaining water for themselves.

Deciding there was no point in continuing this useless ex-

change of signals, Easterwood asked for a list of wounded and
missing, as well as the names of the survivors from Major
Robinson's squadron. He explained that the wives in the fort
were concerned over lack of information concerning their husbands. After some delay, the names were signaled.

As soon as the "no more" flashes came, Easterwood ordered
Fanshawe to sign off. "Post the casualty lists on the front of
headquarters," he said to Jonas. "You and Fanshawe are both
dismissed for dinner. The sentry will take over the signal
watch."

When he came down the ladder he was surprised to see a
detail of men hard at work policing the grounds of every scrap
of dried vegetation, every piece of bark and sliver of wood.
Sergeant Connors was doing his best.

That afternoon, Easterwood buried the dead—two troopers
and Baird Stuart's cowboy—leading the little procession outside the fort to a small knoll used as a burying ground. Guards
were posted, and no time was wasted in reading the services.
Later that same day, the three men—Easterwood, Campbell,
and Greenslade—sat once again around the box table in the
corner of the surgeon's quarters. Blue smoke from their cigars
curled in a beam of late afternoon sunshine slanting to the floor
through one of the small windows.

"The Sioux and Cheyenne," the surgeon was saying, "are the
aristocrats of the plains. Proud, brave, independent, the best of
fighters. They honor bravery among their enemies, and seldom
take prisoners. They seldom torture."

"What do they fear?" Easterwood asked. "What above all do
they fear?"

Campbell drew on his cigar. "Mystery," he said. "They fear
only mystery—that which they cannot understand."

Easterwood's eyes were half closed, fixed on the smoke-filled
beam of sunshine. "That's what I was getting at. Something
mysterious. Something so awesome they cannot comprehend it,
and therefore must fear it."

"They live and move, sir, only at the mercy of multitudinous
associations. What may be fearsome to one Indian may not be
so to another. One warrior may have signaled out some mystery
symbol, an object representing that which is most feared or
worse hated among his surroundings. I recall an incident of

years ago, out in the Crow country. We were camped with the Crows; old Jim Bridger was scouting for us then. One morning I killed a black chickensnake outside my tent, a good six-footer. A young brave rushed up and protested that I had destroyed his medicine. He wanted to kill me, and I do believe he might have done so forthwith, had not old Bridger interfered. I think Bridger convinced the Crow I was crazy in the head, and was therefore not responsible for my actions."

Greenslade chuckled softly. "I've heard they also worship the sun. Is this different from their animal worship?"

"Professor, to these people the sun *is* an animal, the mightiest of all animals. Only the thunderbird, which you see painted on their tipis, is a rival in power to the sun. Thunder, to them, is the flapping of the wings of the Great Ancient Eagle, the thunderbird. The sun and the thunderbird are great mysteries, and there are mystery places, too. The Canyon of the Horse Bones, a few miles to our east—created by our Colonel Quill when he slew the Sioux horses two years ago—has become a sacred place of mystery. Skeletons' Rock where yonder fumes our colonel, is a place of mystery—desecrated now, in their eyes, by our comrades' unwilling presence."

"I've heard them speak of these mysteries," Easterwood said. "They call them *Wakanda*."

"Ah, yes. The sun is *Wakanda*, the moon is *Wakanda*, the thunder, the sacred cedar trees—" Campbell tossed his half-burned cigar across to the fireplace, and then reached up to the wall shelf above the table. He pushed aside a pair of old beaver gauntlets and took down a cigar box half filled with smoking tobacco. He began packing his pipe.

"A balloon," Easterwood said quietly, "an enormous gas-filled balloon, rising suddenly into the sky from nowhere—"

Campbell put his pipe down, his jaw slacking, and then suddenly his lined face broke into a broad grin. "By God, man, what a *Wakanda* that might be!"

Professor Greenslade began brushing nervously at the gray curls on the back of his head. "But Captain," he said, "the iron filings we must have to generate gas for the balloon are sitting on a wagon, a couple of miles beyond the Yellowhorse. For all the use we can make of them, they might as well be on the moon."

The surgeon's smile vanished; he shrugged and said sadly:

"Well, who knows, the Indians might have looked upon your fanciful balloon as a good *Wakanda,* a fortuitous rather than a bad omen."

Easterwood pushed back his chair and began pacing up and down the floor, the boards creaking as he walked. "None of them has ever seen a balloon. I think they would read a balloon in the sky as a bad sign from the Great Spirit." He stopped in the middle of the floor, his thumbs hooked over his belt. "I'm so sure of it I'm going to make a try for that wagon. As soon as the sun is down."

Campbell shook his head. "You'll never make it, Captain. They'll be watching every move around this fort, and even if you're lucky and find your wagon, you'd never be able to drive it back in here."

Leaning forward over the surgeon, Easterwood smiled suddenly at him. "I'll wager you give your wounded men better encouragement than that, sir. Thanks to our farsighted little professor here, we're going to bedazzle and bamboozle our redskinned friends this evening. And maybe conjure up a wagonload of iron filings to gas-fill our empty balloon skin."

Campbell rubbed his sideburns and frowned perplexedly at Greenslade. The professor's white goatee bobbed up and down. "The man is mad," he said, with a note at exasperation. "I don't know what he's talking about."

Easterwood grinned back at them. "What time will the moon rise tonight?" he asked.

"Last night it was up about half past eight," Campbell replied. "It'll be shining like a beacon before ten o'clock."

"Four to five hours of darkness. More than enough." Easterwood picked up his hat. "Professor Greenslade, I shall require your presence at the main gate immediately after dusk. Excuse me, gentlemen." He was smiling when he went out the door.

During the time before retreat, Easterwood studied the hand-drawn map on the wall behind the command desk, memorizing the position of the stockade and the gate in relation to the land lying on the south and west. He noted the curving line of the Yellowhorse, the estimated depth of an upper crossing, and the directions in which the ridges and coulees ran on the north side of the stream. Later, he sent for Fanshawe, questioning the scout for several minutes in regard to some unmarked features of the surrounding topography.

After Fanshawe left, he called in Sergeant Connors and gave him several orders to be carried out immediately after retreat ceremony. Among the orders was one to saddle the Appaloosa and three other horses, and to put two mules into full harness for drawing a heavy wagon. Another order was to remove a box from the balloon supply wagon to the main gate, the box marked FIELD SIGNALS.

At the end of the retreat ceremony, Easterwood was not surprised to find Mellie Quill waiting for him on the headquarters porch. She was still wearing the yellow scarf. "Supper is waiting," she called gaily.

"Ready in five minutes," he replied. "If you don't mind waiting here on the bench?"

She nodded, her eyes smiling up at him for a moment, and then turning serious. "You're up to something, Tom Easterwood. It's written all over your face."

Without reply, he went on into the inner office. He hung the dress saber, donned for retreat, back on its hook, and then went over to the foot of the horsehair sofa where his saddlebag lay. Opening the bag, he took out his rolled buckskin jacket and the pair of old moccasins he had worn on the journey from Frenchman's Creek to Goldfield. He changed quickly, wiggling his toes into the comfortable moccasins. He buckled his wide belt over the jacket, checked his knife, revolver, and the loads in his bandolier. After taking one last look at the hand-drawn map on the wall, he went back outside, his moccasined feet treading silently.

Mellie gave him a surprised glance: "I was right," she said solemnly. "You are up to something. You look like one of Matt's scouts in the old days."

"Like Bratt Fanshawe maybe? Before he put on cavalry blues?"

She frowned at him, her eyes puzzled by the question, her dark skin coloring. "Bratt Fanshawe and some others. They all dressed like wild Indians."

He took her arm. "Let's go," he said roughly. "There isn't much time."

As soon as they were inside the tiny storm vestibule of her

quarters, she shut the door and caught him by both arms, pressing her body close against him. "Why must you do it, Tom?"

He sighed. "I came for supper, Mellie. Not to discuss plans concerning the fort."

She kissed him lightly on the cheek, and led the way into the living room. The center table was covered with a cloth and was set for two, with a tall wine bottle standing between the opposite plates. He could smell boiled beef and the sweet yeasty odor of baked bread.

While she lighted the oil lamp, he poked up the fire on the hearth. They sat down, facing each other across the table, she offering him wine from the tall bottle. When he shook his head, she pouted. They began eating in silence.

He ate rapidly, thinking of what was immediately ahead of him, recounting in his mind a dozen small details.

"You're not even aware that I'm here," she complained petulantly. "I might as well have dined alone."

"I'm sorry, Mellie."

She pushed her chair away, and stood with her hands pressed hard against the table top. "I know you're going to try to save Mathew from the trap he's blundered his way into. He isn't worth it, Tom."

Easterwood put his fork down. "We're all in the trap, Mellie. Not just Matt. The troopers up there on the Rock, the men and women here in the fort. You and I. None of us can escape without the others."

"I don't care, not for myself, I don't care what happens. You don't know him, Tom. He's horrible, he's completely mad." Her mouth was twisted, distorting her facial muscles so that she looked like a stranger.

He went over to her, touching her gently on the shoulder. "Don't say anymore." He kissed her on the lips, and she moved against him, shuddering, whispering.

"It's turning dark outside," he said, releasing her. "Goodbye, Mellie."

"Oh, Tom!" Tears suddenly filled her eyes, and she clung to him as he moved toward the door. "Why can't it be the way it was? You loved me once, didn't you, Tom?"

"Yes," he said. "I loved you, Mellie. Maybe I still do."

She kissed him, passionately, clinging, and he had to pry her arms from around his neck. "Goodbye, Mellie."

He could hear her sobbing when he closed the door, and faced the darkening parade. The sky was cloudless, with the first big stars beginning to show pale against a dull, slate-gray background.

At the gate he found Connors waiting with Fanshawe, and two other troopers who were wearing forage caps. Asahel Greenslade was sitting, like a round and merry bird, on the box of field signals, his crutches propped beside him. Four saddled horses, including Easterwood's Appaloosa, and two harnessed mules were at the hitching post.

"Everything in order, Connors?"

"Yes, sir, I believe so." Connors stared at Easterwood's fringed buckskin jacket, glanced down momentarily at his worn moccasins.

"The trace chains well greased?"

"In the gunny sack, sir. I inspected them myself. They won't jingle."

He turned toward the troopers. "You men understand what you are to do?"

The two men saluted. One of them said: "Everything except the routes we are to take, sir."

"You'll get full orders later."

Fanshawe moved in closer; his lean face was gaunt-looking in the dusky light. "Sir, I know the routes north to Goldfield better than any man in this command. I beg to volunteer."

Easterwood replied sharply: "You will ride with me, Trooper." He turned toward Greenslade. "Professor, I suppose you know what you're sitting on?"

"Enough signal fire to light up the whole heavens," Greenslade replied dryly. "The captain wouldn't be planning to make a big *Wakanda* for the Indians, would he?"

Easterwood laughed. "Just a small *Wakanda*, Professor. If you will stand by and give the instructions, the troopers will set up a dozen colored lights and a mortar for candle bombs, just outside the gate. How much time will you need?"

"Maybe ten minutes."

"It should be solid dark by then." Easterwood ordered the main gate opened wide enough for the men to pass through, and then moved over quickly toward the hitching rack. "Bring the lantern, Connors." The sergeant came up quickly, holding the lantern high so that Easterwood could examine the harness on the mules. Easterwood walked around the horses, examining the pair selected for the messengers. One of them was skittish, high-spirited. "Whoa, boy, let me look at your hoof. Hold the lantern closer, Connors. Are these the best mounts you could find?"

"Yes, sir. Not much to pick from, sir."

"This one's got a sand-crack. It needs to be grooved out, filled with pitch, and reshod. Run him back and get another mount. In ten minutes. And tomorrow morning, we'd better order a stable and mount inspection."

Connors' round face was red with embarrassment. He saluted awkwardly, took the horse's bridle and led it off toward the rope corral.

Easterwood went out through the opening in the gate; Greenslade and the two troopers were setting the last fuses on the field signals. The land was dark now except for the small fires glimmering high on the Rock, and one big fire down on the sand flat where the Indians were camped. He could see shadowy figures of dancers in circle around the blaze.

The Sioux medicine men were beating on drums, and he guessed they were blowing their eagle-wing flutes and bone whistles. Beat, beat, beat, and then a mournful wailing chant. Maybe one night, or two nights, or three nights, he thought, before their frenzy became so unbearable they would hurl themselves against the stockade. A coyote howled somewhere, and a dog yelped in pain. The smell of woodsmoke was heavy on the air, which already had a frosty sting in it.

"First messenger," Easterwood said. The two troopers looked at him, one moving forward uncertainly. He gave the man his orders, directing him to ride slowly around to the opposite side of the fort and then head straight west for ten miles before turning south to cross the Yellowhorse for the dash to Goldfield. "Stay off trails until you get into the ranching country. Then pass the word to the cattlemen. They'll help you on your way to Goldfield."

Fifteen minutes later, Easterwood, Fanshawe, and the second messenger rode slowly out the gate, leading the harnessed mules and keeping a tight formation all the way around to the west side of the fort. Their shadows blended with the dark stockade. As they came to the corner turn beside the closed stable corral, Easterwood glanced back. Across the river the Sioux fire burned bright; he could hear the rhythmic war chant, faint like a faraway meaningless song.

After they turned the angle, the fire could no longer be seen, but he could still hear the beat of the drums, slow and ominous. He checked his horse, waiting for the others to come alongside. "Stand your mounts quiet."

After another moment, the professor's colored lights in front of the east gate flared up suddenly, red and green and white.

"Wait," Easterwood said.

Almost as he spoke, the first candle bomb was whistling in the sky. It burst with a loud explosion, high over the river, scattering a myriad brilliant stars. When the last glittering light vanished, the night seemed darker by contrast. The drums and the chanting had stopped; the silence was complete.

"Let's go," Easterwood said. "At a walk."

12

They rode to the west, single file away from the fort, Easterwood taking the lead. He followed a short winding path up the small knoll where he had buried the soldiers and the cowboy that afternoon, then skirted a clump of unmarked and sinking mounds, and moved down past a line of box elders. Here there was no trail; the grassy land sloping away toward the river was scarred by streaks of yellow earth.

He urged the Palouse to a faster walk, feeling the tug of the unwilling mule he was leading. Somewhere behind, a hoof struck a stone; the noise seemed incredibly loud against the silence of the night. He ordered a quick halt, and the three men sat motionless in their saddles, listening. It was so quiet they could hear the river running below. After a full minute, Easterwood relaxed his reins, and they went forward again, angling toward the upper ford he had seen marked on the map.

He was wondering if they had overshot the crossing when he saw the river ahead of them down a draw, a flat black surface shining only where the starlight struck occasional ripples. A dozen willow saplings marked the bank, a gentle breeze rustling their branches. He turned back to Fanshawe, asking in a whisper: "Is this the place?"

Fanshawe's long narrow head moved up and down.

Easterwood pulled the Palouse over beside the trooper who

was to ride as messenger. The man's horse shied away, hoofs dancing nervously. "You know your orders. Keep going west five miles, then look for a shallow crossing. Head for the nearest ranch, then for Goldfield."

"Yes, sir."

"And God's luck to you, boy."

"Thank you, sir." The big horse moved away, prancing; he would have broken into a gallop had the trooper not held him in check.

Easterwood waited until mount and rider were swallowed up in the night, until the silence pressed down again upon the lonely land, a silence broken only by the purling of the river. Then he led the way down the draw until they were among the rustling willows. Here the animal's hoofs began sucking against the muddy river approaches. He held up his hand, halting Fanshawe, and slid out of his saddle, searching for dry ground with a moccasined foot.

"Fanshawe," he said softly, "get down to the river and take a smell around." While the scout went forward, Easterwood began unstrapping a canvas bag from his saddle. As soon as he got it unloosed, he moved quickly into the shadowy willows and tied it securely to one of the lower branches. When he returned to his saddle, he peered back into the willows until he was satisfied that the bag could not be seen from the trail.

The scout had vanished without sound, but after a minute he was back, crouching beside Easterwood's horse. "No sign," he whispered.

"Let's cross." As soon as Fanshawe remounted, they urged the horses down through the mud, forcing the mules to follow. The damp pungent odor of decaying vegetation rose above the sweated leathery smells of the harnessed animals. Then they were in the stream, moving slowly to avoid splashing. The river was deeper here than at the lower ford. In midstream Easterwood felt cold water stinging suddenly against his ankles and soaking into the bottoms of his wool trousers.

They came out of the river in the shadows of a cottonwood that had been twisted and tortured by repeated floods. The mules shook themselves, jerking at their tow lines. As soon as the mules could be quieted, the two men pulled their mounts close together.

"We could never get the wagon in through this thicket," Easterwood said. He was looking up and down the bank at the heaps of tangled driftwood. "The map showed a coulee opening somewhere in here."

"Coulee's about a hundred yards upriver."

"You're certain?"

"I scouted it yesterday, remember?" Fanshawe's voice had a bitter note in it.

Easterwood turned his horse upstream.

"No need to take the coulee way, Captain. The wagons lie in a beeline right across there. Shorter." Fanshawe's long forefinger pointed toward a low ridge, barely visible through the brake, the ridge from which Young Elk had led his Sioux warriors down upon Quill's column.

"All right," Easterwood replied in a sharp whisper. "But we'll get the grain sacks on first."

They dismounted, and Fanshawe untied a bundle of empty grain sacks from the back of the mule he was leading. He tossed half of them to Easterwood. They worked rapidly, wrapping the sacks around the hoofs of the four animals, securing them with strips of rawhide. Fanshawe finished first and was sitting in his saddle when Easterwood swung up.

The scout's head was cocked at an angle. He edged his mount closer to Easterwood, his hand reaching out for the captain's saddle pommel as if he had suddenly lost his balance. Then he grasped Easterwood's service revolver out of its holster, at the same time spurring his horse back in the clear. "Don't try for your carbine, Captain!"

"What in damnation has come over you, Fanshawe?"

"I'm cutting loose, Captain. Got no choice. If Colonel Quill comes down off the Rock, I might as well be in hell." Fanshawe's voice was high and nasal. A lock of his long hair had spilled out from under his hat over his bony forehead. In the starlight his eyes looked wild.

"If you run away, it'll be worse." Easterwood kneed his mount, trying to edge in closer to the scout, but the Palouse resisted stubbornly, shying away from the led mule. "Wherever you are, Quill will find you."

"He won't find me." His arm holding the revolver stiffened. "Don't try nothing, Captain. Just keep it steady. I don't hold no grievance against you, and I'd like to see you get the men off the Rock." His voice whined slightly: "Why, I could've just run away on you cold, made believe I was scouting and kept on going. Reason I didn't, I know'd you would waste time searching for me, thinking I got lost or killed. You should of let me make one of the rides for Goldfield."

Easterwood was still trying to figure Fanshawe's actions. "Why did you come back to the fort last night, after you escaped from Robinson's ambush? Why didn't you run away then, Fanshawe? The army would've posted you as missing, presumed dead. Now you'll be reported as a deserter."

"Not if you report me dead."

"I won't do that."

"No, I reckon you wouldn't, Captain." His narrow head leaned at an angle; he moved the revolver back and forth, keeping the muzzle centered on Easterwood. "Maybe I ought to kill you now."

"Why didn't you shoot me in the back while I was working with the grain sacks?"

"I never shot a man in the back yet. I wouldn't even shoot Horse-Killer Quill in the back."

Easterwood whispered harshly: "Why did you come back last night, Fanshawe?"

The scout hesitated; in the faint light his thin face looked tortured. "I thought I had a reason, Captain. But things had changed. Maybe you know what I mean. I got more than one good reason to kill you, Captain."

"Mellie Quill maybe?"

"I figured you might know." Fanshawe's voice was choked.

"You're wrong Fanshawe. She's not any man's woman. His, or yours, or mine."

Fanshawe sat motionless in his saddle, the revolver still held tightly in his long-fingered hand. The silence was broken only by a rising wind, rattling the branches of the trees and rustling the dead foliage of the underbrush. A cloud scud was building up in the southern sky. Frost was beginning to bite against flesh.

"Words don't mean nothing, Captain," Fanshawe said in a hollow whisper. "We're both wasting time talking."

"I won't stand much chance getting that wagon back by myself."

"I'm real grieved about that, Captain, real grieved. But now I got to go." He slipped his own revolver out of its holster and then tossed Easterwood's weapon into a grass hummock a

dozen yards away. "You might need that after I'm gone." He
slapped his bridle gently, keeping his revolver steady on Easterwood.

"Wait a minute, Fanshawe. I'll need that led mule." He could
see the scout's eyes blink back at him in the starlight. Then
Fanshawe's free hand dropped the bridle and slipped a knife
from his boot. He reached back and slashed the rope on the
mule, flinging the end to Easterwood.

"You'll not try a wild shot after me with that carbine." It was
a half statement, half question, his voice whining again.

"I wouldn't count on that, Fanshawe." But then the scout
was gone, the hoofs of his horse muffled by the grain sacks,
turning leftward in an awkward run down the riverbank toward
the coulee. Easterwood reached for his carbine. He could try for
Fanshawe, but more than likely he would miss, and the firing
would surely alert every Indian within range of the sound. With
Indians on the prowl, chances of bringing the wagon in would
be reduced to nothing. He slid wearily off the Palouse, retrieved
his revolver, and then started angling across the broken unfamiliar terrain toward the wagon trail.

Easterwood found the wagons as they had left them, pushed
back from the trail under hanging willows. The canvas cover of
the balloon supply wagon was gone from its hoops, and one of
the black barrels had been overturned, the end smashed in.
Some of the iron filings were scattered beside it. He could imagine the Indians smelling and tasting the stuff, and then aban-
doning it in disgust. The remaining seven barrels and the
twenty carboys of sulphuric acid remained untouched on the
wagon bed. But everything else left there was gone; he saw a
heap of empty tomato tins, broken in by knives, lying in the
ditch.

While he was tying the Palouse to the rear of the wagon, he
listened to the sounds—the wind in the high grass, the scream
of a panther somewhere along the river. He read the stars, yet
unobscured by vapory clouds moving in from the south, and
reckoned on two hours before moonrise.

From his saddlebag he took a can of axlegrease that Connors
had packed for him and smeared the metal rings and swivels on
the singletrees and the wagon tongue. He worked as rapidly as
possible, but the mules were uncooperative in taking hitching

positions. With another man to help, to stand watch, to listen, the job could have been done in half the time, and he silently cursed Fanshawe for the time wasted. A sense of failure nagged at him; he was angry with himself for trusting Fanshawe too far.

In the shadows of the willows, he had to feel his way in the dark while he hooked up the greased trace chains and harness. He fastened the lines through the hames, crossed them, and looped the ends to the whip stock. Then he went around to the front to check breast and choke straps.

Satisfied that all hitches were secure, he was just starting around the side of the wagon when he saw the Appaloosa's head go up sharply, ears lifted. Easterwood dropped in a crouch, balancing on his moccasined toes, alert to every sound. He heard nothing and saw nothing, but the Palouse's ears were still twitching. *He's got the smell of something new, man or animal,* Easterwood thought, and he rocked over beside one of the wagon wheels, hugging the deeper shadows.

He heard something then, the faintest of sounds, something more than the sighing of wind in the grass, interrupted, and beginning again. The back of his neck tingled and he shivered involuntarily. The fear would last until he knew what had made the sound; it was the unknown that always bothered him. He crouched in the murky shadows, sorting out the smells of dry grass and axle grease and leather. For five minutes he stayed motionless, breathing silently. Whatever it was, the mules were indifferent to it, occasionally shaking themselves and impatiently stamping their sack-bound hooves.

And then he saw a slight movement blurred against the trunks of the willows, and through the wheel spokes he watched a pair of booted legs approach from the other side of the wagon, moving slowly, uncertainly. Was it Fanshawe? Had the scout reconsidered, turned back? He started to call Fanshawe's name, but thought better of it. He had let his guard down once tonight; how did he know Fanshawe had not returned to kill him as he had halfway threatened to do back on the river bank?

His fingers gripping the hilt of his knife, Easterwood slid under the wagon. He sprang outward from his toes, lunging violently against the legs, throwing the unknown visitor to the ground. He came down on top, his knife balanced against the stranger's throat.

He almost dropped the knife, then, rolling away and coming up on his knees, one hand still grasping the other's shoulder that was so unexpectedly soft and yielding, resistance gone with laxness of fright or unconsciousness. She still lay where she had fallen, her yellow hair disarranged, her face streaked with dirt, and as he bent over her he smelled the sour scent of burned wood; her hair and clothing were saturated with the odor of wood smoke.

"Alison!" he called, in his urgency forgetting to keep his voice down, and repeated softly: "Alison."

Her eyes opened slowly, and she tried to rise. He put his arm about her, but she shook away from him and came up on both knees facing him. "Captain Easterwood, thank God it's you!"

"Anybody ought to know better than to come up to a wagon in the dark like that," he said angrily.

She gasped for breath. "It doesn't matter now," she replied. She pushed her disheveled hair back, her eyes wide as she looked at him. The man's shirt she wore was ripped across the front; she tried to fasten the shreds of it together, ended by standing up and tucking the tails into the trousers that were too large for her and rolled up from the boot heels.

"You're not hurt?"

"I'll be all right," she said. "Breathless, that's all." After a moment she asked: "Where is my father? Has anything happened to him?"

"He's all right." He touched her arm gently. "Let me help you on the wagon. Then you can tell me what happened." He could guess what had happened. Some of Young Elk's braves, drunk on victory, had paid Stuart's Ranch a visit. He wondered how she had managed to escape, and what had happened to Lee Bowdring.

She drew away from him suddenly. "Where are you going?"

"Back to the fort. We'll have to hurry to beat the moonrise."

"We can't go without Lee. We'll have to go back for him."

"Bowdring escaped, too?"

"I'm afraid he's been injured, he doesn't seem himself."

"Where is he?"

"Back toward the ranch. Hid out in a sort of cave in some rocks."

Easterwood caught her elbow. "We can't go back for Bowdring until this wagon's in the fort."

She pulled away from him, flinging her yellow hair back, breathing hard. "No."

He moved toward her. "Listen to me," he said. "What this wagon is carrying may save your father's life, the lives of a squadron of soldiers trapped on the Rock, the lives of everybody in Fort Yellowhorse. I can't risk losing the wagon to try to save one man."

Her head turned slowly. She looked at the barrels and crated carboys stacked in the wagon bed. "So my father is in danger, then? He's not all right."

"Trapped on the Rock, with Colonel Quill and two troops of cavalry." His voice had turned urgent. "We'll send a search party back for Bowdring."

"They'd never find him without me to guide them."

He stared down at her for a moment, blowing a sigh through his lips. "All right, we'll have to risk driving the wagon in by moonlight."

She touched his arm gently in a gesture of gratefulness, then began shivering—from the frost, or nerves, or both—her hands clutching at the torn shreds of her shirt. He removed his buckskin blouse, insisting against her protests that she wear it.

Before they started back for Bowdring, he pulled the wagon off the road and down into the entrance of the winding coulee that led back to the upper river crossing. He tied the mules securely to a cottonwood sapling, mounted the Palouse, and lifted the girl up behind his saddle.

She directed him across a treeless valley broken by gullies. They climbed a steep embankment studded with clumps of brush, and then descended into a boulder-strewn badland, where in the starlight every upright rock assumed the shape of an enemy. Haste was impossible, and Easterwood resigned himself to the steady plodding of the Palouse.

As they twisted back and forth through the broken terrain, she began to tell him of what had happened. The Indians had come that morning, not many, she thought not more than twenty, all young bucks naked and painted on their war ponies, circling the ranch house. One of them had jumped his pony up on the porch, demanding whiskey. Lee Bowdring shot him at close range through one of the loopholes; the Indian fell flat on his face right in front of the door, dead. That was when the fighting started. Bowdring and Steve Faulkner and the boys

couldn't hold all of them off; enough of them got in with
torches to fire the roof. And while the cowboys were trying to
extinguish the fires, some of the warriors broke in through a
window.

"When my father built the ranch house," she continued
calmly, "he had a small cellar dug under the kitchen. I made
Lee get in there with me. We almost smothered from smoke, but
the heavy boards overhead didn't burn. We waited until we
thought it was dark, and forced the door up. It wasn't quite
dark then, but there wasn't a sign of life anywhere. What was
left of the ranch house was still smoking. We waited down there
in the cellar until we could see the first stars. Then we walked
over to this old badland. I remembered stories about it from the
time I was a girl, stories about how Indians were afraid of it. I
thought we'd be safe in here, and maybe somehow could get on
to the fort."

The passage they were following narrowed, and seemed to be
ending up against a low wall of sandstone. Easterwood wondered what had happened to Bowdring; the Texan could not
have been so badly injured if he had made it this far from the
ranch. "Stop here," she said, relaxing her hold on his belt. She
slid easily off the Palouse and called softly: "Lee, Lee!"

Echoes came back whispers in the night. The horse snorted
and shook his head. Easterwood dropped down beside the girl.

She led the way up through natural rock steps to a ledge in
deep shadow from overhanging rocks. As he came up on the
ledge, Easterwood heard a low sibilant growl, repeated rhyth-
mically—a man snoring.

Alison had gone forward so that he could barely see her in
the blackness, leaning forward and repeating in a whisper:
"Lee, Lee!"

When Easterwood bent down beside her, he got the strong
smell of whiskey and sweat and rank wood smoke. Lee Bowdring lay sprawled on his back, his powerful arms outflung. One
of Easterwood's moccasins nudged a bottle; it scraped and
clinked down the slope of rock. He pulled off one of his gauntlets and felt Bowdring's forehead. The skin was moist with perspiration. A *man who's hurt bad,* he thought, *wouldn't sweat
and snore like that.*

"Bowdring!" he called. "Wake up."

The big Texan moaned, turning away. Easterwood slapped his cheeks sharply. "Wake up, Bowdring!"

The girl put one arm out, shielding Bowdring's face. "He's been injured, I told you."

"Injured where?"

"I'm not sure. When we got this far, he said he could go no farther. He was not himself."

"Where did he get the whiskey?"

She was silent for a moment, then said dully: "There was whiskey in the cellar. He may have drunk too much of it. Before that, he complained of his head hurting."

"We'll have to get him on the horse," Easterwood said. He caught the man's wrists and pulled him to a sitting position. Bowdring groaned complainingly, but Easterwood brought him up to his feet, supporting his swaying body with one arm tight around his shoulders. "Walk," he commanded, "walk!"

Bowdring's head lolled; then as they came down the rocks, the girl on one side of him and Easterwood on the other, he opened his eyes, blinking uncertainly in the starlight. "What is it?" he asked thickly, "what do you want?"

"Keep walking," Easterwood said.

Bowdring turned his head steadily then, fixing his eyes on the captain: "Who're you?"

"It's Captain Easterwood," the girl said gravely, as if she were addressing an unwilling child. "He's come to help us."

"Easterwood, is it? Too late, Captain. Too late." He grimaced. "They burned us out, the bastards. Too many, Captain." He resisted movement, but Easterwood pressed him forward, kept him walking down toward the Palouse.

Just like in the old days back in Kansas, Easterwood thought, like when he had to sober up that old drill sergeant, what was his name? Every Saturday night. Men got drunk for various reasons, he knew, and wondered what Bowdring's reason had been. An incubus of fear, like Major Robinson's?

"Let me sit down just a minute," Bowdring protested.

"Keep walking." Easterwood forced him on. "You've got to mount and ride out of here."

Bowdring turned on him. "You think I can't ride? I'm all right, Captain, I'm fine. Nothing wrong with me."

Easterwood tightened his grip on the man's shoulder, and

could not resist lashing at him: "You're all right, you're fine, but you hid out here while this girl went to find help for you."

The Texan tried to draw away, angry, his breath coming heavy with the effort. "I had no idea what she'd done, I swear, I didn't know she'd gone. She was foolish to do so."

"She was foolish enough to try to save your life."

Ahead of them among the ghostly rocks, the Palouse whinnied softly. Easterwood replied with a low whistle. In another minute they were down the rock shelf, the horse stamping a hoof as if in greeting.

When he learned there was only one mount, Bowdring insisted on walking out. The liquor—and perhaps Easterwood's remarks—had turned him stubborn, and only the pleading of the girl finally brought his consent to ride the Palouse. They got one of his boots in a stirrup, and pushed him up into the saddle.

"Climb up behind him," Easterwood said to the girl. "And for God's sake, don't let him fall out of the saddle."

He went forward to take the Palouse's bridle. The frost was beginning to bite through his woolen shirt, and he started off at a rapid walk to get his blood moving for warmth. Having lost track of time, he searched the sky; the cloud scud was spreading slowly but stars still glittered in the east, and he knew the rising moon would soon overtake them.

13

When they were within fifty yards of the coulee entrance where he had left the wagon and mule team, Easterwood halted. Bowdring had slumped forward in the saddle, but he was still conscious. After cautioning him to keep silent, Easterwood helped him to the ground, while Alison dropped down on the other side. He handed the reins to the girl, and then started forward to reconnoiter the wagon.

In the east the sky had brightened above the Rock; the moon was rising. He found the mules, waiting like patient sentinels, in the shadow of the coulee's rim; he saw no evidence of their having been disturbed, but he circled the area carefully, searching for tracks in the sand.

Finding no sign of unwelcome visitors, he returned in a jogging trot to the place where he had left the others. Bowdring was lying with his head in Alison's lap. Easterwood came up behind them, noiselessly in his moccasins. "Idyll by moonlight," he said caustically. She almost cried out, startled by his unexpected presence. When she shook her yellow hair away from her face, he remembered keenly the night at the spring when he had kissed her.

He kneeled and grasped Bowdring's wrists, bringing him to his feet, urging him toward the Palouse. Once again the big Texan was lifted to the saddle, and with the girl riding behind, they went on to the wagon. Easterwood pulled the horse in close alongside the tailgate.

"Slide off into the wagon bed," he ordered quietly. "You can stretch out real comfortable on the boards."

"You think I can't sit a saddle," Bowdring complained, his tongue thick, his tone belligerent. "I'll ride as I am, Captain."

Easterwood tightened his grip on the big man's arm. "Keep your voice down!" he whispered savagely. "And come out of that saddle!"

Bowdring growled unintelligibly and slid awkwardly toward the wagon, stumbling against the gate. Easterwood gave him a boost, but Bowdring fell forward between the barrels and the crated carboys.

The girl moved in close to Easterwood. "I wonder if you'd do that," she said, "if he were not at a disadvantage, if he were himself." She was breathing hard. "I ask no favors for myself, Captain Easterwood, but if you have a blanket, give it to me for him."

"Use the buckskin you're wearing," he replied shortly. "I have no blanket."

He lifted her into the wagon, and then hitched the Palouse behind the tailgate. Bowdring still lay where he had sprawled against a barrel, and Easterwood climbed in beside the girl, helping her pull the Texan forward to an empty space behind the driver's seat. While Bowdring moaned and protested repeatedly that he could sit the saddle of any horse, she covered his shoulders with Easterwood's jacket, and then lifted his head into her lap.

After dropping down and untieing the mules, Easterwood climbed back into the seat and slapped the team gently across their rumps. The wagon jerked forward, then rolled smoothly for a few yards over hard ground.

But as the coulee widened, they had to cross a rocky passage where the wagon wheels bounced over piles of round washed stones. Bowdring began swearing in protest against the jarring of the wagon bed, and when Easterwood turned to order him to silence, he was surprised to see the barrels rocking dangerously. He pulled in, seesawing on the lines. After a minute the struggling mules were digging their padded hoofs in the sandy bed of a dry wash, and the wagon began running smoothly and silently except for the low rumbling rhythm of axles against hubs.

As they moved steadily toward the river, the coulee curved with the roll of the land, shallowing gradually. On the east the Rock seemed to be receding, and after a few minutes the moon came into view, dim under a layer of thin clouds.

Again Easterwood could feel the frost in the air. The long brisk walk had warmed him, but now the sweated cloth of his woolen shirt felt cold and clammy.

The shallow coulee began curving sharply; he braced one leg against the footboard, swinging hard on the lines to keep the team in the middle of the wash of sand. Abruptly then, the mules halted, rumps jamming back against singletrees, the left animal rearing and trembling.

Easterwood struggled with the lines, standing erect, speaking softly to the team. A few yards ahead, flattened against the moonlit sand, was a dark object, darker and larger than the numerous stones strewn along the sides of the wash. He called softly, urging the team forward, slapping the leather firmly, but the mules refused to move.

He glanced around quickly. The coulee had deepened, but from his standing position he could still see the rolling land, bare of trees with only a few greasewood bushes crowding along the rim of the depression. There was no sign of movement, no sound except from the restless mules.

Alison was looking up at him, her face alarmed and questioning. "I'll need you to hold the lines," he said, and she lowered Bowdring's head gently to the boards, and stood up behind him. "Climb over," he ordered in a rough whisper. He handed her the lines, slipped his revolver out, and started to step down from the wagon. "My carbine is under the seat," he said. He looked at her for a second, their faces close together. Her lips were trembling slightly. He got down and walked close beside one of the mules, soothing them with his voice, watching the dark huddled thing in the trail, his revolver ready. Then, glancing once more at the low bushes along the ledge, he walked slowly forward, his moccasins sinking in the white sand.

Fanshawe had come this way, he knew, and it could be Fanshawe. And if it was, more than likely the Indians were still around somewhere. It was a man, all right, with his face in the sand, and Easterwood was watching not the body but the bushes when he turned it over with his foot. He could feel his stomach tightening and a cold numbness running from his back muscles to his neck. As he bent forward he smelled animal grease and sweetgrass in the braided hair before he saw the face, or what was left of it—a young Sioux with his throat criss-crossed in two wide knife slashes. Fanshawe had come this way all right; the crossed gash was his mark.

He kneeled and caught at the Indian's loose shirt, dragging him away from the center of the trail. The mules, getting a fresh scent of blood, backed against the wagon again, shaking their harness, and they would have lunged in terror had not Alison reined them back with fierce jerks on the lines.

Easterwood rolled the dead Sioux against the coulee wall. One of the long braids fell across the smashed face, and again he smelled the faint scents of grease and sweetgrass. He had blood on his hands, and he bent down to clean them with loose sand. At the rear of the wagon, the Palouse began stamping nervously, tugging at its tie rope, ears aquiver.

As Easterwood climbed back into the wagon, he reached under the seat for his carbine, handing it to Alison, and then took the lines from her. "Bowdring will be all right back there. Keep that carbine at ready." He could see her eyes, big in the moonlight, as she clutched the weapon.

He slapped the mules' rumps viciously with the leather, and the wagon lurched forward, wheels bouncing against stones as they began a gradual descent toward the Yellowhorse. Just before they reached the river, he halted, stepped down, and cut the grain sacks from the mules' hoofs. Marking his position by the twisted cottonwood where Fanshawe had left him, he urged the team into the stream at a downward angle toward the oppo-site bank.

About halfway across, the front wheels dropped suddenly, water pouring in across the foot boards. Lee Bowdring yelled out hoarsely when cold water splashed up through the wagon bed planking.

Alison tried to sooth the big man, talking quietly to him. Easterwood interrupted her with a sharp reminder to keep the carbine at ready. His eyes scanned the dark willows along the bank, and as the mules began to pull up out of the shallow channel, he turned them leftward to meet the muddy opening where he and Fanshawe had started their first crossing.

In another minute they were out of the river, the team strug-gling in the muddy approach. Not until the wheels were on dry ground did Easterwood ease up and permit the mules to come to a halt. He shifted the lines roughly into Alison's hands, and took the carbine.

"I'm going to set off a candle bomb," he told her. "Brace yourself to hold the mules when it goes off." The animals were almost exhausted, but he feared a sudden explosion might frighten them into a mad run.

Dropping to the soft ground, he hurried back to the willow where he had hung the canvas sack. His fingers fumbled at the strings, then he slipped out the loaded bomb mortar. He squirmed through the undergrowth to a clear strip along the riverbank, his moccasins squelching in the slippery mud. He set the mortar at a sharp angle, remembering that Greenslade had assured him the bomb was good for at least three hundred yards, enough to take it across the river and beyond the fringe of cottonwoods.

Shielding a sulphur match in his hands, he lit the fuse and then hurried back toward the wagon. Before he was halfway there, he heard the swish of the bomb. A second later the explosion came from across the river, and the tired mules sprang to life. The Palouse tugged nervously at his tie-rope, but quieted when he felt Easterwood's soothing palm.

Bowdring was half standing, supporting himself against one of the barrels of iron, light from the bright stars of the candle bomb on his amazed face. Apparently the cold river water and the frosty air had sobered him; his eyes turned hostile when he saw Easterwood approaching, then the bomb flare was gone, and he was only a silhouette hulking over the wagon bed.

Alison was holding the mules steady when Easterwood climbed back into the seat and once again swapped the carbine for the lines. He thought of giving his revolver to Bowdring but decided against it. The Texan was sitting on the flooring again, his back against the seat, breathing heavily. The man's voice came vaguely, questioning: "That signal wouldn't be bringing us a cavalry escort, would it, Captain?"

"No," Easterwood replied. He tightened his fingers around the lines, and for the girl as much as for Bowdring, he replied: "It was a decoy, or we can hope that. And to let the boys in the fort know we've crossed the wagon."

He whipped the tired mules up the slope until they were riding in bright moonlight. The wheels were rattling too loud on the hard ground, but he was gambling that any enemy in the vicinity would have all attention turned to the point across the river where the candle bomb had burst.

Not until they were over the last knoll, circling the cedar thicket and the line of boxwoods along the old burying ground, did he glance again at Alison. She was turned in the seat with the carbine's stock resting against her shoulder, the barrel balanced on the back rest, alertly watching the unmarked trail behind them.

The fort's watch had seen them now; a lantern was swinging on the south bastion. As they rolled around the jutting angle of the stables corral, Easterwood saw the gate beginning to open. Between him and the lantern, steam was rising from the backs of the sweated mules. The moon had come out crystal bright from between frothy wisps of clouds.

As they entered the open gate, he saw Connors coming up with a lantern, Asahel Greenslade just behind him. Both men were grinning happily. A group of curious troopers stood respectfully to one side.

One of the men ran forward to take the lines, and Easterwood dropped over the side. He reached up for Alison's hand and helped her down beside him; she blushed suddenly in the lantern light.

"Drive the wagon by the hospital, trooper. The man in back needs medical attention."

Bowdring started to get up, mumbling a protest, but apparently he reconsidered, and dropped back against the seat.

Connors came forward. "The last messenger is ready to ride out, sir."

"Hold him another hour," Easterwood replied. He felt suddenly exhausted as the tension drained away from him.

He turned toward the girl. Her eyes were watching the wagon rolling away down the line toward the hospital. She looked frail and vulnerable, her fingers twisting in her torn shirt, the oversized trousers drooping over her boots. For the first time, he felt sorry for her.

He touched her arm gently. "You're safe now," he said, and started walking with her across the parade toward Mellie Quill's quarters.

14

Hands were shaking his shoulders roughly, and Easterwood lunged upward out of a deep sleep at his wakener. It was Sergeant Jonas, wearing a blue forage cap, his thin features sharpened and elongated by yellow light rays beamed from a lantern.

Disentangling his twisted blanket, Easterwood mumbled an apology and got his feet off the horsehair sofa and into his moccasins.

"Five minutes before reveille, sir," Jonas said, and sucked in the sad hollows of his cheeks. "Shall I light the lamp in here?"

"Yes, thank you, Jonas." Easterwood yawned and stretched. He hadn't slept like that since leaving Frenchman's Creek, he thought, but he didn't like the odd stiffness in his knees; that usually meant bad weather. He could hear the wind rushing against the eaves outside the dark window.

"How's the weather this morning, Sergeant?"

Jonas frowned, carefully trimming the wick until the flame in the ceiling lamp stopped smoking. "Cloudy, sir," he replied gloomily. "Looks some like rain."

Fastening his jacket, Easterwood crossed over behind the desk, took down the dress saber from the wall, and buckled it on. A sudden gust rattled the window. Maybe it would die down by daylight, he thought, maybe the rain would blow over, at least hold off until the balloon could be inflated and put in ascension.

The reveille call came, muted and wavering in the wind. He went out through the orderly room; the door and windows were all closed tight, the air stale and close. When he opened the front door, the wind almost took his hat off; he dropped his chin and pushed his hat down tighter over his ears, sniffing the damp air. It was so dark outside he could not see the men, only the fluttering lanterns of the noncoms ordering counting-offs. Sergeant Connors began taking reports; he turned to face Easterwood: "All present and accounted for except Trooper Bratton Fanshawe, sir."

Easterwood ordered the men dismissed to quarters, where they were to remain alert for a dawn call. He wheeled and started back toward the yellow-lighted headquarters. Sergeant Jonas came up suddenly out of the darkness into a splash of light from a window. His morning-report book was clasped tightly in one hand. "How shall I post Private Fanshawe, sir? I believe he went out with the captain last night."

Easterwood stepped through the open door, Jonas hard on his heels as if propelled by the blasting wind. The sergeant closed the door with an effort, almost dropping his report book. He turned to stare glumly at the captain.

"You know damn well he went out with me last night," Easterwood replied sharply. "Report Trooper Fanshawe without leave." He went on into the inner office to discard the awkward saber.

Taking the bugler with him, Easterwood climbed to the north bastion just before dawn broke. He fixed his field glass on the Indian camp. Several breakfast fires were already lighted, but the cold slaty light revealed no mounted warriors or other signs of warlike activity. It was normal, he thought, to see only the women outside the tipis so early in the day, but something was missing. He ran the glass back and forth, straining his eyes against the colorless gray. The horse herd? Where were the horses?

He swung around facing south, and almost at that instant he heard the warning call of a sentry, somewhere to his left inside the stockade. The Indians were coming across the shallow ford, an endless line of warriors in feathers and paint, their mounts splashing and churning against the yellow waters.

The bugler had seen them, too, his lips tightening as he glanced at Easterwood. "To arms!" Easterwood cried, and dropped down the ladder, the scream of the bugle following him as he burst out upon the windy parade. A trooper brought a drum out from the guardhouse and began beating the long roll; the men were pouring from their quarters toward assigned loophole positions. He met Sergeant Connors, red-faced from running, in front of the main gate. "Connors, pass an order around, reminding the men that fire is to be held until the enemy approaches within one hundred yards."

After checking the gate to see that all its heavy traps were secure, Easterwood stepped up to a loophole. The Indians were already on the slope, massing about three hundred yards out, horses still moving at a walk. He guessed there were at least three hundred warriors, mixed bands of Sioux and Cheyenne. Their irregular ranks began opening slowly like a fan, the lead warriors urging their mounts to greater speed, one file spinning off to the left, the other to the right.

In the brightening but sunless morning, the spreading circle became a flow of changing colors—shields and lances dangling, feathers and pennons streaming in the wind. The distance between each horseman lengthened gradually as the entire body circled the fort at a gallop two or three times, the warriors whooping, lifting their rifles in threatening gestures toward the fort. But they came in no closer.

Then, as if by some unseen signal, the circle broke, the Indians quickly massing their ponies flank to flank with the animals' heads facing the gate. Easterwood held his breath for a moment, his muscles tightening, listening, expecting the inharmonic yelling to increase in pitch and volume. Instead the babble of voice sounds died away to a murmur, and from the center of the close-packed rank, a single horseman emerged, riding slowly toward the gate, holding high a bent ramrod from which rippled a strip of ragged white cloth.

Easterwood's tight lips relaxed, but his eyes did not leave the approaching rider until he was halfway in to the gate. "Hold your fire!" he shouted. "Pass the order!" He could hear the words echoing along the east side of the stockade, repeated, and called again.

"Open the gate," he said to the sentry, and then louder to the riflemen on either side: "Keep him in your sights. If it turns out to be a trick, shoot him out of his saddle."

He knew that the Indians knew he was the only soldier-chief in the fort, and there was risk in this. Long ago their war parties in the field had learned to pick off the soldier-chiefs, knowing that afterward the troopers would often scatter in confusion, easy prey in disorganized flight. There was a risk in this, he knew, certainly if the approaching horseman was Young Elk.

The gate creaked open, a foot or more, and he held it there, stepping out into the gray morning, his eyes narrowing, watching the horseman moving forward. The horse's head and neck were covered with a buckskin hood as heavily beaded as armor, the saddle and other gear ornate with quill and hand embroidery, with silver work, and rows of elk teeth.

The Indian was not Young Elk. He wore a cavalry major's blouse, buttoned closely up to his throat. Sylvanus Robinson's blouse, Easterwood knew, and he folded his arms and waited until the emissary halted.

Easterwood returned the man's cold stare; he was a finely formed Sioux, the left side of his smooth coppery-skinned face covered with a thick coating of vermilion clay. From the coup feathers in his warbonnet, Easterwood guessed he was an *akicita,* a subchief.

As soon as the formalities of pantomime greeting were finished, the Indian spoke, in a sort of metallic-sounding English mixed with Dakota: "Spotted Wolf speaks to Tall Man with the tongue of Red Leaf."

Easterwood concealed his surprise. *If Spotted Wolf still holds his power,* he thought, *there is still hope for all of us. "Washte!"* he said, speaking in Dakota. "Tall Man's heart is glad to hear words from his friend Spotted Wolf even from the tongue of another."

"Spotted Wolf say white man break promises." Holding out one hand, Red Leaf flicked his fingers open and shut several times. "So many moons past, soldier-chiefs say if Spotted Wolf lead his Oglala people to reservation, bluecoats then leave sacred hunting grounds forever. This thing was done. Oglala live on reservation. They are like children in the care of an old woman. They go and hunt only when agent of Great Father say so. But this promise was kept. And now the bluecoats come back to the sacred hunting grounds, swarming like gnats about a she-buffalo at calving time." The emissary stopped his slow-speeched introduction, his eyes shining belligerently.

"Spotted Wolf has spoken truly," Easterwood replied calmly. "What is it he would ask of his friend Tall Man?"

"Spotted Wolf say Tall Man must lead bluecoats away from fort on the Yellowhorse. Lead them back north to place where white men dig the yellow metal."

"Eyayo!" Easterwood cried, and made an upward gesture of his palms. "What will happen then to Colonel Quill, the head one of the bluecoats?"

"Killer-of-Horses," Red Leaf answered, using the guttural Sioux name, "Killer-of-Horses must die. Spotted Wolf has seen this in a vision from *Wakan-Tanka,* the Great Spirit. Killer-of-Horses must stay on the Rock of the Skeletons until his tongue thickens for water, until *Wakan-Sica* the Bad Spirit, takes away all but his bones. Until the bones of Killer-of-Horses become as white as those of the horses of the Oglala in the sacred canyon."

Folding his arms, Easterwood began speaking slowly: "Go back to Spotted Wolf. Tell him three things. Tell him Tall Man is strong with the power of the Great Thunder Bird. Tell him the Great Thunder Bird will come flying from his lodge at the top of the sky and bring death to the Oglalas. And last of all, tell him Tall Man can make no promises until he has talked on the sun mirrors with the bluecoat chief, Killer-of-Horses." He turned on his heel, and went back through the opening into the fort, not looking back until the gate was closed. Then he stepped up to the loophole, watching Red Leaf ride slowly back to the main body of warriors. He adjusted his field glass on the center, but could find neither Spotted Wolf nor Young Elk in the painted, gesticulating group. After a moment the Indians were in motion again, the young braves dancing their ponies back and forth along the front, and then two files of riders broke away, moving at a trot toward the ford. Only a few rear stragglers showed any warlike intentions; they chanted their individual war songs and some of them fired their rifles sky-ward, but at last they also rode down the slope, to cross the ford and disapper into the wind-twisted willows beyond.

For the first time since he had taken command of the fort, Easterwood felt a slight sense of elation. He knew that the re-straining hand of old Spotted Wolf was still a power in the

Oglala councils. He knew the fear and respect the Indians held
for the Great Thunder Bird. And he believed his demand for
time to exchange messages with Quill would make another parley almost mandatory; that is, if Spotted Wolf could hold Young
Elk and the hotheaded bucks in check. At least he had gained
time, time enough to get the balloon in ascension.

When he climbed to the north bastion, he found Sergeant
Jonas and two troopers waiting beside the swivel gun. The wind
had diminished, though it still blew in occasional gusts, and
black threatening clouds lay in the northwest.

Under the heavy sky the heliostat was useless. He sent one of
the troopers back to headquarters for signal flags, and the other
to the south bastion to summon Sergeant Connors. While he
was waiting, Easterwood fixed his glass on the top of Skeletons'
Rock. Several troopers were gathered along the brow of the
upper ledge. Doubtless they had been watching the Indians'
demonstration around the fort.

He turned his attention to the Indian camp; the demonstration party had not yet made its way back around the Rock. But
off to one side of the tipi ellipse was a new burial platform, with
three horses lying where they had been slain at the foot of the
scaffold. The body of the dead Indian lay wrapped in red blankets stoutly bound with cords. A warbonnet of eagle's feathers
fluttered from an upright pole above the platform.

"There's one with nothing more to worry about," Jonas com-
mented gloomily. "I reckon our chances ain't much better'n his,
are they, Captain?"

Easterwood's reply was brusque: "Goddamn it, Sergeant,
you're a melancholy old lady. Our chances are improving." He
was going to add: *If the boys on the Rock don't stir up the kettle
again with that buffalo rifle.* But the trooper was back with the
flags.

It was awkward getting the signaling started. He missed Fanshawe's speed and efficiency. Jonas knew code well enough, but
had little flag experience, and the wind made things no easier.
To add to the difficulties, Quill's man was using a flag made of
undershirts which whipped around so erratically in the high
breeze that it was almost impossible to read signals.

As briefly as he could, Easterwood reported his conversation
with Red Leaf. He added that three messengers had been dis-
patched to Goldfield during the night, that Stuart's Ranch had

been burned, but that Alison Stuart and Lee Bowdring were now safe in the fort. Taking no time for details, Easterwood then informed Quill that he planned to inflate the balloon and make an ascension in hopes that its sudden appearance would create fear among the Indians.

Quill was interested in the balloon. He wanted to know if it could be raised over the Rock to drop water, food, and ammunition. Easterwood replied that there was not enough rope cable in the Territory to reach that far, and if they cut loose they would need a slow south wind to have any chance of moving above the Rock. The wind at that moment was gusty from the west. Quill's response was an order: If the wind shifted to the south. Easterwood was to make an attempt to transport supplies to the besieged Rock. Acknowledging the order, Easterwood requested permission to sign off.

Jonas was signing off, fighting the wind, when Sergeant Connors' red face appeared at the top of the bastion ladder. "A message for the capt'n, sir. From the colonel's lady." The sergeant's usually solemn eyes held a glint of humor in them. "She requests the honor of the capt'n's presence to breakfast with her and Miss Stuart, sir."

"I'll make a reply to that in person, Sergeant. And you'll be needing a bite of breakfast yourself. As soon as that's done, relieve the men on the loopholes, and select the best twelve-man squad of the lot—lively sharp-witted boys. Put them to littering straw in front of the quartermaster storehouse, and have them bring up all the balloon wagons and the water-cart. Everything to be ready within the hour. In the meantime get some army bacon under your belt." He returned Connors' salute, and went down the ladder.

Mellie Quill answered his knock. Her face was freshly powdered but there were traces of shadow under her eyes that were not artificial. As soon as the door was closed, she kissed him. He was not expecting this, and drew back.

She frowned, and then broke into a smile when she saw that he was peering beyond her into the living room. "Alison is at the hospital," she said, her voice huskier than usual. "She's looking after that beau of hers, Mr. Bowdring. Was he hurt badly?"

Easterwood shook his head. "No, not badly." He noticed the

center table was set for three. "I'm sorry but I have only a few minutes, Mellie."

"Alison should be back any moment. That must have been a terrible experience for her, but she looks as fresh as a daisy this morning." She dropped with a sigh on one end of the mattress sofa. "Do sit down, Tom. You must be all of a frazzle yourself." She was working her fingers together, and her teeth clenched nervously at her bottom lip.

"Not so much of a frazzle as yourself, Mellie."

She looked up at him, her dark eyes widening slightly. "I think one reason I didn't marry you, Tom Easterwood, was because you could read my thoughts." She turned away from his direct gaze, and asked softly: "Tom, tell me what happened to Bratt Fanshawe."

He moved over in front of the fireplace, staring down at her. "Fanshawe means a lot to you, doesn't he, Mellie?"

Her face flushed as she looked up at him again. "He is all that was left of the old days, Tom. I know there have been misunderstandings between Bratt and Mathew for some time—all that silly business about scouts being in uniform—and other things." Her fingers moved along the edge of the buffalo robe on which she sat. "Mathew would never take the field without Bratt Fanshawe, you know that."

"Why is Fanshawe afraid of Matt?"

She came up off the couch, her hands clasped, her dark eyes full of apprehension. "Bratt ran away. He ran away, didn't he?"

"Yes. He's posted without leave."

To his surprise, she seemed suddenly relieved. "He's threatened to run away before. But he'll come back. Where could he go? What could he do—away from a cavalry post—anywhere else?"

Easterwood shook his head, and the corners of his mouth twisted in a wry smile. "I've often asked myself the same questions, and could never answer them."

The front door opened suddenly, cold wind sweeping into the room from the vestibule, and then banged shut. He turned as Alison Stuart came into the room. "Why, it's Captain Easterwood," she said pleasantly. He stammered slightly over his reply. He had never seen her eyes so blue. *Her hair is yellow as the morning,* he thought, remembering old Spotted Wolf's words the night they had visited his tipi. She was wearing a

dark dress, one of Mellie's belted tightly at the waist so that she
looked as slender as a boy. She whirled about, almost dancing
as she went over to the couch and sat down beside Mellie. "I
hope the captain likes this costume better than the one I was
wearing last night," she said, almost shyly, holding out her feet.
She wore deerskin slippers decorated with colored beads and
porcupine quills dyed bright colors.

He smiled his approval. "How is Mr. Bowdring this morning?" he asked politely.

She sighed. "When the Indians came up to the gate, it was all
I could do to keep him from getting right off that hospital cot
and rushing out to help defend the fort—"

"Fortunately, it turned out we didn't need his help," Easterwood said dryly, his face not changing expression. He noticed Mellie frowning slightly, looking at him with a sidewise
questioning glance. She stood up and began smoothing her
skirt. "We'd better start breakfast," she said. "Tom tells me he
can spare us only a few minutes of his valuable time."

Alison arose, moving lightly toward him in the slippers.
"Have you had any news of my father this morning, Captain?
Mrs. Quill tells me you can exchange messages with the men
trapped on the Rock."

"The colonel and I were in communication just a few minutes
ago. Except for a shortage of water, they're all right."

"You don't know my father, how impatient he can become.
I'm afraid he may attempt some foolish action."

Mellie called them to the table, and as they ate, Alison kept
up a continual round of questions about possibilities of breaking
the siege and the chances of the Indians attacking the fort. As
he listened to her and made careful replies, Easterwood realized
they were questions that would never have occurred to Mellie
Quill. Long accustomed to frontier army life, Mellie had never
shown any interest in regimental talk, or in what was happening
beyond the range of her own circumscribed activities. He wondered if she had ever cared, or if the passage of the years and
her life with Quill had deadened whatever interest she may have
once had.

His thoughts were interrupted by the trumpeter sounding
troop call. He excused himself hastily, and when Mellie invited
him to return for dinner at noon, he found himself reluctant to

decline. "I'm hoping to have the balloon ready for ascension about noon," he said. "But I have enjoyed this breakfast."

"Yes," Mellie replied, her voice growing huskier as she spoke. "Miss Stuart is an entertaining conversationalist, isn't she?"

In spite of the shifting wind which blew in irregular swirls and gusts, Sergeant Connors and his detail somehow had managed to spread straw across the flat stretch of ground in front of the commissary storehouse. As Easterwood came up from the parade, he found Professor Greenslade hopping about on one crutch at the end of the nearest balloon wagon.

"How does it look—the weather I mean?" Easterwood asked.

"Not good." The professor pushed his spectacles back, squinting upward at the turbulent clouds. "Too much wind."

Easterwood's head was angled so that his hawk nose seemed to be sniffing the air. "Out here I've seen it threaten like this for two, three days running, and nothing ever happens. We can't sit on our hands waiting. If you say it's safe to inflate, we'll do it."

"If it blows no harder than this, we may ride it out." But the professor wagged his goatee dubiously. "We'd best use the short cables, in case of sudden gusts."

Easterwood swung around toward the wagon and began loosening the straps that bound the canvas. "If anything goes wrong, we have enough iron and acid for another inflation." He looked across the littered ground to where the men were still scattering hay; the wind was whipping the straw into tremulous eddies. "Connors!" he called. "Bring the men up!"

Following Greenslade's careful instructions, the troopers removed the bulky muslin envelope from the wagon and hauled it across to the center of the littered space. A few minutes later, cordage and netting, pulleys and snatch-blocks, and the rattan ascension car were laid out in proper order. The generator wagon was pulled into position adjoining the envelope, and cooler and purifier boxes were placed a few feet apart in front of the generator. Hoses, couplers, and a hand force pump were laid alongside.

While this work was underway, Easterwood took one of the men and went into a dirt-floored shed adjoining the quartermaster storehouse. This was a temporary structure used as a blacksmith shop during the fort's construction, and was well stocked with tools hanging along its walls. He selected several that would be needed in assembling the inflation equipment, and then, because it was very cold in the shed, he ordered a fire built in a woodstove that stood in the middle of the bare room.

Greenslade appeared in the doorway, his face red from cold and exertion. "She's ready to be connected, Captain," he called cheerfully, and hobbled over toward the roaring stove to warm his hands. "Wind's dying."

Easterwood picked up a handful of wrenches. "Maybe this is our lucky day." As he turned toward the door, he saw Alison Stuart standing there, a brown woolen shawl drawn tight around her neck and shoulders.

"Ah, Miss Alison," Greenslade cried. "And prettier than any picture on this gray morning."

She came in curtseying politely to the professor. "My curiosity overcame my feminine reticence," she explained. "I simply *had* to see the balloon go up."

"We could use another good crewman," Easterwood said lightly, and then added seriously: "At best you'll have a two or three hours wait, miss, and the wind's cold out there."

As soon as the iron filings and water were sealed in the generator, they brought up ten carboys of sulphuric acid and started syphoning the chemical into the tank through a lead funnel. Professor Greenslade stood by with his pocket watch, timing the pourings. After six carboys had been emptied into the tank, he flung up his hand. "Hold it there—about half an hour," he called to Easterwood. "If the acid goes in too fast the gas might strain the tank walls and force a leak."

During the delay, they went into the blacksmith shop. The wind had veered to the north, blowing steadier and colder, and the men welcomed a chance to warm their hands by the stove. While they waited, Alison kept both Greenslade and Easterwood busy with questions about the balloon. "As soon as we complete the pourings," Easterwood told her, "there'll be time for an exchange of signals with the men on the Rock. It might be possible for you to communicate with your father."

Her blue eyes brightened immediately; she reached out, touching his sleeve with a gesture of gratitude, and thanked him.

Greenslade, keeping an eye on his watch, finally announced it was time to finish pouring the acid. He led the way outside, bowing his head against the freshening breeze.

Easterwood leaned over the cooling box, placing a bare hand against the copper elbow connection. "Heat's coming through all right," he said.

They finished the pouring, and put a rotation crew on the hand pump. After a glance at the sky, Easterwood nodded to Greenslade. "It's up to the weather now, Professor. If you'll stand by, I'll inform the colonel we plan to ascend about twelve o'clock noon."

Greenslade wagged his goatee. "Providing the lot of us haven't been blown out of here by this young norther."

Easterwood called to Alison. They crossed the parade against the wind, and climbed up the steps to the bastion. Sergeant Jonas, waiting in the sentry box, came outside. He saluted, and immediately began shivering in the cold.

"A little flag work will warm you up, Sergeant, but you'll be needing your greatcoat when we've done with this trick."

"Yes, sir." Jonas added pessimistically: "Looks like we're in for some bitter weather to add to all our other troubles."

They roused the signal watch on the Rock without difficulty, and as soon as Easterwood finished reporting the probable time of the balloon ascension, he asked if Baird Stuart could be brought up to the signaling station. A few minutes later the old cattleman appeared suddenly in the field glass, tall and angry-looking with his white beard tossing in the wind. "Here he is, miss—your father."

She caught at the glass, and Easterwood had to steady her hands and fix the position again. She gasped, smiled, and then murmured something to herself. "He was looking at me, too, through another glass." She laughed lightly, then added in a serious tone: "He's got his blood up. I've never seen him look so furious. But I do feel better, knowing he's all right."

On the way back to the balloon, Easterwood left the girl at the hospital entrance. She wanted to tell Lee Bowdring about seeing her father. "But I'll be out there to wish you luck when you go up into the sky," she assured him.

When he walked around the hospital toward the quartermaster storehouse, he was surprised at how rapidly the balloon envelope was filling out. The lettering of its name, *Intrepid,* stood out boldly through the loose netting.

A small crowd of spectators had gathered; all were standing at a respectful distance, excepting Surgeon Campell who was with Asahel Greenslade, one hand cupped behind an ear as he listened intently to the professor's explanations of the inflating procedures.

"Good morning, Surgeon," Easterwood said as he came up. "I'll wager you've never seen the likes of this in all your years of frontier duty."

"Indeed I have not," Campbell replied. "Reminds me of the tales of Jules Verne. The snout of that thing, Captain. Weird enough to give a man pause. Shouldn't be surprised at all if one of these days our military geniuses don't have you horse soldiers flying through the air."

"A saddle is far enough from the ground for me." Easterwood glanced again at the mushrooming envelope. "She isn't filling too fast, is she, Professor?"

"Everything is going well," Greenslade replied, "except this wind." He had already put the men to work on the basket car; they had attached ring and stay hoops and were adjusting the mooring cables.

Easterwood turned back to Campbell. "By the way, Surgeon, I've had no medical report from you on the condition of Mr. Bowdring. Not too serious, I hope?"

Campbell hooked his thumbs in the collar folds of his greatcoat. "Unusual medical case, sir." He frowned. "Mr. Bowdring complains of fever. But my instruments show normal temperature. I told him this morning the only cure for his type of fever was to plunge him into a tub of the coldest water procurable, hold him there until his teeth began to chatter, then haul him out, wrap him in a blanket and place hot bottles at his feet."

Easterwood kept a straight face. "What did he say to that?"

"He assured me he had internal injuries," Campbell continued solemnly, "and could never survive such treatment."

"You're certain he has no internal injuries?"

"The man eats like a horse. If his were a military case, I'd put him on report as a malingerer." Campbell sighed. "I can understand *him*, sir, but not *her*. That fine, high-spirited, yellow-haired lassie wasting her time and good looks on a man such as that one."

Time passed slowly, the *Intrepid* filling by imperceptible degrees until it was tugging against its ropes, huge, tan, pear-shaped. Word had been passed around among the men that there would be no break for dinner call.

Around noon they started removing the anchoring ballast
from the netting, and hooking ascension ballast to the rattan
car. The wind had calmed at ground level, but clouds still
boiled turbulently in the sky. "I don't like the way it looks up
there," Greenslade warned, "but if you say the word, everything is ready for us to board her, Captain."

"I'm going up alone," Easterwood said.

Greenslade caught at his sleeve. "It's been a long time since
you had a try at this, Captain. If anything goes wrong, if the
wind should snap the craft loose from its mooring, you might
end up in Omaha."

"In that event I'll pay a call on General Sheridan's headquarters and tell him what I think of this Army Department." He
grinned, and waved to Sergeant Connors to put the ground
crew on the cables.

"Two men are always better than one," Greenslade insisted.
In his excitement, he dropped his crutch. Easterwood shook his
head firmly. "Your job, Professor, is to get me off the ground
safely." He turned his back and stepped over into the fragile-
looking basket.

Greenslade hobbled back out of the way and began checking
the pulleys and snatch-blocks. "Stand by your cables!" Easterwood ordered. A moment later a gust of wind whipped
across the parade, whirling straw and dust high in the air. The
balloon swayed and stretched lazily.

Instead of blowing itself out, the wind began gathering
strength, whistling eerily against the eaves of the blacksmith
shed. Easterwood gripped the rim of the basket, frowning down
the length of the fort at the flag that was whipping itself into a
frenzy, its staff bending under the wind's force.

"Anchoring ballast!" he shouted. "Ballast on the netting!
And draw in on the cables!" He leaped over the edge of the
basket, racing for the nearest pile of sandbags. The cable crewmen were struggling desperately to tighten the ropes around the
grappling irons used for ground anchors.

But the wind was howling now, twisting the balloon until
several strands of cordage around the lower section of the envelope snapped under pressure. It lifted sidewise like a windblown
bubble, pulling netting and basket along, knocked over two of
the cablemen, and then dragged helplessly against the sharp-
poled roof of the blacksmith shed.

A second later a ripping explosive sound burst against Easterwood's ears. The *Intrepid*'s envelope collapsed, sighing like a wounded animal knifed across the belly. Sleet and cold rain began beating against his face.

15

It has all come to nought, Easterwood thought. *After all the strain and sweat and careful preparation, it has all come to nought.* He stood there staring at the crumpled, useless bag with its ripped netting and dangling cables, watching the sleet rattling against the cloth. For at least a full minute he was oblivious to the cold downpour, to the presence of the others, to the troopers watching him, half curiously, half resentfully because he had not given them an order to take shelter, to Greenslade standing with his shoulders hunched forward against the upturned collar of his shiny green coat so that only his white goatee was visible.

Somebody touched his elbow, and he turned mechanically, surprised to find Alison Stuart standing beside him, a wisp of yellow hair plastered against her forehead, unmelted sleet clinging to the brown shawl she wore.

"You'd best be taking cover, miss," he said dully, and waved his arm then toward the men, storming out at them angrily: "Get into the blacksmith shed, damn it, you can do no good standing out here in the weather."

He took the girl's arm, urging her toward the shed. They had to turn aside to avoid trampling on the crumpled balloon skin.

From beside the stove Surgeon Campbell greeted them

sourly: "I was wondering when the military would come in out of the wet. Hospital's full now, no room for exposure cases."

Easterwood moved the girl in close to the dusty stove, ignoring Campbell's remarks. Tempers were getting ragged, he thought, and he didn't like the dour looks on the troopers' faces either.

Greenslade was the last to come inside. He wiped dampness from his goatee carefully with a handkerchief, and then said to Easterwood: "Wind is a tricky thing, Captain. The balloonist's friend and treacherous foe."

"Our luck just plain ran out today." Easterwood held his voice low, but he could not keep bitterness out of it.

"All is not lost, Captain, all is not lost." Greenslade propped his crutch against the wall, and smiled cheerfully. "I've been risking my neck with these gas bags for a long time, and a storm is no novelty to the good old *Intrepid*. She'll live again."

Easterwood kicked the stove door open savagely, and tossed several sticks of wood inside. *Everything has come to a dead end,* he thought. *I've failed because I left no margin for error. Damn the responsibility of command. Damned the forced cheerfulness of Greenslade. Damn the stupid, arrogant ambition of Quill, the cause of it all. If I could only be alone where I could think again, out of this stinking trap, back in the hills along Frenchman's Creek . . .*

He turned abruptly and walked over to the single unglazed window facing the parade, and looked out at the gray slanting rain. The girl followed him there; he could smell the wet wool of her shawl before she spoke. "I know how you feel," she said. "I felt the same way when I came up out of the cellar and saw the smoking ruins of our ranch house. Part of me had gone with it, and the only thing I could think of was to run." Her voice became hesitant, as if she were wondering whether he was listening, or cared to listen.

"Keep on talking," he said. "You wanted to run."

"When I thought of running, I thought of you," she said. "I told myself that Captain Easterwood would know what to do. You were always right, nothing ever went wrong for you. Whatever you decided to do would be right—like cutting the ambulance loose and leaving my wedding trunk to the Indians."

He turned and looked at her, and he thought it was like seeing her for the first time in his life, her blue eyes full of some communicated meaning he had not read in them before that moment. "You'll never forgive me that trousseau trunk," he said slowly. "You'll tell your grandchildren about the time Captain Easterwood left your wedding finery to the squaws."

"I'm glad you said that," she said. "About the grandchildren, I mean. From the look on your face since that happened out there, I've been wondering if there was any likelihood I'd live long enough to have grandchildren."

His head went back, and he laughed softly and put his hand over hers resting against the window casement. "Thank heaven for you, miss."

"Look," she said, "the storm's breaking up."

As if in echo, Greenslade called from the doorway. "It's blowing over, gentlemen. We can get back to work."

"Speaking as post surgeon," Campbell cut in tartly. "I prescribe hot tea or coffee for all hands before another lick is hit. At my quarters, Captain?"

"If Miss Stuart is also invited."

"My honor, miss." Campbell bowed politely.

But Alison excused herself. Mellie Quill would be expecting her, she explained, and besides she should change into dry clothing.

"Give my regrets to Mellie," Easterwood said, "for not being able to accept her dinner invitation."

He watched her as she crossed the straw-laden ground, her beaded moccasins flying, her lithe figure hurrying against the cold spray of the dying storm, and he wondered in mild astonishment what it was he had seen in those blue eyes to drive all despair from his heart.

"She'll need drying out a bit, Captain, before we can begin repairs," Greenslade said, and paused to inhale steam from his cup of tea.

Easterwood looked out the dusty window of the surgeon's quarters. "If the sun breaks through, the cloth should dry this afternoon. Granted we can manage the drying, how much time will we need for repairs?"

"Well, she's damaged in two places, one long tear and a big hole. I took only a quick look at her, and there could be some smaller breaks. Netting's cut up rather badly, too, and that'll take time, reknitting out of sailmaker's twine. If we had some people who knew how to knit and who could sew with sailmaker's needles, we could do the job by bedtime."

"We have several women in the fort—troopers' wives and the ones in haybag row. Most of them know how to sew."

Greenslade wiped a dribble of tea from his goatee, and pursed his chapped lips. "They'd need to learn how to handle the big needles and palms. Maybe they could be shown how."

Campbell chuckled, and reached up on the wall shelf for his cigar box. "Professor Greenslade's School for Balloon Seamstresses," he said. "Cigars, gentlemen?"

Easterwood took one of the long black stogies, and went over to the fireplace to light it against a coal. "You can teach them while the skin is drying out. I'll ask Mellie Quill to recruit the women."

"I'll do my best, Captain. But we'll need a place to stretch the gas bag. Lots of floor room."

"I'd thought of that. It'll have to be one of the storehouses. Quartermaster is not as full as the commissary, so we'll use quartermaster. I'll order Connors to put the men to moving everything into other buildings." Easterwood, still standing, picked up his teacup and drained it. "I'll meet you at the storehouse inside half an hour, Professor."

When he stepped outside, shafts of sunlight were beginning to slice through the thinning clouds. But the air was chill, with a smell of winter on it, and he felt the bite of the wind as he crossed the parade to Mellie Quill's quarters.

He stopped long enough only to impress on Mellie the urgency of her task, explaining that only the most expert needlewomen should be chosen, and that they were to report to the quartermaster storehouse for instructions within the hour.

During the next few minutes. Easterwood ordered Connors to put a large detail to work at cleaning out the quartermaster storehouse, and a smaller detail to the tricky task of lifting and stretching the balloon skin on poles so the cloth would dry more rapidly. He also took time to signal Quill a brief noncommittal message informing him that the balloon ascension had been temporarily delayed.

Returning to the storehouse, Easterwood found Connors standing in a cloud of dust, barking orders, and futilely attempting to suppress a series of explosive sneezes. "As soon as the floor is cleared, Sergeant, put a detail in here with brooms. This place will need a good sweeping out."

"Yes, sir. It sure is surprisin' how much clutter can be packed into one of these storehouses." He sneezed, and motioned toward a collection of miscellaneous objects piled against an end wall. "Tootin' horns and drums. It looks like the colonel aimed to have him a band out here, sir."

Easterwood followed the sergeant over to examine the instruments—several clarinets and fifes in new cases, a drum, triangle, bells, and even a violin. "Bought with regimental funds, I'll wager," Easterwood said. "See that these things are stored in a dry place, Sergeant."

"Captain Easterwood! Captain Easterwood!"

He swung around. A soldier carrying a rifle stood in the doorway. "Right here, trooper."

"Sir, the sergeant-of-the-guard sent me. Something is doin' in the Indian camp."

Easterwood crossed the room in long strides, the messenger falling in behind as he hurried outside and turned up the parade to the guardhouse. The sergeant-of-the-guard was waiting for him beside the gate. "A big Indian party just mounted up and rode off around the Rock, sir. Some others seem to be gathering along the riverbank."

Easterwood stepped up to the nearest loophole, adjusting his field glass on the Indian camp. In the brightening sunlight, a hundred or more braves, mounted and painted for war, were riding along the sandspit. "You say a larger party went off around the Rock, Sergeant?"

"Yes, sir, a few minutes ago."

Easterwood turned to the messenger. "Get back to the storehouse on the double and tell Sergeant Connors he's ordered to pull out a twenty-man platoon from his work detail. He's to report with them here at the gate as soon as possible. Twenty men, mounted, fully armed. And my horse is to be saddled and brought up with the platoon." The messenger saluted and ran off in a jog-trot toward the storehouse.

For another minute Easterwood watched the Indians along the sand flat. Their restlessness seemed to be increasing; they were rearing and prancing their ponies, and their high-pitched war cries were becoming more frequent. He shifted the glass toward the village; the tipi flaps were all closed, and except for an occasional plume of smoke from a blackened smokehole there was no sign of life. Was it the dropping temperature that had driven the women and children inside, he wondered, or was it something else?

"Sergeant, keep a close watch on that bunch along the sand-spit. If they start across the river, have the trumpeter sound to arms. I'll be on the north bastion."

He summoned Sergeant Jonas from headquarters, and a few minutes later they had opened communication with Quill's signalman: LARGE PARTY INDIANS MOVING AROUND ROCK. GIVE US POSITION.

They had to wait several minutes for a reply, then it came: HOSTILES BEYOND UPPER PASS. HEADING YOUR DIRECTION.

Easterwood flicked the heliograph closed. Sergeant Jonas' face had turned a dirty gray color; he began rubbing his hands together to warm them. "I reckon the captain will be wanting me to stay here on the swivel gun, sir," he said.

"That depends. Whether it's a war party or another parley. We'll know when we see them." He leaned against the parapet, staring upriver toward the shallow ford.

A few minutes later a bugle call cut across the stillness, blatant and urgent in the crisp air. Easterwood swept his glass downstream, picking up the first wave of warriors slashing their ponies into the river. The leader was holding a pennoned lance high over his head; a shield strapped over one shoulder bobbed up and down. The sunlight caught the warrior's face clear for an instant, the jet-blackness of his stiff hair, the daubs of yellow paint. He was Young Elk.

"Here come the others, sir." Jonas' voice was breathless; he pointed up toward the ford. "The whole damned Sioux nation." He bent over in a half crouch, moving toward the swivel gun. "She's ready to fire, sir. Sentry, give me a hand here."

"Wait your orders, Sergeant!" Easterwood shouted, and waved the sentry back to his post beside the box. He wondered if the men running to their loopholes inside the fort were as close to panic as Jonas. He whirled and saw Connors coming down the parade at the head of the mounted platoon. He megaphoned his hands, shouting to the sergeant: "Hold fire! Hold fire, Connors!"

What game Young Elk was playing, he did not know. But his first glance at the column crossing the ford was reassuring.

Three horsemen were in the lead, riding abreast. In the center rode Spotted Wolf, blanketed against the cold, his chief's war-bonnet of golden eagle feathers trailing over his mount's rump. On his left was Red Leaf, the subchief of the morning's demon-stration, still wearing Major Robinson's blouse and carrying the long ramrod with its truce symbol, a fluttering white rag. The third rider looked like a medicine man, probably a leader of the *Wakan-wacipi,* the secret society of the Oglala band. He wore a buffalo horn headdress that covered almost the whole of his forehead.

Easterwood slung his glass. "Jonas," he said, speaking rap-idly, "you'll find the quartermaster sergeant on the south bas-tion. Get over there and tell him to assign four men for special detail. Pack a dozen gunny sacks with sugar, coffee, and to-bacco. Have the packs ready at the gate in no more than fifteen minutes. On the double-quick!"

Young Elk's party was almost across the river, the barrels of their upraised rifles glittering in the sunlight. Easterwood watched them until the first mounts came floundering up out of the yellow mud. Young Elk was shaking his lance in a forward gesture toward the fort. They did not stop to re-form, the first ones to cross coming on at a gallop.

It was an act of defiance, he thought—the young braves swimming the deep part of the river—defiance of Spotted Wolf's authority and power. Most of the warriors in the old chief's party, crossing at the ford, wore blankets against the cold; they rode slowly and with dignity. But the bucks follow-ing Young Elk on his white-faced pony wore only their breech-clouts and the necessary trappings of war. Their half-naked bodies and the wet coats of their mounts glistened as they rode wildly about, singing their war songs. Single warriors darted in toward the fort, but they always swerved back to join the rag-ged line of the others.

Spotted Wolf came steadily up the slope, his head thrown back, ignoring the challenge of the young bucks, his long line of blanketed Sioux curling all the way back to the river. Behind them rode the Cheyennes, and when Easterwood saw these other tribesmen he guessed that there was hope, that there was yet time to be bought. The Cheyennes knew where the power of the Oglalas lay and were riding with that power. As yet, the defiance of Young Elk was only the challenge of youth. But what would happen, he wondered, if Young Elk chose this occasion to press his rebellious demands?

He thought of these things as he crossed the parade to the gate, where Connors was waiting with the mounted platoon. From the gate loophole he watched the main body of Indians forming into a double-ranked semicircle fronting the fort. Young Elk had drawn his braves off to one side; most of them had stopped their war songs and seemed to be waiting to see what Spotted Wolf would do.

A few minutes later, Sergeant Jonas and his detail arrived at the gate with a dozen gunny sacks bulging with sugar, coffee, and tobacco. As soon as the bags were handed up to the troopers and secured to their saddles, Easterwood mounted his Appaloosa and signaled for the gate to be opened wide.

When the heavy portals swung apart, he felt suddenly naked and defenceless, shrunken in size, facing the immense power of the panoplied tribesmen. The shimmering colors of their war paint and blankets seemed to be closing in upon him, diminishing the horizon.

Flanked by the buffalo-horned medicine man and the subchief in the blue cavalry blouse, Spotted Wolf advanced his horse a few paces, then halted, his right hand upraised.

Easterwood gave the forward command then, riding well out ahead of the platoon. As he passed the end of the open gate, he drew his carbine from its boot and tossed it to the sentry. He kept the Palouse going at a fast walk straight ahead, watching the chief's face intently, trying to break through its impassivity into the thoughts hidden beneath. He was close enough to get the smell of them, that strange feral smell of men who have reached that emotional pitch wherein death becomes meaningless. From lances and shields, scalps dangled—some of them fresh, others old, dried and smoked and decorated with bead work. Several of the blanketed warriors had painted their faces black.

In response to an almost imperceptible gesture from Spotted Wolf, the long double rank of Indians suddenly dismounted, each man tossing his rifle or bow to one side. Easterwood had not expected this. His muscles tightened for an instant as he glanced sidewise at Young Elk's party. None of them had dismounted, and their weapons were still held at ready.

Young Elk kneed his white-faced pony, and circled toward

Spotted Wolf's escort party, leaving his followers behind. On
his left arm, and supported by a belt over his shoulder, he carried a shield at least two feet in diameter, of thick buffalo hide
with a soft-dressed elkskin cover. As he came up to Spotted
Wolf, he threw the shield cover back, a gesture of going into
battle. He then reined his pony in beside the subchief, facing
Easterwood. Spotted Wolf ignored the intrusion.

Easterwood slowed the Palouse, raising both arms high,
empty hands extended, palms outspread. He halted the platoon
and rode forward until he was within a few feet of the four
Indians. Spotted Wolf loosened his red-and-yellow blanket; he
was wearing a long wide breechcloth, high leggings over his
moccasins. The folded wrinkles of the old chief's face moved as
his lips moved in some unformed, unspoken words. His old eyes
looked sadly out at Easterwood.

"Only seven sleeps past," he began in his cracked guttural
voice, "Spotted Wolf and Tall Man met as friends. On this day
they must meet as enemies. Spotted Wolf's heart is sad for this
thing."

"It is a bad thing when friends must meet as enemies," Easterwood agreed. He stole a glance at Young Elk, but there was
nothing to be read on his face.

Spotted Wolf moved his horse in closer, solemnly extending
an offering stick to Easterwood. The golden eagle feathers in his
warbonnet rustled softly as he nodded his head several times.

Easterwood accepted the offering stick silently; then he beckoned quickly to the platoon, ordering the men to bring up the
bulging gunny sacks. "Sugar, coffee, tobacco," Easterwood
cried, "for my friend Spotted Wolf and his Oglala people!"

The old chief bowed gravely and made a swift gesture with
one hand. A dozen braves ran forward and took the bags eagerly.

"There is plenty sugar and tobacco and good beef waiting for
the Oglala people on their reservation. Why is it that Spotted
Wolf keeps his people camped on the sand flat to eat fish and
roots? Why does he let his young men dance the scalp dance,
and prepare themselves to die for nothing?"

For a full minute, Spotted Wolf sat silent in his saddle, his
arms folded, his wrinkled lips working over his gums. His voice
was harsh when he replied: "Spotted Wolf will lead his people
back to the reservation in the moon when the deer copulate—

before *Waziya,* the god of the north, blows snow out of his mouth. But *Wakan-Tanka,* the Great Spirit, has shown Spotted Wolf a vision, a vision of many Oglala horses in the land of ghosts. The spirits of our horses cannot rest while Killer-of-Horses is in the land of the living. Killer-of-Horses must join his victims in the land of ghosts. *Wakan-Tanka* has shown this thing in a dream. It must be so."

"Colonel Quill, the one called Killer-of-Horses, is a soldier-chief," Easterwood replied sternly. "He will not die like a rabbit. If he must go to the land of ghosts he will take with him many of Spotted Wolf's young braves."

"Ha-eye-ya! Is the heart of Killer-of-Horses so black he will not go alone to the land of ghosts? Is his heart so black that he must take with him all the young bluecoats and the young warriors?"

"So? Then it is Killer-of-Horses the Oglala demand as their price for peace?"

The wrinkled face of the chief relaxed slowly, his old eyes shining brightly. "When the Oglalas have Killer-of-Horses and the fort in their hands, they will be at peace." He paused dramatically and then continued, his voice rhythmic, a harsh almost monotonous cadence: "The long-nosed white men have become as numberless as leaves of the forest, they are *owanchaya,* all over everywhere. The Oglala have been swept to where the sun sets. To an old chief remembering the splendid days of his fathers, it is like a whirlwind. He has seen the smokeman come that runs on iron rails faster than the swiftest pony. He has seen the wires on poles, so that the white man who lives at the rising sun talks with his brother who lives at the setting sun. The white man has taken our land, the white man who walks on heavy feet instead of the dewy feet of the moccasined Indian."

"Perhaps *Wakan-Tanka,* the Great Spirit, has willed it so," Easterwood said.

Spotted Wolf shook his head slowly. "It is not the way of *Wakan-Tanka,"* he said. "Not many moons past we sat here under the treaty, Spotted Wolf and the other chiefs and the Great Father's soldier-chiefs. We put our marks on the treaty that was to last as long as the grass shall grow. Now the long-nosed white men are digging in our hills again for the yellow metal, now the bluecoats are back in the fort on the Yellowhorse. The white men have put all our heads together and covered them with a blanket. It seems as though they take the head from my shoulders. The Great Father promised that he would not take the heart of this land. The heart of this land is big and good, and Spotted Wolf has camped all around it and watched and looked after it."

Easterwood felt the emotion in the old chief's voice, in his words. He knew that whatever might be said in answer would bear an echo of hollowness. The whirlwind of time could not be spun in reverse. He replied slowly: "The heart of the land is no good without buffalo. Maybe it would be better for the empty hunting grounds to be filled with white man's cattle."

At this remark, Young Elk made his first movement, a gesture with his shield. He drew himself up straight in his saddle, his vermilion-stained cheekbones glistening in the sunshine. *"Eyayo!"* he cried. "Tall Man speaks with the tongue of a traitor chief. Like an old chief who grows fat and lazy on a reservation and councils the young braves to take the white man's road." Young Elk glanced slyly at Spotted Wolf and continued bitterly: "We do not want to walk in the tracks of the white man's sheep and become like them. We do not want to dig in the heart of the land to grow corn and wheat for grasshoppers to eat!" He spat in disgust.

Spotted Wolf sat silent, gazing straight ahead, as if considering Young Elk's speech. The medicine man raised his hand then, shaking his buffalo-horn headdress. For the first time, Easterwood noticed that the medicine man was wearing split tomato tins over his wrists, the paper labels still on them. They had been taken from one of the raided wagons.

The medicine man broke the silence with a sing-song voice: "Those of the *Wakan-wacipi* have listened to the spirit of *Tatanka,* the great buffalo bull. With our magic we have heard *Tatanka* speak of many mysteries" He touched his medicine sacks with his fingers. "In the moon when the green grass comes, the *Wakan-wacipi* will stretch out their arms and strike the white men to nothingness. The earth will open and swallow them up, and the buffalo will come back as numberless as stems of the green grass."

Young Elk grunted at this, moving restlessly. He started to speak again, but Spotted Wolf waved him to silence. "The Oglala have not come here to make speeches for the ears of Tall

Man." He motioned toward the sky. "Where the sun stands now, Spotted Wolf promises peace when Killer-of-Horses and the fort come into the hands of the Oglalas. If these things do not happen before the sun rises once more to turn darkness to the yellow of morning, there will be war!"

Easterwood gathered his reins, his head coming erect. "Tall Man always talks straight to his friend, Spotted Wolf. Tall Man talks straight now, as friend to friend. Colonel Quill, the one called Killer-of-Horses, commands this fort. Tall Man is small *akicita,* not a head warrior. Tall Man cannot give you the fort."

Young Elk banged his shield angrily against his saddle. "Tall Man lies!" His voice was almost a snarl. "Tall Man carries marks on shoulders of clothing. He is soldier-chief."

Deliberately keeping his voice calm, Easterwood retorted: "Tall Man is like the one here called Red Leaf who wears the coat of my dead friend, Major Robinson. Like Red Leaf, Tall Man can speak only with the tongue of his chief. Killer-of-Horses is my chief, and Killer-of-Horses will not give away this fort."

"Then the Oglala and their Cheyenne friends will take it!" Young Elk threw his shield over his back—a gesture of distrust. With a knotted bridle rope he slapped his white-faced pony into movement. "When a great thirst burns their throats and makes them mad for drink, Killer-of-Horses and all the bluecoats will fall into our hands." Kicking the pony into a trot, he moved away toward his band of followers.

Easterwood's fingers tightened on his bridle. He glanced back at the platoon. Sergeant Connors was watching Young Elk suspiciously.

"On some days the young men speak with foolish tongues," Spotted Wolf said calmly. "But there is truth this day in the words of Young Elk." He dropped his hands wearily to his saddle pommel; their veins stood out like twisted ropes under the bronze skin. "It is bad to live to be old. It is better to die young, to fight bravely in battle." His voice suddenly became stronger: "Go now and tell Killer-of-Horses on the sun mirrors to come down from the Rock of the Skeletons. Under a white flag, riding alone on his pony, to come down and surrender himself to the Oglalas. When he has done this thing, all the bluecoats can go north in peace. Leave the heart of the land in peace. If Killer-of-Horses does not do this thing, Spotted Wolf will knew his heart, is black as the night when there are no stars in the sky. If Killer-of-Horses does not do this thing, there will be much fighting with the rising of another sun. Many good warriors will go to the land of ghosts. Where the sun is now is witness to what Spotted Wolf has said."

As he finished speaking, the old chief brought his blanket together, then turned abruptly in his saddle, making a sweeping gesture with one arm. Gathering their weapons from the ground, the long ranks of Indians mounted their ponies. The sounds of their concerted movements, the creaking of leather and the rattle of accoutrements, was like a sudden rush of wind against treetops.

Spotted Wolf wheeled his horse, his golden eagle feathers training after him.

"Before the Oglala cry their war songs with the next rising sun," Easterwood shouted warningly, "let them remember the bluecoats can make strong medicine, too! If the Oglala make war, the Great Thunder Bird will come flying with arrows of death from the top of the sky!"

Spotted Wolf held his horse momentarily, muttering angrily: "The Oglala have no fear of the white man's medicine."

"Remember the words of Tall Man. The Great Thunder Bird will come, hovering and striking with its glance of lightning!" He had said enough, he told himself. Let Spotted Wolf and his medicine men worry with the threat of the Great Thunder Bird. Perhaps in the night of ceremony and dancing to come, the threat would be repeated, would whisper itself disquietingly in the minds of the medicine men. Perhaps they would not wholly believe, but the idea would be there, formed or formless among the visions they would compel themselves to see and then chant around the circle of the dance.

With majestic dignity, Spotted Wolf and his flankers moved away down the slope toward the shallow ford, the line of blanketed Oglalas and Cheyennes following. Young Elk still held his white-faced pony steady, his braves glaring disdainfully at the cavalry platoon.

"Deploy the men, Sergeant," Easterwood commanded. He danced the Palouse sideways, watchful of Young Elk, until he was at the end of the ranks. "By twos. Incline to the right!"

Young Elk raised his shield, jeering at the troopers. His followers joined in the taunting, adding obscene gestures when the cavalry file veered in toward the fort's gate.

As Easterwood passed the gate sentry, he leaned out of his saddle for his carbine. Over his shoulder, he saw the heckling war party breaking away, galloping their ponies back toward the deep waters below the small rapids.

For a few moments he held the Palouse in the entry, watching the flowing colors of the flying Indian ponies. This was the final turning of time's sandglass, he thought. The grains trickling now, the passing seconds, would be the last. Time was coming to a stop.

After ordering the platoon to fall out and return to regular duties, Easterwood went directly to the quartermaster storehouse. During the parley, the building had been cleared and swept clean; the ripped envelope of the balloon *Intrepid* was already spread across the pine flooring.

Around a long table against one of the end walls, a group of women was gathered, and in the center of the table sat Asahel Greenslade, cross-legged like a tailor. The professor was demonstrating how to hold a sailmaker's needle and the methods of stitching sealing patches to balloon cloth. "Now if one of the ladies will volunteer," Greenslade was saying, "we shall proceed to the next—" Looking over his spectacles he saw Easterwood coming across the floor, and he paused in mid sentence, holding his long needle in front of his nose.

"As you were, Professor, continue as you were," Easterwood said, and the grim lines around his mouth relaxed into a smile.

Alison Stuart moved toward him out of the group, her blue eyes brightening. "So they've gone away again." There was relief in her voice, and as she came closer she added softly: "I was praying for you, Captain. We all wanted to go outside to watch the parley, but Professor Greenslade refused us permission. He insisted that duty must keep us here."

Mellie Quill's low confident laughter interrupted, her voice drawling as she came up from the left. "The professor has been a tyrant, Tom."

The other women of the group overheard her; some laughed in polite appreciation, others glanced shyly at Easterwood. "We'll all be needing the professor's strong hand," he said, feeling suddenly ill at ease. His voice turned solemn as he continued: "The balloon is the important thing now. It *must* be repaired before morning."

"Don't fret yourself about that balloon, Captain," the professor said firmly. "With these fair ladies to assist, the old *Intrepid* shall be fit again before bedtime. You can wager that."

"My thanks to you, Professor, and please accept my apologies for interrupting." Still embarrassed from having had to face and encourage the group of women, Easterwood hurried outside. He was glad to find Connors waiting beside the door, but was surprised to discover the sergeant's ruddy face wrinkling into a gloomy frown. "For God's sake, Connors, you're beginning to look like the sergeant-major. One Jonas is enough for this post."

Connors' face flushed. "Beg pardon, sir. But there's somethin' the capt'n should be knowin' about."

"All right, speak your mind."

"It's the men, sir. They've seen and heard just enough it's got 'em low-spirited. I didn't like their talk as they was unsaddlin', and there was more of it just now among the ones in the barracks. They're beginnin' to think we're done up for, sir."

Easterwood stared down at the ground. "Yes, I suppose they would be beginning to wonder." He thought a moment, then said in an almost quizzical tone "At a time like this a post needs a parade review, eh, Connors?"

Connors' face looked startled. "The capt'n wouldn't be funnin' me, sir?"

"No. Where did you store those musical instruments?"

"In the loft of the commissary. But if the capt'n is thinkin' of a band concert—"

"A band concert, good and loud. We have a pair of trumpeters on the roster and at least one flutist. I heard him playing in the barracks the other evening. What instrument do you play, Connors?"

Connors shook his head slowly. "I'm afraid the good Lord passed me by when he was dealin' out parts for makin' music, sir."

"Well, at least you're an Irisher and you know good music when you hear it. I want you to muster a volunteer band before retreat time. If they don't volunteer, just pick the windiest-looking troopers out of the lot."

The sergeant still looked dubious. "If I may say so, sir, the boys may think it mighty queer doin's at a time like this."

"Let them think anything except what you tell me they've been thinking." He tightened his hat against the wind. "It doesn't matter a damn if they can keep time or carry a tune we can recognize. Just noise, Connors, noise. Get to it."

"Yes, sir." Connors forced a slight smile, and turned off toward the barracks.

Continuing across the parade, Easterwood roused Jonas out of the warm orderly room. As soon as the sergeant had buttoned himself into his great-coat, they went on to the north bastion.

It was very cold up there, facing into the north wind. And it was colder on the barren Rock, judging from the looks of men, huddling together, swinging their arms to keep warm. Quill was waiting beside his signalman, his face raw and blue-looking through Easterwood's field glass.

The signaling went rapidly under the bright afternoon sun, Easterwood outlining briefly the terms offered by Spotted Wolf: CHIEF OFFERED US PEACE ON TWO CONDITIONS. CONDITION ONE, FORT TO BE ABANDONED. CONDITION TWO, COLONEL QUILL TO SURRENDER SELF TO HOSTILES. IF CONDITIONS MET ALL SOLDIERS FREE TO MARCH NORTH UNMOLESTED. IF NOT MET BY TOMORROW MORNING SPOTTED WOLF WILL ATTACK FORT.

Easterwood waited for the reply. It came quickly: SPOTTED WOLF CAN GO TO THE DEVIL. Quill then proceeded to send a lecture on the treachery of Indians, the perfidiousness of their promises, and warned that the promise of peace in exchange for his personal surrender was only a cunning trick to render the command leaderless. He concluded: ALL OUR CANTEENS SQUEEZED DRY. WATERS OF YELLOWHORSE TANTALIZING OUR THIRSTS. WE HAVE NO RATIONS. FIREWOOD ALMOST GONE. BUT WE SHALL NEVER SURRENDER.

When Quill had finished, Easterwood informed him of the accident to the balloon, expressing confidence that it would be repaired before morning.

Quill replied: HAVE NO FAITH IN YOUR BALLOON. MY MEN CAN ENDURE ONLY ONE MORE NIGHT ON THIS CURSED ROCK. BUT WE CAN STILL BEAT THEM. WAIT MY ORDERS. The sun mirror on the Rock blinked out for two or three minutes, then

continued: YOU WILL ATTACK HOSTILE CAMP IMMEDIATELY
BEFORE DAWN WITH EVERY MAN WHO CAN CARRY A FIRE-
ARM. AS SOON AS I HEAR FIRING WILL LEAD MY SQUADRON IN
BREAKOUT TO YOUR AID REGARDLESS COST. THIS IS AN OR-
DER. REPEAT BACK.

Easterwood read the words mechanically, Jonas scratching
the letters down on his pad. He told himself he might have
expected this; it was the normal reaction of a man trapped and
insulted by an enemy he despised. He took the message pad
from Jonas and flashed back a repetition of the attack order.

Quill's man waited only a few seconds, then signaled: ORDER
STANDS. THAT IS ALL. QUILL.

Easterwood's jaw was clamped shut. *Any attacking party I
can muster from Fort Yellowhorse couldn't keep a fight going
long enough to light a pipe,* he thought. Jonas' face was blue
from cold and gray from fear. "The colonel sure dealt us a dead
man's hand, sir," he said. "I guess it had to come." He glanced
fearfully over the parapet at the Indian camp down river.

"Sergeant," Easterwood said slowly, "I wouldn't suspect you
to be a man to make free with talk around the barracks, or
anywhere else. What you've written on this message sheet—
forget it. You never saw it, remember?"

"Yes, sir. Does the captain mean—"

"I don't *mean* anything, Sergeant," he said sharply. "Take
the heliostat back to headquarters."

He heard a movement behind him, a light step on the ladder.
Alison Stuart's yellow hair bobbed in front of him. She was
wearing a buffalo coat, several sizes too large for her. "How do
I look, Captain?" She smiled brightly. "Like an old cayak buffalo?"

He grinned, rubbing his chin with his gauntleted knuckles.
"Balloon repaired so soon?"

"The professor sent us away for early suppers. He said we
knew more about sewing than he did and could finish the work
after supper." Her face became serious. "I knew you were up
here signaling. Did you see my father again?"

"No, only the colonel."

"How are they faring?"

"Not too comfortably."

"Lack of comfort won't annoy Father Stuart. It's his temper
that'll hurt him."

"Temper is hurting the colonel, too," he said. She moved over to the parapet, resting her arms on the log railing, and he joined her. A hundred yards out, a covey of prairie chickens was running before the wind across the beaten brown grass.

"You know," she said, "there is something else I wanted to say to you, Captain Easterwood."

He looked at her, at her yellow hair blown by the cold wind across the translucent pink skin of her cheeks. "Yes?" he said.

"I don't think of you as a cayak anymore." She laughed, almost gaily, and the young sentry beside the box could not resist a quick turn of his head, but the boy faced away again, straightening himself rigidly, staring down the river. "Until this morning," she continued, "I thought of Captain Easterwood as someone beyond flesh-and-blood, a man made of iron, someone not quite a human being. Then suddenly this morning I discovered the captain was fallible, real, a flesh-and-blood human being. I knew it when I looked at your face, after the balloon wrecked in the storm."

He started to speak, then glanced at the sentry's rigid back.

"You're thinking I'm a bold and forward young lady, aren't you?" she asked, looking up at him.

"No, I was thinking that maybe it was fortunate the balloon got ripped, after all."

They leaned against the parapet railing again, and he was surprised at how rapidly the sun had dropped in the sky. Against the face of the Rock, the golden light was changing to bronze, and along the northwest horizon long streaks of cloud had turned carmine, dull red, and pale yellow. The land had a quality of tranquillity in it that was unusual; even the barking of the dogs in the Indian village seemed only a peaceful overtone.

But suddenly it was all gone, with the blasting of brass horns and the beating of a drum, discordant and brazen. Alison swung quickly around, startled.

"That's only Sergeant Connors and his concert band," he reassured her, "preparing for parade review."

"You're a surprising man, Captain Easterwood," she said softly. He reached out for her, and one of her heavy sleeves went up around his neck, her warm lips seeking his.

16

Under a wintry sky filled with racing dark-bellied clouds, the soldiers and noncombatants of Fort Yellowhorse prepared for a parade review. Even the gloomy Sergeant Jonas had entered into the spirit of the occasion, unearthing several long strips of faded flag bunting which he had wound around the log posts of the porch, and which were now flapping festively in the breeze.

Captain Easterwood's guests for the reviewing party—Surgeon Campbell, Asahel Greenslade, Mellie Quill, and Alison Stuart—were waiting with him inside the orderly room. The fireplace crackled merrily and the talk was merrier still. To a casual observer, the little group would have appeared completely free of care. It was only during occasional lulls in the conversation, or whenever one of them stood too long in silence, unheeding another's remark, that their true feelings were revealed. Each of them, at one time or another, was conscious that he was waiting for something more than a post parade. They dreaded the waiting, hating the expectancy, all of them rejecting with their light bantering words the fear that hovered and grew and would not go away.

Sergeant Jonas—standing watch by the door that was opened just a crack so that he could see up the empty parade—was obsessed with the fear. His whole body seemed shrunken and twisted out of shape. "Here they come, sir!" he called, his voice unnatural and louder than necessary.

Easterwood tightened his dress sword, and picked up the ladies' coats from the bench. They all went outside, the cold dry air stinging into their faces. Drums were beginning to roll at the south end of the fort. Along the plank sidewalk the women of the fort were gathering in small groups, their heads wrapped in woolen shawls.

The low sun, breaking through the clouds, caught the polished instruments of the pathetic little marching band. To the beat of the drums, the bandsmen moved down past the whitewashed hospital. And then they began to play, the trumpets blaring uncertainly, the clarinets screeching reedily. But at last they all got together, after a fashion, and the tune came loud and spirited: "Garryowen." Behind the bandsmen marched the thin ranks of the garrison—with Sergeant Connors leading the first platoon of troopers in yellow-turned jackets and brass-mounted forage caps. After them came the quartermaster boys, unable to repress their grinning appreciation of the amateur musicians; and bringing up the rear were the wagon drivers, marching raggedly but doing their best. Connors had shrewdly spaced platoons well apart so that the parade seemed more impressive than it was.

As the flag-bearer came by, eyes left, and straining to hold his staff firm against the wind-tossed banner, the fifer and flutist broke into a duet, playing "Yankee Doodle." Easterwood held his salute longer than necessary, listening to the women applauding along the sidewalks, watching the faces of the marching men, and he felt a sudden fierce pride for them, for what they and the sounds and symbols represented.

The paraders swung on down to the north end, wheeled and marched back, the band halting and facing the reviewing party. Sergeant Connors stepped forward, saluting briskly. He inquired if the captain would care to request a favorite tune.

Easterwood replied that he would defer to the ladies, and Mellie Quill requested "Dixie Land." The men blew a few discordant notes and looked apologetic. Then the flutist, a tall lanky boy, stepped forward and volunteered to try "The Bonnie Blue Flag" as a solo. "That's a rebel tune, also, ma'am," he drawled politely, and when Easterwood laughed, the men in the ranks roared. But the flute player performed beautifully.

After the band attempted two or three other tunes—with little success other than to produce merriment among the listeners—Easterwood raised his hand for silence. "When I ordered Sergeant Connors to organize a band on short notice, I might've known he'd pick a bunch of Irishers," he cried. "There's only one piece of music you Irish troopers know. Sergeant Connors! March them back to their warm barracks, and let's hear them play the hell out of 'Garryowen'!"

They marched and they played, and Captain Easterwood and the others stood there in the cold wind with the faded bunting flapping around them, watching and listening until the last beat and note had vanished in the clear air. All of them had forgotten—for a time—the waiting, the dread, and the fear.

The lightheartedness induced by the band concert persisted into the evening, by which time the scene of major activity had been transferred to the quartermaster storehouse. In that bare rectangular building, empty of everything but one long table and the crumpled balloon, Asahel Greenslade was the chief actor. Wearing a farrier's apron, he looked somewhat like a dwarf shoemaker from a fairy tale as he darted back and forth with the aid of his single crutch.

Rows of oil lamps hung from the overhead crossbeams, lighting the emptiness with an unreal saffron glow, and the hollow reverberations of mingled voices added to the quality of fantasy within the place.

After some experimentation, the professor had discovered that the sewing could be performed most efficiently by placing the volunteer seamstresses in a semicircular line along the floor. Mellie Quill and some of the others had provided cushions, and they all sat cross-legged, sewing patches with their big sailor's needles over the long split in the balloon cloth.

Greenslade checked each woman's work carefully, showing them how the pieces should overlap to prevent leakage. When the sewing did not suit him, he would shake a forefinger, wag his goatee, and lecture the offender with such geniality that none seemed to mind ripping out seams and starting over again.

Captain Easterwood wandered in and out, keeping to the background so as not to disturb the workers. He noticed the off-duty men were as interested as he was in the unusual activity inside the storehouse. The men walked aimlessly along the plank sidewalk, stopping to peer into the yellow-lighted doorway. One of the curious was the lanky flute player. Recognizing the young soldier's face in the light, Easterwood stopped him and asked if he would mind playing for the ladies. The boy ran off eagerly to the barracks, and was back in a few moments with his flute. Easterwood took him inside, and the trooper sat down at one end of the table and began to play.

Mostly he played long slow ballads out of his memory, weaving one into the other, mournful and haunting. Only occasionally did he break the monotony with a short rollicking tune. Easterwood leaned against the wall, in the shadows, listening, and watching the women sewing.

Alison glanced up at him once, smiling, and he knew that Mellie Quill had noticed the exchange. Mellie's dark eyes regarded him seriously for a moment, then she shook her head slowly and returned to her sewing. He let his thoughts wander with the music, wondering why all of time past seemed to have been compressed into the days since that afternoon when he had come down to Sun River Cantonment on his Appaloosa, the last day of his ride from Frenchman's Creek. He had an odd feeling that nothing important had ever happened to him before that day. But what about Mellie and the time in Virginia? Had he loved her then? Did he love her still?

He grew restless, disturbed by the music and his thoughts, and he walked out of the storehouse, through the parting crowd of off-duty men gathered there silent before the door, they too seeking something in the music.

When he came back, after walking without purpose or direction in the bitter cold air, the balloon envelope had been rolled back against one wall, and an impromptu dance was underway. Some of the bolder men had wandered inside; the flutist was playing a gay Irish reel, and Asahel Greenslade was keeping time by beating his crutch against the flooring. When he saw Easterwood, the professor called cheerily: "She's all whole again, Captain! The *Intrepid* is good as new. Ah, these wonderful seamstresses, the best in the world."

The dancing had stopped, the men drawing away, avoiding Easterwood's eyes. The flutist looked embarrassed. "A celebration is in order, then," Easterwood said. "Take your places, everybody!"

For an hour they danced, until the flutist was exhausted. As the sets broke up, Mellie took his arm. "What a grand evening, Tom. We should do this every evening. But suddenly I feel very tired. Will you walk me home?"

Then Alison was there in front of them, wrapped in her borrowed buffalo coat, her blue eyes sparkling. "I see Mellie Quill has prior claim on the captain. Would it be presumptuous of me to ask if I might walk with you two as far as the hospital?"

The sparkle in her eyes held a glint of fire, Easterwood thought. "It's rather late to go calling on a hospital patient," he replied.

"Dr. Campbell won't mind, and I promised Lee I'd come by."

He bowed slightly. "Since this seems to be ladies' night on the post, I shall offer no objections." He took her arm, walking between them.

After Alison left them at the dimly lit entrance to the hospital, Easterwood and Mellie cut across the parade toward the commander's quarters. The wind had died away, leaving the sky swept clear; the glittering stars seemed close enough to touch. From down river the monotonous sound of the Indian drums still persisted.

She walked very close to him, her arm linked in his. "I suppose you know that Miss Alison has a case on our handsome captain," she said, with a little tremolo of laughter in her voice.

He was so surprised by the remark that he made no response. His only indication of having heard it was a lengthening of his stride and a quickening of pace. Mellie pulled hard on his arm, bringing him to a quick halt so that they faced each other under the cold starlight. "You can't run away from her or from me," she said, her voice low and throaty. Her lips were half parted in a smile.

"Females," Easterwood said. "Why must they always be fashioning romance?" He was embarrassed, realizing suddenly that they were standing in the middle of the empty parade in the attitudes of lovers.

"Alison told me about my daguerreotype portrait," she said triumphantly. "If a gentleman keeps a lady's portrait for ten years, Tom Easterwood, is that fanciful romance?"

He drew away from her. "She told you about the portrait, did she?" He choked off an oath, and turned, starting her walking again toward her quarters.

"She wouldn't have told me," Mellie continued, "if she hadn't been so jealous. She wanted to know how I still felt, of course."

"The reasoning of women," Easterwood replied.

She was still laughing softly as they came up to her door. "I think it was sweet and gallant of you, Tom, to keep my likeness. You'll come in for a while, won't you, for a hot drink?"

"Good night, Mellie," he said, releasing her hand.

"At least come in for a minute. I'll lend you some of the new *Harpers* and *Leslies* that came in the mail. You can read yourself to sleep."

His mouth relaxed slightly. "All right. I suppose I should find out what's been happening back in the States."

But as he reached up to open her door latch, he heard his name called: "Captain Easterwood! Captain Easterwood!" It was Connors calling, and there was urgency in his voice.

"Here, Sergeant!" A streak of lantern light splashed across the narrow porch in front of headquarters. He could see the silhouetted form of Connors, and dimly in the background a second figure. "I'd best see what this is about, Mellie." He opened the door for her, touching her hand gently. "I'll be back."

In a dozen long strides he crossed over to the bobbing lantern. "What is it, Connors?"

"I hope it's nothin', sir." Connors stammered slightly. "But I been thinkin' maybe the capt'n should be hearin' this man's report."

Easterwood had thought the other man was Sergeant Jonas, but he was one of the sentries. He stepped forward, saluting with his rifle. "Speak up, trooper," Easterwood said sharply, squinting against the lantern light.

"Something odd happened, sir, on my post. I thought I should report it to the sergeant-of-the-guard, and he passed me on to Sergeant Connors, sir."

"All right, what was it?"

"I was on Post Number Four, sir—that's on the southwest corner, and takes in the closed gate running to the stable corral. I was just walkin' past the gate when I hear this queer noise, like a man fallin' on the ground, sir."

"Did you see anyone?"

"I think I did, sir, but the light is tricky tonight, I'm not certain. It was so quicklike, sneaky like an Indian."

"Whatever it was you saw, was it on this side of the gate?"

"Yes, sir, when I heard the noise, I opened the gate and sang out the challenge. I couldn't hear nothin' then and it was dark-like in that corral runway. After I closed the gate I thought I saw some kind of movement out the corner of my eye, sort of a sneaky movement off toward the last house on officers' row."

"You called the sergeant-of-the-guard then?"

"Yes, sir."

Easterwood turned to Connors. "When did all this happen, Sergeant?"

"Not over thirty minutes ago, sir. I took the lantern and went up to search the ground around there."

"Find anything?"

"Tracks around the gate. But they don't mean much because a bunch of our men was in there this afternoon haulin' supplies out of the storehouse down into the corral stables."

"No moccasin tracks?"

"None I could find, sir."

"Let's go up and have another look."

At the corral gate, Easterwood took the lantern and searched the ground carefully, but as Connors had said, there were too many boot markings to mean anything, both inside and outside the gate. The center passage was bare and beaten down by the passage of men and horses, and only at the edge of the stockade was the fresh yellow clay soft enough to take a moccasin track. He searched there but could find nothing.

After commending the guard for his alertness, Easterwood walked back along the plank sidewalk toward Mellie Quill's quarters. On a night like this, he thought, a man's imagination could play tricks on him. Any sound or shadow could assume a shape of danger against the dark unknown that lay beyond the dubious sanctuary of the stockade, the dark unknown where the Sioux drums continued their monotonous beat.

He knocked on Mellie's door. For a full minute he waited, then knocked again. He was rapping insistently when she opened the door. There was an odd brightness in her eyes, a vivacity in her movements that seemed unnatural after her le-thargic calmness of a few minutes past. "I'll have the weeklies for you in a moment," she said, her voice low, almost a breathless whisper.

He followed her into the living room. A single oil lamp burned fitfully on the writing desk in the corner, leaving most of the room in shadows. "Anything wrong, Mellie?"

She turned, facing him too quickly, and he caught the flash of alarm in her dark eyes. "No," she said, one hand at her throat. "Why do you ask?"

"Nothing," he said. "I suppose we're all kind of spooked tonight."

She had turned away from him again, and he saw her shoulders relax at his words. "I'll bring the weeklies," she said, and went through the green calico curtains without looking back. He sat down on the mattress couch, frowning at the smoking lamp. Beside the lamp, atop the writing desk, was the pile of weekly magazines that had come in the mail from Goldfield.

Easterwood hunched forward, staring into the dull orange glow of the fireplace. He saw something else then, near the edge of the rug, something out of place in the neat orderliness of the room. He dropped down, squatting on his haunches, and touched it with his fingers. Yellow mud, still damp. Two feet away was another small lump, shaped as if crushed and fallen away from a boot instep.

He was standing erect with his back to the fireplace when Mellie returned through the curtains. "I suppose Alison must have brought the magazines back in here from the bedroom," she said. Her laugh was forced and unnatural. "Here they are on the writing desk."

As she crossed the room, Easterwood moved over toward her. "Mellie," he said heavily, "I'm going to ask a question I don't want to ask."

She looked at him, her eyes almost pleading for a second, then her face calmed as she picked up the bundle of magazines. "You seem strange, Tom."

"Is there anyone else in this house?"

He could see the tortured movement of her throat muscles, then she replied: "What on earth do you mean?"

"It's my duty to search your rooms if you don't answer the question," he said steadily. "Is there anyone else in this house?"

She gripped the bundle of magazines tightly in both hands,

her mouth growing tight and angry. "Tom Easterwood, have you lost your reason?"

"You haven't answered the question," he persisted.

"Of course there's no one here," she cried spitefully. "If you don't believe me, search the rooms!"

He reached out and took the magazines from her. "I believe you," he said. "And I apologize. Forgive me. Good night, Mellie."

She refused to answer him. As he went out into the vestibule and put his hand on the door latch, he glanced back at her. She was still standing beside the desk, ignoring his departure. "If you need me, I'll be next door, in headquarters," he said gently, and stepped outside into the cold clean air.

Just before midnight, Easterwood was propped up on the horsechair couch in Quill's office, reading, or trying to read, the old *Harper's Weeklies* that Mellie had given him. He wondered how he could have been mistaken. He and Mellie had walked from the quartermaster storehouse directly across the parade. And after the windy day, the parade ground was as dry as the plank sidewalks.

The yellow mud had come from beside the stockade where the fresh-turned earth was still damp. He'd seen other tracks there beside the stockade where the sentry had been so certain he'd heard something like a man falling and had seen some movement in the starlight at the end of officers' row.

That Mellie Quill was a creature of small deceits, he could believe. But he could not believe she would lie deliberately. Perhaps Bratt Fanshawe (it had to be Fanshawe) had been waiting in her quarters when she had come in, and she had warned him away. But why would Fanshawe have come back to the fort? Mellie had said he would return, she had said there was no place else the scout could go. With her woman's intuition she had known he would come back.

Moving restlessly on the lumpy sofa, Easterwood turned the pages of the magazine, staring dully at the drawings of boat races at Saratoga, at a cartoon involving General Sheridan—the political meanings of which escaped him.

I should order a thorough search of the fort and corner Fanshawe like a trapped rat. Why don't I do it now? Is it because I still love her, this woman who is Matt Quill's wife, is it because I still love her that I believed her so readily when she said there was no one in her rooms? Is it because I am afraid of finding Bratt Fanshawe that I lie here stewing in my thoughts? Is it because I'm afraid to discover the truth?

He turned a page, and a drawing of a balloon seemed to leap from the folded paper: DONALDSON'S FATE. ASCENT FROM THE CHICAGO HIPPODROME. The picture showed a balloon drifting above a pennanted tent before a crowd that held thousands, if the artist's sketch was to be believed. The terse account told of an aeronaut named Donaldson who had ascended in his balloon to entertain the crowd. Caught in a sudden storm, he was swept out over Lake Michigan and drowned. "The departure of the balloon, according to the Chicago papers, was full of evil augury."

Full of evil augury, he thought, mulling the phrase over in his mind, closing his eyes and listening to the wall clock ticking away in the orderly room. He had set the balloon's inflation time to begin at two o'clock in the morning. He wondered if he should try to snatch an hour or so of sleep. *Full of evil augury.*

The wind had died completely, but above the ticking of the clock he could hear occasional snapping sounds of roof nails reacting to the freezing cold. The men on the Rock would be having a bitter night. He could almost hear Quill's voice, using the men's discomfort as a weapon to prime them for the ordered dawn attempt to break through the down-pass.

Quill would have everything planned to the last detail, probably had already formed a phalanx platoon to lead the breakout charge; he would have outposts listening for the first rattle of gunfire from the Indian camp. *Only there wasn't going to be any gunfire from the Indian camp. There wasn't going to be any sacrifice surprise attack led by Captain Tom Easterwood against the Indian village.*

By the time the balloon got up, Quill would be raging. *But suppose something goes wrong again, suppose the Indians . . .* He shut his mind against the possibility of failure. He could not lead fifty men down on that sand flat to die, orders or no orders, not as long as this other choice—the balloon—was possible.

The clock struck midnight, slowly and haltingly as if its springs needed mending, and he got up and opened the back window to let in fresh air. The moon was up, and sounds carried clear in the frosty night. The Sioux drums had quieted, but he could hear the guards calling: "Guard House Post Number One. Post Number One, twelve o'clock and all is well!" "Post Number Two, twelve o'clock and all is well!" The calls echoed around the stockade.

He lay down again, pulling his blanket over his shoulders. All is well, he thought, and full of evil augury . . .

Sometime later, on the inward drift of sleep, he heard a sudden wild bleating of a bugle, and then the drums. Fire call! "Corporal of the gua-a-ard! Number Five! Turn out the guard!" The voice came hoarsely out of the night.

Easterwood's feet hit the floor. In a matter of seconds he was in the outer office, snatching off Jonas' blankets and shaking the sergeant awake. As he ran out to the narrow porch, he saw low flames burning in the southeast corner of the stockade, below haybag row.

The south end of the moonlit parade was alive with men, rushing out of their barracks in nightclothes; and he could hear the clatter of fire buckets around the water barrels.

Easterwood ran directly toward the gate. "Connors!" he called, "Sergeant Connors!" A dozen lanterns were moving outside the guardhouse. The trumpeter in his long underwear was darting back inside for his breeches and boots.

The sergeant-of-the-guard came forward with a lantern. "Sergeant Connors is down on Post Number Five, sir. Icehouse on fire!"

"Any sign of an attack?"

"No, sir. If the hostiles fired the roof, they pulled away fast."

"Keep a sharp watch on all outside approaches, Sergeant."

Easterwood turned up the parade toward the fire, running at a fast jog-trot. As soon as he reached the row of enlisted men's family quarters, he could see that the fire was out of control. The roof of the half-completed icehouse was crawling with flames.

A bucket brigade had formed along the narrow street, passing filled water pails. Other groups were mounting ladders to the roofs of the quarters nearest the burning icehouse. Behind Easterwood came the water cart, drawn by several half-clothed men, the wheels rattling as they swung around a corner.

Easterwood turned and stood with his legs wide apart in the middle of the street. "Halt the wagon!" he called sternly. The men broke their forward motion and slowed the cart to a standstill. "And hold up the fire buckets!" he shouted to the bucket brigade. "We need that water worse than we need the icehouse!"

Smoke boiled down around him. "Connors!" he called.

"Yes, sir." Connors had come up out of the smoke, his red face streaked with soot and perspiration.

"Goddammit, Connors, we'll need every drop of water we can muster to inflate the balloon!"

The sergeant stammered for words.

"I know," Easterwood continued patiently, "the men were only doing their duty." He choked in a sudden downdraft of smoke. "Keep the details standing by. No water is to be used. But get some more men up on the roofs with dry blankets to beat out sparks.

"Yes, sir."

Holding his hat in front of his face as a shield against the heat and smoke, Easterwood moved in closer to the burning icehouse. Around the entrance the packed earth was illuminated as if by daylight. He saw bunches of straw there, and wondered if the morning wind had blown it all the way from the litter in front of the quartermaster storehouse. The heat was almost unbearable, but he forced himself forward until he could see into the doorless entry. There was a mass of burning straw inside, small tufts of it smouldering on the heavy sill.

His buckskin jacket was smoking when he backed away and turned down the crowded street. In the windless air, the roof details were having no trouble keeping flying sparks under control.

The fire had been purposely set, Easterwood knew, not with arrows shot by Indians out of the moonlit night, but by someone inside the fort, someone who knew where to find a bundle of hay. He wasn't sure yet why it had been set, but he guessed that it was meant to draw attention away from some other part of the fort.

He hurried up past the quartermaster storehouse, cutting across behind the troopers' barracks, and passed the rope corral that held the horses. He stopped beside the closed gate that led to the stables, waiting for the pacing sentry to come up to him. The sentry was the same man who had reported hearing something unusual earlier in the evening.

Easterwood returned his salute and asked quickly: "Have you seen anyone around this gate since fire call?"

"No, sir, no one who shouldn't have been here."

"Someone was here then?"

"Yes, sir, a detail went down to the stables for extra fire buckets."

"Did you notice anything unusual about any of them?"

The guard hesitated a moment. "I did not, sir."

"Is there a lantern on your post?"

"Yes, sir."

"Fetch it, unlighted."

Easterwood lifted the trap in the gate and let himself into the runway. The high stockade shut off the moonlight, leaving the passage in deep shadow. He stood listening until the sentry returned with the lantern. "Follow after me, trooper, and keep it quiet." Walking silently in his moccasins, he led the way down into the stable corral.

As he came to the end of the runway he thought he heard low voices, and he stopped in the edge of shadow, trying to place the source of the sounds. Motioning the sentry to follow, he crossed a splash of moonlight to the end of the first line of stables.

He flattened himself against the log wall, and looked down the dark narrow strip of ground between the stables and the corral stockade. Two human figures and that of a single horse were dimly outlined against the corral exit, the gate he had ordered permanently closed after his first inspection of the fort.

Turning back to the front of the stables, he hurried down the empty street to the end of the unit, the sentry following close behind him. Here the corral widened; the closed gate was directly on his right. He slipped his revolver out and whispered to the sentry to light the lantern.

As soon as he heard the scratch of the match, he slid around the corner of the end stable. "Stand where you are!" he commanded. One of the figures at the gate dropped in a crouch. The other backed against the stockade, frozen in an attitude of surprise. "Bring up the lantern, trooper."

The saddled horse shied away from the light, and he could see the man crouching on the ground. He was Bratt Fanshawe. "One thing you didn't know, Fanshawe," Easterwood said. "I ordered this gate nailed shut the first night I took command."

Fanshawe began to rise, balancing with his arms, his long fingers curving like claws. "Don't try it, Fanshawe," Easterwood said coldly. The scout relaxed slowly, his long jaw

slackening, but his eyes were shiny and shifty in the lantern
light. "Take his weapons, trooper, and keep clear of line of
fire."

Easterwood did not look directly at Mellie Quill until Fanshawe was disarmed. When the sentry stepped back, his lantern
swinging slowly, Easterwood turned to face her. In the dancing
light she looked unreal, her dark eyes blazing fiercely at him,
her lips curled with loathing. She wore a clinging riding habit of
coarse army cloth, a jockey cap with the eartabs turned down
and tied beneath her chin, a rough fur cape about her shoulders,
and long beaver gauntlets. She screamed out at him: "How do I
look to you now, Tom Easterwood!"

He pushed his revolver down hard into its holster, and
crossed over to take the lantern from the sentry. "Lead off with
your prisoner, trooper."

Mellie Quill had not moved, and when he started toward her
she pressed back against the stockade like a cornered animal.
"How do I look to you now, Tom Easterwood?" she repeated in
a savage whisper. "Like the girl whose photograph you carry
next to your heart?"

"Mellie," he said gently, "Mellie."

"You could never leave me alone, could you?" Her eyes
burned at him. "You thought I still loved you." Her voice broke
into a tortured sob. "Why don't you let us go? If you love me,
Tom, you'll let us go." She fell against him, sobbing wildly.

He forced her forward, her legs moving unwillingly, his arm
supporting her. Gradually her resistance changed to lethargy,
and after what seemed to him an eternity they reached the gate
at the runway's end. The sentry was waiting there with Fanshawe, the scout staring off into space, disdainful, lost in his
own private world of studied indifference to the actions of others.

Easterwood straightened the fur cape around Mellie's shoulders. "You'll be all right now," he said. Under the ludicrous
jockey cap her face was tear-streaked.

She turned away from him, the coarse cloth of her riding
habit rustling as she ran toward officers' row. He watched her
until she reached the plank sidewalk.

Although the icehouse fire had burned itself out, the excited
voices of firefighters and spectators still carried loud from the
southeast corner of the stockade, and an occasional spark

drifted overhead. The smell of woodsmoke was heavy in the still air.

"Take your post, sentry," Easterwood said, and added wearily to the scout: "You know the way to the guardhouse, Fanshawe."

17

When Easterwood returned to the icehouse, the building was vanishing into a heap of fitfully glowing embers. Sergeant Connors and Professor Greenslade were seated together on a barked log with their backs to the warmth that still flowed from the remains of the fire.

Connors rose as Easterwood approached. The sergeant's face was soot-smeared, his eyes bloodshot and watery from smoke. "Everything's under control, sir. I dismissed the men back to quarters, exceptin' a small detail to watch for flyin' sparks."

"Very good, Connors. But there's no rest for the weary. It's time to start the balloon inflation. Summon out the balloon detail and a platoon for special duties. Have them fall out by the tool shed."

After Connors had gone to carry out the order, Greenslade stood up and stretched his arms, yawning sleepily. "Any idea how this fire started, Captain?"

"It doesn't matter now," Easterwood replied, and glanced at the moonlit sky. "We have less than five hours to ready that balloon."

From across the river, the monotonous beat of the Sioux drums rose and fell.

"Time enough," Greenslade said, and added wearily: "Judging from that unceasing racket, the Indians should be as fagged out as we by morning."

Easterwood drew in a deep breath. "They'll be wrought-up to where pain or death is meaningless, Professor." He turned toward one of the fire ladders standing by a scorched shed, and climbed it to the top rung.

On the sand flat, tiny silhouetted figures were dancing around the brightly burning campfire of the Sioux. Easterwood watched them through his glass for a minute or so. An old man was beating a skin drum, another was shaking a rattle. A squaw, slow-dancing behind the flames, waved a hoop on which was stretched a fresh scalp. He wondered, with a tightening in his throat, if there would be other fresh scalps in the camp of the Oglala before another sun had crossed the sky.

He searched for Spotted Wolf, for Young Elk, and the chief medicine men, but saw nothing of the leaders, and he guessed the soldier societies were still holding council in the *akicita* lodge. By now they should have done with feasting on choice bits of buffalo put by for this occasion; already they should have rubbed their bodies with sage, smoked their pipes to the four directions, and cried out for visions. Perhaps some were singing visions that warned of the Great Thunder Bird's wrath. Or perhaps it was only a struggle for power between the chief and Young Elk that was keeping the leaders from joining the scalp dancing.

What does it matter now, he muttered to himself, *they will come anyway.* He looked at the streak of river flowing below the small rapids, and guessed they would cross there, come splashing across the river within a few short hours, as Young Elk had come that afternoon.

He hurried down the ladder, glanced once at the remains of the fire, and nodded to Greenslade. "Let's get ready for them," he said.

By the time they reached the tool shed, the platoons were forming in the moonlight. Connors called the men to attention, and Easterwood in a few crisp words explained what was expected of them. The balloon detail was to repeat the operations of the previous morning; the special platoon was to collect all water barrels within the fort and bring them up for use in the generator wagon.

Although the rising moon brightened the sky, shadows still

marked parts of the inflation site, and a number of lanterns were set at intervals around the area to furnish light to work by.

While Greenslade directed the placing of the netting and the balloon envelope, Easterwood began putting the generator into operation. After bolting and locking the drain gateway at the tank's rear, he ordered the men to break open one of the barrels of iron filings, and so began the slow process of lifting and pouring the filings through the top manhole. "Ease the stuff in and spread it evenly," he repeated, and went over to see how Greenslade was coming along with the balloon.

"Skin's good," the professor declared, "but the net may not take high altitude strains. I recommend we use the short cables again."

"Agreed. The short ropes should give us height enough to be seen clearly, and if the ground crew walks the balloon along a ways, that should furnish enough movement to make an effective Thunder Bird—if they see it as a Thunder Bird."

"Doubt corrodes the soul, Captain." Greenslade shook a forefinger chidingly. "They'll fear it, whatever they see in it."

The night was windless, frost-chilled, and silvered with moonlight. The work proceeded without a hitch until water ran short. After the last barrel was drained carefully into the generator manhole, Easterwood climbed up and took a measurement. "Three feet from the top," he called gloomily to Greenslade. "At least a foot short."

"We'll need a sprinkle more, Captain, a sprinkle more to be certain."

"Sergeant Connors!"

"Yes, sir."

"Take every man here, except those with their hands occupied, and go through barracks and hospital, knock on every quarters door. I want every pitcher, bowl, pan, and chamberpot emptied into firebuckets and brought back here in twenty minutes. On the double."

The water foray produced enough liquid to raise the tank's level several more inches. As soon as the last drop was in, Easterwood closed the manhole and fastened the wing knobs securely.

"Ready to syphon acid!"

The next hour dragged. Now they had to wait for the acid to work, carefully spacing the pourings to prevent too rapid generation of gas. The stench of sulphur floated in waves around the wagon.

At last gas began flowing slowly through hose connectors to water cooler and lime purifier, and Greenslade gave the word: "Hydrogen pure. Connect the balloon when ready, Captain."

In another half hour they should know whether the patched envelope would hold.

Easterwood spent most of that interval alone, watching from the north bastion. Only one tiny fire was burning on top the Rock, and there was no sign of life around it. *Quill already has moved his men down toward the pass,* Easterwood thought. *He's waiting for me to make the next move. If I were following Quill's orders I should be sneaking my men out of here right about now. Even now, it's not too late to lead the men down there and die obediently.*

He turned toward the Indian village. The dancing had stopped. The camp was quiet as death. He could hear only the gurgling of the little rapids in the river. The warriors would be supplicating the Great Spirit now, or painting their bodies for battle.

When he returned to the balloon, it had taken the shape of a huge pumpkin, about as wide at the base as the top, the loose net screening it like a silvery veil under the moon's light. Two men were working the hand pump between the purifier and the balloon, and Greenslade was down on one knee beside the valve in the connecting hose.

"Anything wrong?" Easterwood asked anxiously.

The professor stood up, straightening his back with an effort. "Some leakage, not too serious."

"She'll lift by dawn?"

"Easily. Only thing frets me is the netting."

Easterwood picked up a lantern and crossed between the anchoring bags that circled the balloon. Lifting the lantern, he studied the twisting pattern of the net. Some of the frost-covered strands were badly frayed.

When he turned away, he noticed someone sitting on one of the earth-filled ballast bags. At first glance he thought it was a trooper in a greatcoat, was about to order him off the grounded netting. Then he stared hard again, bringing the lantern around. Alison Stuart smiled at him from out of the upturned collar of her oversized buffalo coat.

"You shouldn't be here, miss," he said. "This patchworked balloon—"

"It's a beautiful balloon," she replied, "in spite of its patching."

He touched her arm. "Come along now. You should be in bed."

"I was in bed. One of your men came and almost battered the Quills' door down, demanding our last drop of water."

"And you couldn't go back to sleep?"

"I haven't been to sleep. When did you last sleep, Captain?"

He urged her back toward the edge of the tool shed, where Sergeant Connors was standing by patiently with some of the men of the detail. Easterwood glanced skyward, measuring the moon's changed position. "Connors," he said quietly, "you can rouse all the men now. Give them their orders in the barracks. No bugles are to be sounded, and each man is to take his position silently. Just before dawn breaks, bring the sentries down off the platforms. I want this fort to appear completely deserted from the outside. Understand?"

"Yes, sir." The sergeant saluted and moved off towards the barracks.

"I wish there was something I could do," Alison said. "Isn't there something I can do?"

Easterwood looked down at her, wishing she were safely out of there, a thousand miles away from Fort Yellowhorse. "You can pray, miss," he said brusquely. Weariness pulled at him, and he watched the balloon anxiously; its spherical shape was pinched in where the patching had been sewed. Would the cloth hold, would the netting hold?

He couldn't stand there waiting, waiting, with doubt and uneasiness tugging at his mind and body. "Shall we walk to the gate?"

She put her arm through his, seeming to understand his need, and he was grateful for her silence as they crossed the frosted grass. By the time they reached the gate, the stars and the high moon were beginning to lose their brightness, the light graying so that the land seemed darker than before.

A sentry moved out of the shadow strip before the gate, saluting, and Easterwood stepped up to the wide loophole. Cold air poured in through the slot, a breeze coming up from the river with the smell of morning on it.

Alison's buffalo-coat collar raked across his cheek. She drew in a deep breath. "My father always says the sweetest perfume a man can breathe is the smell of a new morning—earth smell and river smell, sage smell and crushed grass smell." Her voice was soft, almost a whisper. "I suppose you'd have to live out here a long time to understand that."

"I understand, miss. It makes a man know how good it is to be alive." He adjusted his field glass on the Sioux village, still a dark irregular mass merging into the hills beyond. Along the lighter, contrasting sands scattered lines of horsemen were moving slowly.

With each beat of his heart, the night drained away. The morning star lost its glitter and vanished, the sky turned neutral. And then through his glass, he found Spotted Wolf riding on a white pony, the chief with his great headdress of eagles' feathers, riding slowly out toward the forming lines of warriors, two lines that reached as far as he could see into the gray mists down river.

Easterwood drew his revolver from its holster, handing it to Alison. "You may be needing this." He slipped a handful of cartridges from his belt and dropped them in the side pocket of her buffalo coat. "You'd best take cover in the Quills' quarters, miss. Mellie Quill will be grateful for your presence."

He swung away from the loophole and started in a long-strided jog-trot toward the balloon, now full-swollen in its tapering shape above the adjacent buildings.

As he came up, he found Greenslade and the ground crew attaching the basket car and the mooring cables to the concentration hoop. Above the hoop, the gray light exposed a jagged gap in the netting. One of his moccasins kicked into a spare snatch-block; he stumbled, choked back a curse, and shouted to the men: "Clear the bags off that netting and fasten ascension ballast!"

He went forward to help in the work, adding quietly to Greenslade: "It's a matter of minutes now."

"Shall I join you in the ascent, Captain?" the professor asked hopefully.

"No. You'll be needed on the ground again." He hooked a bag of sand to the basket rim. "As soon as the balloon lifts, start the crew to towing me along the parade. All the way to the gate unless I wave my scarf."

A minute later he climbed into the basket, bracing himself in a crouch. The balloon tugged powerfully, like a trout on a tight line. He glanced at the colorless sky, listening for hoofbeats, listening for the first war cries. A hand touched his shoulder, startling him, and when he turned, Alison Stuart's blue eyes were looking directly into his.

"I ordered you to take cover, miss," he said harshly.

"Not until I wish you godspeed, Captain." Her gloved fingers gripped the basket rim as she tried to stand steady against the uncertain swaying of the craft.

"I'm grateful to you, but—"

She touched one gloved hand to her lips, and waved to him as she backed away.

"Stand by your cables!" Easterwood shouted. "And pay out slowly."

Foot by foot the balloon lifted, not too evenly in spite of the professor's earnest efforts to direct the inexperienced crew. A slight upper current rocked the basket, and for a second roofs spun dizzily beneath him. He dug his elbows against the rattan siding.

When the basket steadied, he was looking out over the high stockade toward the river. Several bands of mounted Indians had already crossed below the rapids; others were forcing their ponies ashore. A horse whinnied nervously down there, then the heavy silence flowed in again until it was broken by the voice of Professor Greenslade far below. The ground crew was beginning to move out upon the parade.

Down on the slope before the fort, the Indians were coming now, in little yelping bands, the leaders crying the battle cry, *hoka-hey!* repeated, and then counterpointed by shrill war screams of individual warriors, all sound-blurred in the hollow drumming of hoofs over dead grass.

Here and there a horseman pulled his mount in sharply, head flung back to stare skyward; a few had seen the balloon, but the others came on like swift ghosts in the dawnlight, ghosts with unearthly voices riding toward the fort in the dawnlight.

Abruptly then, one side of the rattan basket lifted higher than the other, flinging Easterwood forward. He scrambled into an upright position, locked his fingers over the rim, and looked directly below.

One of the crewmen was dangling from a cable, free of the

ground. He was kicking his legs and yelling. The man let go
suddenly, dropping like a bag of ballast, flattening out when he
struck the ground. He lay there a moment as if stunned, then
got up limping.

Instead of leveling, the rattan car angled even more. On the
ground, Professor Greenslade was hobbling in a circle, waving
his arms and shouting to the cableman. Acting on impulse,
Easterwood reached for the dangling cable, was on the point of
leaping free of the basket for a quick slide earthward. But a
moment later, the balloon shot upward as if propelled by some
sudden force.

He looked down again. All the cables were free, with grappling irons still fastened to the ends, swinging lazily to and fro.
Greenslade's face was turned upward, his arms widespread. He
had ordered the cables released to relieve pressure on the
twisted basket and the ripped netting.

The professor probably had saved his life, Easterwood
thought, but he had also cut the commander of Fort Yellowhorse loose from his post of duty. The fort was without an
officer.

A sound like wind blowing through dried reeds, then like a
great thrumming of wings, rose from below. Easterwood
whirled inside the rocking car, stared down at the slope thick
with mounted Indians. A cry of relief choked in his throat. The
noise was from the beating of hoofs as the warriors lashed their
ponies in panic flight back toward the river. And then from
inside the fort, a cheer burst over the echoing hoofbeats.

Yet, one horseman still held steady below—Spotted Wolf all
alone on the deserted slope. As if in fear of the Great Thunder
Bird above him, as if in prayer for deliverance, the chief's head
was bowed. At last he turned his mount about, and with unhur-
ried dignity shook out his train of golden eagle feathers so they
trailed over the rump of his white horse. Then, with the Great
Thunder Bird hovering above him like an evil spirit, he galloped
after his terror-driven warriors.

18

From the swaying rattan car of the balloon, Easterwood
watched the Indians swarming like wind-stirred leaves. For an
hour or more, the *Intrepid* floated in a gentle west wind, with
the morning sun silvering its dull tan surface.

Before the fleeing warriors recrossed the river, the women
were dismantling the tipis, stripping them to bare skeletons of
poles, and then forming the poles into travois. In their precipi-
tate haste, only a few remembered to leave the customary farewell feasts for the ghosts. The flight became a panic; they
heaped blankets, clothing, pots and pans, children, dried meat
—whatever came to hand first—upon their travois and fled
eastward.

As the *Intrepid* drifted down the valley of the winding Yellowhorse, the morning breeze picked up velocity. Easterwood
discharged ballast gradually and the balloon lifted higher and
higher until he could see for miles across the flow of land. To
the south the grassy hunting grounds were grayed out from
frost; to the north the broken ridges were marked with dark
green splashes of pine. And on the east he could see the trailing
dust of the Indians' travois as they fled for the sanctuary of the
reservation. When they reached the level uplands, their trail
spread out like a fan, a measure of their hasty flight.

When the fort behind him on the west had shrunk to a tiny

brown square in the distance, he pulled the control cord opening the gas valve and began a slow descent. He chose his landing place carefully, a wide grassy slope, and brought the *Intrepid* down without mishap.

As soon as he had secured the cables by driving a pair of grappling irons into the ground, he disconnected the rattan basket, and waited until all the gas escaped from the envelope. Then he rolled the cloth and netting together and lashed them between the grappling irons.

He had made his way back within a mile of the fort when he saw two mounted men, one leading an extra horse, galloping toward him. He dropped the greatcoat and heavy fur cap which he had been carrying for the past few miles and sat down to wait.

In a minute or two he recognized the riders, Sergeant Connors and Professor Greenslade. Connors was standing in his stirrups, grinning and waving his hat. "She worked like a charm, sir," the sergeant cried warmly, as he pulled his mount to a quick halt.

"It's a grand day for the Signal Service," Greenslade added proudly, "in spite of our little accident with the cables."

Easterwood stood up, mopping the sweat from his face with the sleeve of his buckskin jacket. "Did the men on the Rock get down all right?" he asked.

"Yes, sir," Connors replied. He was still grinning. "You would've thought they'd won a war the way they come marchin' in the gate." He glanced back nervously at the fort. "The colonel's tearin' up mad about somethin', sir. I thought the capt'n should know."

"Thanks, Connors. It's no surprise." Easterwood mounted the spare horse, and Greenslade pulled up alongside him.

"The balloon is in good shape, Captain?" the professor asked.

"Good as ever. About three miles east. I roped everything down securely. We'll try to arrange a wagon detail to get out there tomorrow."

Greenslade nodded with satisfaction. "Now at last perhaps we can get to our real work."

Easterwood did not reply. The sun was noon high, and he felt numb from hunger and weariness.

As they rode through the gate, he returned the sentry's salute mechanically. *Hail the conquering hero comes,* he thought to himself. There was no welcoming party to meet him as there had been on the night he brought in the generator wagon. The feel of the place had changed; only physical objects in the fort remained the same. The tension of waiting was gone, and he saw only a few men, busy at routine details at the south end of the parade.

"Surgeon Campbell is expecting us," Greenslade said. "He promised he'd get out a bottle he's been saving for a proper celebration."

Easterwood kept his mount headed straight across the parade toward headquarters. "The celebrating will have to wait," he replied, "until I've reported to the colonel."

"Surely you can stop in first and share a wee nip with old Campbell and me?"

Easterwood shook his head. "I'll have to report to the colonel first." He pulled in on his reins. "Sergeant, will you stable this horse?" He swung out of the saddle, and tossed the bridle to Connors. "Thanks for everything, Connors."

"It's been a pleasure, sir, soldierin' with the capt'n in command." The sergeant saluted and rode away down the parade toward the stable corral.

Easterwood stepped over beside Greenslade's mount. All the merriment was gone from the little professor's face; he looked almost crestfallen. "You see, Professor," Easterwood explained quietly, "I disobeyed a direct military order this morning."

Not fully understanding, Greenslade stared down at him, puzzled, as if wondering whether the captain was being serious or not. "We'll be waiting for you down at Campbell's place," he said.

"Save part of that bottle for me." Easterwood slapped the professor's knee, and turned and walked on to the headquarters porch where a new sentry was already on duty. Easterwood began buttoning his jacket as he came up, and he returned the guard's salute awkwardly.

Inside, a lieutenant serving as Quill's adjutant was sitting at the desk which had been occupied by Jonas, and the sergeant-major was back in his old place in the far corner. Jonas gave Easterwood a glum look, and turned back to the morning reports spread over his desk. Easterwood dropped his greatcoat and fur cap on the bench beside the door.

The lieutenant stood up. "Captain Easterwood. Glad to see you again, sir."

"Bad time up there on the Rock?" Easterwood asked.

"Not easy to take, sir."

"The colonel in?"

The lieutenant nodded slowly, his eyes hardening a little. His lips pushed out slightly and he seemed on the point of saying something but changed his mind. "Go ahead, sir."

Quill was waiting behind the command desk, and as Easterwood walked in he caught the familiar smells of chocolate and pomade mingled with the sour-sweet odor of new-cut cedar.

"I came to report, sir," Easterwood said.

Quill pushed a pile of army forms aside, and began gnawing on his red moustache. Then, with a grimace of displeasure, as if he did not like having to look up at Easterwood, he pushed the whirligig chair back and stood facing the captain. He rocked back and forth for a moment or so, then balanced himself with his knuckles pressed down against the desk top.

"I have no questions, Captain."

Easterwood remained silent, expecting Quill to storm out at him, awaiting the shrill voice in anger. But Quill continued calmly: "Captain Easterwood, I charge you with disobedience of orders and violation of the Forty-second and Sixty-second Articles of War. You are also out of proper uniform. Charges and specifications for a court-martial will be drawn up later. For the present you will confine yourself to quarters within the garrison. That is all, Captain."

Easterwood moved into the quarters formerly occupied by Major Sylvanus Robinson, a tiny room in a log hutment midway down officers' row. From the single window he could watch the activities of the fort. By midafternoon he wearied of pacing from the fireplace to the window, and he lay down on the wall bunk to read from the late major's small library, books for the most part dealing with various campaigns of the Civil War.

After retreat ceremonies, a trooper brought his supper. As he had had no food for almost twenty-four hours, he ate every scrap on the tin plates.

Shortly after dark there was a knock on his door. He lifted

the wooden latch, and looked out through the door crack at Asahel Greenslade. "I have the colonel's permission to visit you," the professor explained, and Easterwood let him in.

There were only two chairs in the room, with barely space enough for them between the wall bunk and the fireplace. Greenslade sat down heavily in one of the chairs, placing his walking stick across his knees, and faced Easterwood, "I must confess I don't understand military matters at all," he said.

"The rules are quite simple," Easterwood replied. "If a soldier obeys orders, he's a good soldier and stays out of trouble."

Greenslade shrugged his shoulders and sighed. "Sergeant Connors explained it to me somewhat the same way. But I thought you might be lonely in here by yourself. I thought maybe you'd want to talk it off your chest."

"I'm glad to see you, Professor, but there's nothing to be discussed about my present predicament. Colonel Quill is doing his duty as any commander should."

Greenslade threw up his hands. "Be that as it may, there is one thing I need to know. The colonel has given me authority to recover the balloon, but you are the only person who knows its exact whereabouts."

"I'll draw a map for you," Easterwood replied. He went over to the drop table at the end of the wall bunk, and on a sheet of Major Robinson's ruled writing paper outlined a rough map, marking the approximate location of the balloon.

He gave the map to Greenslade, adding a few explanations, and shortly afterwards the professor excused himself.

The next morning, Easterwood stood at the window watching two wagon parties form on the parade. The smaller group was Greenslade's, and he guessed from the rolls of blankets piled in the second wagon, and the mounted platoon accompanying it, that the latter was being sent north of the Rock to recover the luckless members of Major Robinson's ill-fated squadron.

Sometime after the wagons departed, he saw Alison Stuart with her father crossing the parade toward the hospital. Once or twice the girl glanced in the direction of his window; then she and Baird Stuart entered the hospital. Easterwood wondered how much longer Surgeon Campbell would permit Lee Bowdring to remain there, suffering his imaginary ailments.

Late in the afternoon, the balloon wagon returned, moving

up the parade to the quartermaster storehouse. About an hour afterwards the other wagon arrived, a canvas draped over its blanketed dead, the small mounted platoon following slowly after it until the grim-faced driver wheeled his mules and turned in toward the rear of the hospital.

Soon after retreat, there was a rap on his door. He thought it was the trooper from the mess, bringing his supper, but when he opened the door, Alison Stuart and Asahel Greenslade stood there, each one holding a napkin-covered platter. Easterwood stepped back, surprised.

Alison's blue eyes seemed to be searching his face. "Well, aren't you going to welcome us inside?" she asked, with an expression like a hurt child's.

"Forgive me," Easterwood stammered. "I wasn't expecting such a beautiful mess boy." He made room for them to enter.

Greenslade chuckled. "Was the captain speaking of me or the young lady?" He took Alison's platter and set both on the drop table. "You sit down here on the end of your bunk and fall to, Captain. Miss Stuart and I will do the talking."

"And I have plenty to say," Alison declared. She sat down sideways in one of the upright chairs, her elbow resting on its back, her chin propped in one hand, her eyes never leaving Easterwood. "I've been to see Colonel Quill," she said, "and I told him what I thought of him for his treatment of you."

Easterwood lifted one of the napkins and poured a cup of steaming coffee from the china pot. "Will you have some coffee?" he asked.

She shook her head. "Father and I are dining with the Quills a few minutes from now. And I assure you, the colonel is not going to enjoy his supper."

"You seem to have a grievance against the colonel," Easterwood said mildly, and raised the cup of coffee.

She began kicking one moccasined foot back and forth. "How can you sit there so calmly after what that man has done to you? You're a hero to everybody in this fort, Captain Easterwood, except that stubborn muleheaded colonel—"

"The colonel is right, you know," he interrupted. "All I had was a fool idea. I risked all our lives to find out if my idea would work. The fact that it succeeded is beside the point. Should I have failed, in my disobedience to the colonel's orders, there would have been no second chance, not for any of us. So the colonel is right."

"Men can be most exasperating at times," she replied firmly. "Talking of what's right and what's wrong. I've been begging Father all day to go to Colonel Quill and use his influence as a citizen. But Father is as bad as the rest of you. He says it is military business and he shan't interfere. Men are such stubborn creatures."

"How is Mr. Bowdring, by the way?" Easterwood asked innocently.

"A deal more reasonable than you, sir," she answered. "At least not so willfully exasperating."

Easterwood threw back his head and laughed. "I admire your spirit very much," he said.

"I'm sorry I can't say the same for you," she retorted.

Professor Greenslade cleared his throat loudly. "If it's any comfort to either of you," he said, "Surgeon Campbell tells me he doesn't believe the charges will reach a court-martial, but if by some chance they should be approved by military authorities, then President Grant will refuse to confirm them."

They talked for several more minutes, Easterwood vainly attempting to steer the subject of conversation from his garrison arrest to other matters. When Greenslade and the girl were leaving, Alison declared that she was going to speak to Mellie Quill and endeavor to persuade her to intercede with the colonel. Easterwood asked her firmly not to do this, but she shook her yellow hair determinedly and insisted that she was going to see justice done.

Two days later, the relief battalion summoned from Goldfield arrived somewhat anticlimactically, marching into the fort without ceremony. That evening Easterwood learned from Greenslade that the three messengers sent from the fort had all reached Goldfield safely, that the telegraph wires had all been reconnected, and that rumors were circulating about the fort that Colonel Quill was planning a winter campaign for the purpose of rounding up all Indians who had not returned to their reservations.

By this time Easterwood was becoming more and more puzzled because he had not heard from Quill. Each day he expected to be presented with the colonel's charges in writing. But the days passed, and he heard nothing. The uncertainty and his self-imposed imprisonment began to annoy him. He devised elaborate physical exercises to pass the time, and found himself eagerly awaiting Greenslade's faithful evening visits. The professor brought over a pack of cards, and they began playing cribbage regularly until bedtime.

One morning Easterwood was awakened as usual by reveille call. He arose to find a wintry sky outside his single window. The men around the guardhouse had donned their greatcoats and fur caps and were threshing their fur gauntlets across their chests for warmth.

He heard the faint rattle of bit and trace chains. An ambulance drawn by four mules rolled briskly down the parade, halting in front of headquarters. A minute or so later, Bratt Fanshawe, dressed in what looked like a brand-new winter uniform with large corporal stripes on the sleeves, appeared from out of headquarters. He walked with a jaunty step and carried himself proudly. With the critical manner of an inspecting officer, he circled the mule team, then ordered the muleskinner out of the saddle. Fanshawe pulled down the earlaps of his fur cap, took over the lines, and mounted the saddled mule.

Shortly thereafter, two troopers appeared and began loading baggage into the rear of the ambulance. A man and a woman, heavily dressed against the cold, came into view. They were Colonel Mathew Quill and Mellie Quill. Mellie was wearing an officer's greatcoat, buffalo boots, and a hood of beaver fur. They both turned and waved to someone outside Easterwood's view, probably a farewell group gathered in the headquarters entrance. Without further ado, Matt Quill helped Mellie into the ambulance and followed after her.

A moment or two later, a trooper came hurrying out of headquarters with a smoking bucket of hot bricks which he dumped into a blanket and passed inside. The soldier stepped back, saluted, and closed the rear door.

Fanshawe raised one of his heavy gauntlets, and after a long slow look around the fort, he slapped the mules to a start. The ambulance wheeled and began rolling at a sharp clip toward the gate, which already stood open.

Lee Bowdring and Alison Stuart had walked down from the headquarters steps and were standing where the ambulance had stood a minute before. But the girl was not dressed for the cold;

she tugged at Bowdring's arm, and they walked back out of Easterwood's angle of vision.

Rubbing his unshaven chin in puzzlement, Easterwood watched the ambulance roll away—to where he could not guess—but knowing that Mellie was inside, riding away with Matt Quill. And for a moment he felt the old empty ache he had known often during the long years since that long-ago time in the Virginia valley. As he watched the gate close after them, he saw a few snowflakes, dry and feathery, slanting across his window glass.

The ambulance could not have traveled farther than a mile when Quill's adjutant, the young lieutenant, appeared at Easterwood's door. His face was red from the cold and his hurried walk from headquarters. "Good morning, Captain Easterwood." The lieutenant's voice was cheery and he smiled broadly. "The colonel instructed me to deliver a message, sir. The verbal charges made against you have been withdrawn. As no charges were recorded, no official action is necessary to void them."

"Thank you, Lieutenant."

"It's good news, sir, for all of us."

Easterwood nodded. "I saw the departure just now."

"Rather sudden, that. The colonel received orders by telegraph last night transferring him back east to duty in the States."

"He seems in a hurry to get there."

The lieutenant smiled knowingly and shook his head. "It isn't that. The colonel could have gone at his convenience. But he made up his mind last night to go immediately to Omaha and convince General Sheridan he is indispensable out here."

Easterwood walked over to the window and looked out at the gray sky and the light blowing snow. "He picked a fine day to start for Omaha."

The lieutenant shrugged deprecatingly. "I imagine Fanshawe will see him through as usual, sir."

"They'll be lucky to make it to the first ranch house," Easterwood said.

Pulling nervously at his gauntlets, the lieutenant backed toward the door. "We shall be expecting you at officers' mess, sir, for breakfast."

Easterwood nodded absently, and frowned out at the dancing snowflakes. The grass on the parade was already turning white.

By midmorning of that day the snow was driving in a dense swirling cloud of white smoke straight across the parade. By noon the flag staff was bending under the fury of the wind. By three o'clock that afternoon the storm had become a raging, snarling blizzard. By retreat time—and there was no ceremony —objects twenty feet distant were invisible to the eye, and a man could scarcely breathe facing the icy gale.

At dawn of the following day the blizzard ended, leaving the parade swept clean, but the lee side of every building in the fort was banked to the eaves with solid drifts.

Epilogue

This brings the Yellowhorse story to the time when I met Tom Easterwood and heard from him what has been told to now. I suppose almost every American knows of Colonel Matt Quill, the famous Indian-fighting cavalryman, of how he and his wife Mellie and the scout Bratton Fanshawe were lost in the great blizzard and were never seen or heard of again.

But there is more to it than that.

Although mystery is still there, it is not so much a mystery as the official army accounts have left it.

To get back to the time I met Tom Easterwood—some years after the incident of the balloon at Fort Yellowhorse.

In those days I was a greenhorn meteorologist fresh out of college, and the newly formed Weather Service had employed me and sent me out with an advance party to set up a station in the Yellowhorse country. By that time the Indian wars were all ended, a railroad had been run through the valley, and the grass country was filling rapidly with ranchers and settlers.

I had heard vaguely of Tom Easterwood. I knew he had resigned his army commission to join the Weather Service, and that after a period of duty in Washington, D.C., he was coming out to direct the experimental observations at the Yellowhorse field station. But I had never given him much thought until the day I received instructions to meet him at Newcomb's Wells, a whistle stop on the railroad.

On the day of his expected arrival, I drove the camp's buckboard over to Newcomb's Wells. The train arrived late in the afternoon, slowing to a noisy stop. As soon as the conductor opened the door of the rear car, I hurried along the cinders, to act in my capacity as a greeting party of one.

A tall man stepped down on the platform. He had a hawk nose that seemed to be sniffing the air, and he stood straight like a trooper on parade. Before he saw me, he turned to take a woman's arm and help her down from the car, and as soon as she was off the steps, he turned back and lifted a little boy all the way to the ground.

I wasn't expecting to see a child or a woman—especially a woman so beautiful, a woman with extraordinarily blue eyes, and hair of a rare yellow quality, like the yellow of sunshine in the early morning. The little boy was slender like the man and he had the same features in miniature, but his hair was the same color as the woman's.

"Mr. Thomas Easterwood?" I asked, a bit uncertain by now as to whether this man was the one I had come to meet.

"That's right," he said, thrusting out his hand.

I told him my name, and he introduced his wife and son. By this time the porter had stacked their baggage beside the tracks, and the conductor was signaling the engineer to proceed. We dispensed with conversation until the train had moved away, leaving us in a cloud of coal smoke and flying cinders.

"My wife's father has a ranch not many miles from here," Easterwood explained. "I hope the weather station can furnish us family quarters for the night."

"We have extra tents," I replied. "If Mrs. Easterwood doesn't mind roughing it."

"Alison has roughed it before," he said, and smiled at her.

By squeezing, we made room for all the baggage and the four of us in the buckboard, and we started off for the camp. As I recall that two-hour journey, I believe the little boy had more to say than either Easterwood or his wife. At first, I tried to make light conversation with them, but they responded so half-heartedly that I gave up and concentrated on the boy. It was not that they were being cold or impolite; they just seemed more interested in looking at the pine-clad hills than in talking.

The next day, Alison Easterwood's father drove out from his ranch in a buggy. Baird Stuart must have been well over seventy by then, but that part of his face which was visible above his whiskers was sun-browned and smooth as an apple, and the beard gave him the appearance of a prophet out of the past.

For a few days after his wife and son left for the Stuart ranch, Tom Easterwood was moodier and more reserved than ever. There wasn't much time for getting acquainted; all of us in the camp were working about sixteen hours a day. In addition to our regular observation duties, we were trying to complete construction of our winter shacks before cold weather set in.

But when Sunday came, we all knocked off our extra work and spent the afternoon lazing around. Easterwood and I wandered down to a nearby trout stream. We fished a little, and smoked our pipes, but for the most part we just talked.

He began telling me about his life in the cavalry, about Fort Yellowhorse, about Professor Asahel Greenslade, and the balloon *Intrepid*. He mentioned Colonel Matt Quill, but when I expressed an interest in that famous Indian fighter's career, he turned suddenly reticent.

During the following week, around our late evening campfires, he added a few more details to his story, but not much, just enough to tantalize me. I was becoming interested in the missing pieces of his story by this time, and every evening after our camp supper, I would try to steer the talk around to Yellowhorse and Colonel Matt Quill. But whenever I probed too deeply, Easterwood would withdraw into that unfathomable reserve of his and change the subject.

Then late one evening—it was a Saturday evening and we were more relaxed than usual—we had an unexpected visitor. We heard him coming before we saw him, the creaking of his old wagon and the noise of his team. The wagon driver turned out to be an old man, one of that strange crew of bone pickers who could be seen occasionally in those days wandering about the plains collecting bones of the long dead buffalo and of cattle that had died from consuming poisonous plants or bad water, or from freezing to death in blizzards. The bones were sold to dealers along the railroad line for shipment east to fertilizer factories.

The bone picker hallooed us, and Easterwood called to him to come over to the fire. As he walked up into the firelight, he looked like an old pirate, his short beard matted and dusty, his long hair unkempt, and his clothing stained with earth and grease spots.

"Coffee?" Easterwood asked quietly.

"Sure don't mind if I do, mister," the stranger replied eagerly. "I could smell it way back there."

Easterwood reached for the big pot and poured a pint tin full. The old man took the tin in his trembling fingers and began sucking the coffee noisily through his lips. He wiped his mouth on his sleeve. "I run plumb outa coffee ten days back. This sure tastes good."

"Finding many bones these days?" Easterwood asked.

"Bones gettin' mighty scarce, mister. Mighty scarce. I been figurin' this may be my last year to work this country."

"You heading for any place in particular?"

The bone picker sucked at his coffee again. "Soon's I finish this sweep, I'm headin' back to Goldfield."

"You live there?"

"Don't live nowhere, mister. But I kind of look on old Goldfield as my base. Ain't much left there now, but we had some mighty fine fandangos in Goldfield back in the old days."

Easterwood lit his pipe and puffed slowly. "I spent some time there myself," he said. "You wouldn't know an old codger name of Domino Ruark, would you?"

"Domino! Hell fire in the mountains, mister, Domino Ruark was my pardner. We started bone pickin' together right after the big blizzard."

"When I knew Domino," Easterwood replied, "he had the Troopers' Rest."

The bone picker blew his nose against his thumb. "Domino sold out right after his wife run away with one o' them railroad men that come in. We went to bone pickin' the next spring." He paused and looked sharply at some leftover sour-dough biscuits in a pan beside the fire.

"Go ahead and eat," Easterwood said. "Whatever happened to Domino?"

"God rest his soul, he took to drinkin' heavy. Thinkin' too much 'bout that runaway squaw o' his'n, I reckon." He snatched up one of the biscuits, wolfed it, and washed it down with coffee. "Old Domino got loaded blind one night when we was up to Miles City. He crossed one o' them mean cowmen up there. Took a knife right between the shoulder blades and died without sayin' a word. God rest his soul, I sure miss that old hoss."

Easterwood made no comment. He just smoked his pipe and watched the old man eat the biscuits. After a while, he said: "I always counted Domino as a friend. He was one of the best Indian scouts of his day."

The bone picker rubbed his fingers against the sides of his greasy buckskin pants. "You bein' a friend of his'n, mister, I got somethin' under my wagon seat you might like to see. I'll fetch it." He got up and shuffled off in the darkness. We could hear him talking to his horses, and then after a minute or so he came back, carrying a leather pouch fastened with rawhide lacing. He sat down and worked the lacing loose with his grimy fingers. "This is all on God's earth old Domino left when he passed on." He slipped two pieces of silver metal out and handed them to Easterwood.

"Where'd you get these?" Easterwood cried, and I could see by the firelight that they were silver spurs of Mexican make. "How did Domino come by these?" he demanded.

"Well, now," said the bone picker, "I can't rightly tell you for sure. They's a ring in here, too, solid gold." He fumbled nervously in the pouch and brought the ring out, balancing it in his clawlike hand. Easterwood took the ring, angling it toward the light, squinting inside the band. His fingers were trembling.

"They's letterin' in there, mister. I forget what they are, but they's some letterin' inside that ring."

"Didn't Domino ever say anything about these, where he got them?" Easterwood's voice was hoarse and demanding, and I could see the cords stretching in his neck as he leaned closer to the old man.

"Well, now, Domino sometimes would say he found the silver spurs and the gold ring that time we hauled all them horse bones outa Box Canyon—the place where old Horse-Killer Quill shot them Sioux mustangs. Lots o' bones in there. We made good money that year. They was some human bones in there, all right, but I allus figured they was Indians gone in there to die. 'Course, Indians could o' had them spurs and that ring on 'em, stole from some place."

Easterwood held the spurs and the ring in his long-fingered hands, staring at them in fascination.

The bone picker hawked his throat clear and spat into the fire. "But like I told you, mister, I can't rightly be sure that's where Domino found 'em. Toward the end he was drinkin' a lot and his mind was a-wanderin' and sometimes he would take them spurs and the ring out and look at 'em, and he'd tell me he got 'em from a man and a woman. Man and a woman was headin' for Canada, he'd say, and they needed money bad, and he swapped 'em a big poke of gold dust for the silver spurs and the gold ring. Did it as a favor, he'd say, and never saw that man and woman since, he'd say, and slap his leg, and laugh like he knowed a plumb good joke." The old man grinned across the fire at Easterwood, showing his ragged teeth, and added: "You never could tell when old Domino was funnin' or talkin' straight. God rest his soul, I sure miss that old hoss."

The next morning, Sunday, the bone picker departed. Not long after breakfast, Easterwood and I took our trout rods and went down to the stream to fish. It was while we were there that he started talking about Fort Yellowhorse again. I suppose it was seeing Mellie Quill's ring and Bratt Fanshawe's spurs that helped break down his former reluctance to talk of certain personal matters. I suppose he had come to realize for the first time that part of his past was gone forever. Perhaps he wanted to reconstruct some sort of word memory around the residue of the spurs and the ring. Anyway he told me that day the whole story of Fort Yellowhorse, the story that has been recorded here.

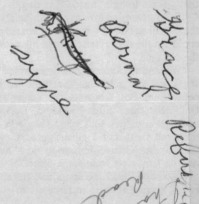